Bringing
S

Jennifer E. Kirk

best wishes

Jennifer Kirk

DS Press

Bringing Home the Stars

978-0-9542455-7-3

First Published 2009
Second edition 2010

Published by DS Press

Bolton
BL7 9YA

Printed and bound by MPG Biddles, King's Lynn, Norfolk

Bringing Home the Stars

Also by Jennifer E. Kirk:

Books:

Homo Superior
Countdown to Extinction
Syndicate Dawn
Daytrippers
Orb of Arawaan
The Atlantic Connection

Visit Jennifer E. Kirk online at:
http://www.jennifer-kirk.com

For Zoë, Mum and Dad.

Bringing home the stars

The salvage Tug shuddered. Sirens wailed penetrating the sleep induced by the stasis quo-fields. Zoë blinked, sluggish. The alarm meant only one thing; their passage within the Rösenbridge was lost and they were hurtling blindly through the vacuum of space.

Zoë was the first to clamber from her pod and stagger to the bridge. She reached a console and keyed in her codes. For a moment the screen remained blank, then text and telemetry scrolled across.

She sensed movement beside her in the gloom.

"What's up?" Dezza asked in a calm twang that never betrayed emotion.

"Core collapse," she said, jabbing at buttons. "It's jumped us out of the Rösenbridge short again."

"Shit. I thought Tubs swore blind he fixed that."

"Obviously not well enough."

He tapped away on the adjacent console activating the holographic display. In any failed Rösenbridge jump, they risked blundering into other ships, planets, stars and moons with fatal results. Space might be infinite and almost empty, but Fate had a habit of testing the reflexes of the unwary.

Static crackled and the computer updated the projected image of what lay outside the hull. An arc of grey became an arc of blue shimmering in the air. With agonising slowness the computer decided that there was nothing of immediate harm and the readouts stopped their garish flashing.

Zoë shook her head grimly and keyed off the alarms. "It's only so long before Lady Luck stops seeing herself clear to keep us from hitting a star. That could have been close."

"It's always close. I'll see what Tubs has to say for himself."

*   *   *   *   *

Tubs lay on an inspection trolley, grappling with the underside of the console panel. Wires stretched out loose either side of

7

him. He studiously ignored the mess to soldier on with careful laser-pen work inside the tangle of electronics.

Dezza leant on the railing, watching him with strained patience. "How long before the core is back online?"

"Just a few hours," Tubs replied, muffled from beneath the panel, "I'm not sure why it croaked this time anyway. It should have held until we could get to dock and have it refurbed."

Dezza held his composure. It was not the first time the tugship had dropped from the Rösenbridge short. For the last two months it had become an increasingly regular occurrence, and one which had become tedious fast. The ship's drive core was old and frail. There were only so many times that ancient electronics could be patched back together. Tubs might be a miracle worker, but eventually even miracles disappoint.

Dezza's communicator buzzed, and for a moment he felt relief that something would break the boredom of this unforeseen stop in deep space.

"Yes?"

Zoë's business-like voice answered, sounding tinny through the old electronics. "Have you checked the scopes?"

He frowned. Something was not quite right.

"No," he snapped.

"This one's the longest yet. According to the navigation sweep, we're not even at the further colonies. The damn core popped us out more than forty days short."

"Forty days? Shit!"

He glared down at Tubs' feet, but the mechanic was oblivious and the gentle buzz of the laser pen drifted from beyond the pair of wriggling legs.

"That's not the only thing," interrupted Zoë.

He heard the concern in her voice. Tubs' work was forgotten and he listened hard.

"What?"

"The sweep picked up something else. About an hour's jag away on the ion drive, we've got a ship floating dead."

"Have you tried to get them on the Comm?" he asked.

"There's no answer. You had both better come to the bridge. If that ship is what I think it is, this drop might just be the break we're looking for."

"How do you mean?"

"It's easier if you're up here and I can show you."

She let the communications channel click dead and nothing more except static came from the speaker. He knew Zoë had a habit for the dramatic. Well, let them humour her. With the main drive core out of commission, it was not as if time was at a premium, for now.

He flicked the device into a pocket and kicked gently at the legs beneath him. A muffled cry shot out from behind the wires.

"Leave that. Zoë wants us on the bridge."

Tubs slid out on the trolley, grumbling. But his griping fell upon deaf ears. When Zoë got one of her ideas they both knew it was best to go along with her.

*   *   *   *   *

The holographic projection shimmered in the hot air of the bridge; stinking of ozone. Dezza wrinkled his nose at the smell. It always filled him with a feeling of unease. Maybe it was because every time he stood here he knew Zoë was going to suggest something that he would feel obliged to argue with. He sighed, hating the conflict that usually came.

Zoë jabbed a finger at a small dot floating at the centre of the display. Ripples of static arched through the projection as the computer struggled to compensate for the untimely insertion of her hand into its image.

"This is what we're looking at," she said.

Dezza scrunched his eyes, trying to focus on what the projection was trying to show him. It was too small to make out and was lost into the hazy limits of the projection's resolution. He was about to say something, to ask what it was they were meant to be looking at, when she tapped a few buttons on the console as if anticipating his struggles. The image suddenly grew exponentially in size.

He stepped back in surprise before remembering that it was only a hologram. It did not matter how many times it happened, he could never get used to this contraption.

The dot grew to the size of a large cylinder and sat suspended in the slight glowing field. He squinted; it was clearly some kind of vessel. He racked his mind, trying to think what it could be so far out from the shipping lanes. The shape suggested it had to be manmade, or else he would have said some kind of comet or asteroid chunk. But it was huge, and that kind of vessel always stayed in the tight shipping lanes on the shortest routes between destinations. Of course, it could always be something that had broken adrift from a tow maybe? But it was not likely.

"Bulker?" he ventured.

She shook her head.

"Not big enough. Some kind of Starliner I think."

He glanced to the reams of data shimmering in the air alongside the main bulk of the projector. She was right: the thing was much longer and more slender than any Bulker could be. With no aerodynamics to constrain a ship's design, their size and girth was always more a function of the cargo they had to carry.

"She isn't going anywhere if she is," he said at last, "Computer says it's holding a stationary position. It can't be docked, we're several light years out into deep nowhere."

"I think it's a derelict," she said.

He was not so sure. A derelict might mean an easy salvage to tow it back to civilisation and a guaranteed ten-percent, but there had to be a reason for it. Out here so far from the shipping lanes, a funny feeling lingered at the back of his mind. Something was not quite right.

"What are you getting on the frequencies?" he asked calmly. If there were distress calls or beacons, that might help them identify the craft, and the reason for her being so far out into deep space.

She shrugged. "Nothing except for a simple docking channel on static."

"Any response to attempts to raise them?"

"No," said Tubs.

"This is going to be our big pay-day. We tow that hulk back to civilisation and that's our pay for the year made in one."

She seemed so sure of herself, Dezza thought. Always rushing in to the task.

Tubs coughed, and they both looked around.

"I hate to be the realist," he began timidly, "But our drive core is offline. We aren't going anywhere near civilisation until we get it fixed."

"How long will that take?" asked Zoë.

Dezza got the feeling that there was going to be a catch.

He shrugged. "Two, maybe three days work. We need a full refit."

"Will it let us tow that hulk?" she probed, as if realising the possibility of defeat after getting so close to success.

"It'll tow," he said after a moment's pause, "But I would be happier not pushing it."

"We can't leave something this big just drifting!" she exclaimed with disappointment heavy in her voice.

Dezza frowned. Why did Tubs have to pick now to err on the side of caution?

"We could come back for it after getting the drive properly repaired," he offered, trying to be diplomatic. He knew Zoë's feelings and whilst he lacked her blind enthusiasm whatever the cost, he knew that Tubs was playing this stubbornly; something was making him look for excuses.

Zoë was not having any of it.

"At the very least, I want to move in closer and scope this baby out. We can do that on the ion drive until the core is back online."

Tubs had to concede they could do that at the very least. It was clear though that he did not want to. Something was bothering him.

*   *   *   *   *

The ion drive fired, bringing gravity swathing through the tug as a change from the peculiar generated variety that never seemed quite right. It pressed the three of them back into the restraints of the bridge seats with a force that had been a while since its last coming.

Through the bridge screen the millions of stars began to slowly revolve as the Tug moved around onto a new course and edged towards the derelict.

Within an hour, one particular pinprick of light grew to be bigger than the rest that set the starscape behind it. They had looked at the long slender form of the Starliner on the computer projection, but now it hung before them for real. The many details lost on the scanner became visible to the naked eye in a way that a computer simulation always seemed to miss.

"Riding and navigation lights are still blinking," said Zoë softly, "It seems they still have power."

Dezza checked the read outs on the screen in front of him. On the gauges he looked for background radiation that would show evidence of reactor core activity. He was rewarded as the scan revealed a blip on the radiation spectrum that correlated with a fusion device.

"Our scan show that at least one of the fusion reactors is still online at a low output."

Zoë looked up from her console, a frown on her face. "All lifepods are gone. Computer systems are either offline or seem to have looped into a system's crash. Other than that, she seems structurally sound."

Dezza paused as he considered this. Something still did not add up to him. "Why haven't we heard about a Starliner being lost?"

He noted that Tubs showed signs of worry again, though he said nothing. Zoë did not seem to have noticed his expression.

"Maybe we've been out of the loop too long in the quo-field," she offered, but seemed unconvinced.

Through the screen they watched the Starliner grow close. Riding lights blinked intermittently, and thousands of portholes glowed faintly. It certainly was beginning to seem strange that a ship this size could go adrift without something coming through to them. Maybe if no-one knew yet? But the shape of the ship seemed wrong, and raised more questions that were left unspoken.

12

The Tug began a flypast, cruising close at a rate of only a few metres per second. The bland metal side of the derelict passed by streaked dull with the dust of space. Occasionally a dulled and deformed mark showed where its navigation field had deflected meteorites.

"Still trying radio frequencies. No response," said Zoë.

Moving upwards they passed along close to the upper decks. Here the monotonous steel wall gave way to clear shielded promenade decks and more complex superstructure. A forest of antennas stretched high into the starscape, twinkling as they cruised by in the dim reflections of running lights.

This was not right. The ship's design was positively out of date. It looked like a museum piece, and none could ever recall having seen a ship like this in service on any port they had ever visited.

"Lifepod bays coming up. All appear empty. What happened?"

One after another, open bays loomed and slid by. Airlocks showed beyond the gloom, but the docking clamps were released and the lifepods were gone.

"Long-range scans show nothing – wherever they went it wasn't local."

"So there's no-one left onboard?" asked Dezza.

"Nothing on the scans, but there's a lot of dense structure in that thing that could be shielding stuff from us."

He nodded. Could it have been a life support problem? But a nagging thought in his mind told him that could easily be repaired without having to abandon ship. A thought occurred to him, another explanation.

"Check for radiation leaks from the drive shielding."

She checked her console. "Already swept. Nothing above normal background levels."

"Hull integrity?"

"Still airtight."

He frowned. What could have made them run away? From the corner of his eye he saw Tubs at his station. Despite the air conditioning of the cabin, sweat glistened on his face.

"What's up, Tubs?" he asked.

Tubs looked startled. For a moment it looked like the man was about to break down. There was a look in his eyes of raw, untamed fear. It was a look Dezza could not recall ever seeing on the face of a hardened salvager.

"Hey! Easy now!" said Dezza, trying to calm the man.

"That ship. I know what it is," said Tubs at last, "It's a myth that has been doing the rounds of the bars and colonies for longer than I can remember. Like an old yarn, this is the *Mary Celeste* story they tell when the lights are low and the drinks have flowed. The story must go back at least eighty years."

"You're kidding, right?" said Zoë slowly, perhaps not wanting to believe that one of her crew could be so easily spooked.

Dezza looked out of the screen at the bulk of the Starliner. Eighty years? Come to think of it, its style did look somewhat dated. But it was still a tall tale. He too wanted to listen; to find out what could have driven Tubs to be this scared. They had salvaged many derelicts together as a crew before now. Some were beaten up to a pulp whilst others grimly still held crew who had not managed to escape explosive decompression. None had unsettled Tubs as much as this one had.

"She went missing. Just disappeared," Tubs continued, never taking his eyes off the bulk of the derelict vessel, "Six months went by and they called off all searches. After two years, one of the lifepods was found out near the outer trajectories, floating in space. It was empty, but the log mentioned contact with something that was enough to make a man drop dead with fear."

Dezza found himself scoffing at the man's tale. Tubs had a penchant for over-reacting to silly stories, but this had to be one of his best yet. How could he let himself be wound up by mere bar stories?

"How come we never heard about it?" asked Zoë.

"Stories change over the centuries," soothed Dezza, trying to be diplomatic, "The *Mary Celeste* story has been around before space travel was ever invented. Everyone likes a good yarn, but you see you never find anyone with actual first-hand experience of the events. It's always a 'friend of a friend'."

Tubs looked past him to the bulk of the derelict easing past silently outside. Their words did not seem to have done much for him and his eyes still glittered with fear.

"Well?" Dezza asked.

"*Cerberus*."

"What?" Zoë said. She seemed taken aback by Tubs' unexpected reply.

"*Cerberus*," he repeated, never taking his eyes off the screen. "If that ship is called *Cerberus* then we go. It's the name of the ship in the stories I heard."

Zoë checked the console in front of her with initial enthusiasm. If Tubs could be proved wrong now, then maybe they could get on with their job. But her shoulders sagged as the system found nothing.

"All computers over there appear to be offline. We can't confirm anything about it, including its name."

"There must be somewhere we can just read it off her hull?" offered Dezza. Sometimes things could be solved by something as simple as looking out of the window.

She thought for a moment, brightening up. "Most 'liners I've seen in dock have it on the prow. We're heading that way so we can take a peek."

"If that name is there, we go?" pleaded Tubs.

She saw in his eyes that he was serious, and laughed. "You're really scared of an old myth?"

He looked hurt.

"Every story gets another leg in the telling of the Chinese whisper," said Dezza with a smile as he glanced down to his console and studied the scrolling read out. They would be at the bows of the derelict in no more than a few minutes. Perhaps then that would appease Tubs' fears.

Deep down he felt the nagging fear that Tubs was going to ruin it all.

*   *   *   *   *

The last few metres of the prow were twisted and scorched. A meteorite had penetrated the navigation field some time in the past and struck a glancing blow. Any further back and it might have stood a chance of compromising the hull integrity. But here nothing more than minor deck fittings had been affected.

There was no trace of the ship's name. Where it had been, the plating was scorched and twisted, then dulled over with a fine layer of silver dust that had accumulated from space. Whatever had done the damage had happened a long time ago.

"No name," said Zoë at last.

"I can see that," said Tubs, "Though I don't like it. We should go."

She turned to him angrily. "And leave this whole thing floating in space? Not likely!"

As much as he wanted to reply, to run, he could not. Deep down he realised that beneath the primordial fear that he felt, she was right. Superstition was getting in the way of the biggest payday this crew had had in over five years of ploughing the shipping lanes and beyond. Right now all he was doing was driving a wedge between their professional relationship, and their friendship.

For a moment there was an uneasy silence in the Tug, then Zoë turned to Dezza and started outlining plans to dock with the Starliner and board her to check her out. With a falling heart he realised there was nothing he could do any more to influence them. He had been sidelined. His fears had cost him their respect, and he knew that it would be hard indeed to rebuild the trust that he had had.

*　　　*　　　*　　　*　　　*

The docking signal was the only computer activity of any sort they could detect on the Starliner. A carrier signal devoid of anything meaningful, once it would have relayed instructions between vessels for an approach to the airlocks. It was a band of static that at the very least would guide them to the docking point. Aside from that, there was nothing else it could give them.

The port was on the forward third of the Starliner. Beside a row of empty bays where lifepods had once been, a larger bay allowed the Tug to circle in and align itself to secure and dock. There were two airlocks to chose from; both seemed equally as easy to approach.

Zoë never had much faith for computer control, not least because all help from the Starliner was missing. They would be coming in blind and she figured that she might as well take control herself than let the Tug's on board computer systems make a hash of it. She had never trusted a machine to do a job a human could do equally as well, if not better.

With eyes glued to a bank of monitors and a hand resting on a small manoeuvring thruster joystick, she guided the craft into place as Dezza called out distance readings to her. For more than a few minutes it seemed like they were going nowhere, then the tug rocked and a metallic grating sound reverberated through the hull. For a moment they felt a series of bumps and bangs as the docking clamps engaged, then silence as the engines powered down.

Zoë relaxed and let go of the joystick. Massaging the cramp from her hands she let out a sigh and looked though the screen to the metallic bulk not more than a foot away.

"We're in."

Dezza nodded. He brought up data on his console and read it off. "Computers all off-line on every frequency. We're going to have to pump up the airlocks manually and go through suited in case our readings on the atmosphere inside are off. We can check out the air with hand-held scanners once we're inside."

There were no prizes for the foolhardy. Without any access to internal systems, they could not be sure of exactly what they were going to find inside.

*   *   *   *   *

In the confines of the helmet, his breathing sounded dry and raspy from the air re-circulation system. Across the airlock in her cream suit, he could tell Zoë only by her slender figure, accentuated by the figure-hugging material. On her back was a pack that contained the workings of the suit, connected to the oversize helmet by a short flexible tube. It made her head look alien and huge. Catching sight of his own reflection in the mirror finish of her visor, he saw he looked equally misshapen.

"Seals show we're seated okay. Let's pump this thing open." Her voice echoed in his helmet, tinny and raspy from the tiny speaker in his ear.

He nodded and they both took up position either side of the airlock door.

"How's it looking, Tubs?" she asked.

Tubs answered, from the safety of the bridge of the Tug. "All systems good. Getting back signals from both of you and your scanning equipment."

It had been a compromise. He had not wanted to step foot inside the Starliner, so they had decided to leave him in the relative safety of a support role on the tug. It was not perfect but, under the circumstances, it seemed the best deal as Zoë had point blank refused to leave this salvage behind. In truth Dezza was inclined to agree with her, but there was always a nagging feeling of uncertainty that had been fostered by Tubs' raw fear expressed in the story he had told.

Faced with the opportunity not to step foot in that vessel, Tubs had taken it.

"When the lights go to green, release the locks," said Zoë.

Dezza nodded and turned to the panel. Three lights turned in sequence from red, to amber, then finally flickered to green. As the last one shone brightly he grasped hold of the white lever recessed into the panel and pulled. It slid easily to half way, and then he found he had to use a little more force on it. For a moment he thought it might not go, so he pushed harder. Just when he thought it was no use the lever slipped and thumped all the way to the bottom, catching him off guard.

Pain shot through his fingers. He yelped.

"What's up?" asked Tubs, his voice thick with fear.

"I just caught my hand. Nothing more."

He checked the glove of the suit. It was fine; nothing was torn. He might have a bruise on his hand come the morning. Despite the throbbing he smiled to himself. Had Tubs really been spooked by the 'bogey man' story?

"Give me a hand here if you're okay," said Zoë.

She was struggling with the release lever on the door. The Tug's door opened okay. He thought he saw a puff of silver dust jet out briefly as air levels equalised. It was probably just debris from space that had collected on the plating.

It rolled back leaving them staring face to face for the first time with the grey steel of the Starliner. He put out his hand and rested it gently on the plating. It felt just like ordinary cold steel and he wondered what it was that made Tubs really so scared.

Zoë rapped her knuckles on the plate a couple of times. Through their helmets they heard the hollow echo reverberate back. She checked her scanner.

"There's definitely some kind of atmosphere in there. However long this hulk has been floating out here hasn't made it leak its guts."

In a panel on the side they found controls for the Starliner's airlock. The lid opened easily enough, but the controls inside seemed dead. He took out a small toolkit and checked the wiring with a meter. A dial flickered on its readout.

"There's still some power but the computer control line is down. We'll have to open by hand."

They found the release mechanism and struggled with it. Unlike the well-maintained mechanism in the tug, this had been exposed to the vacuum of space for who knew how long. It was stiff and even when the locking bars finally slid out the door did not seem to want to move.

Dezza put his weight against it and heaved. Zoë added her weight too, but for a moment nothing happened. Then there was a grating and they felt something move.

"It's coming!"

The door slid a little more, and a jet of dust and gas appeared from the edge accompanied by an eerie moan.

"What was that?" came Tubs' alarmed voice.

"Just gas venting. Nothing to worry about," Zoë soothed.

With a bit of work, the door slid back in stages, revealing a black hole beyond. They switched on their helmet lights and played them over the interior. The beams cut into a scene of dirt and decay. Whether Tubs was right or wrong, their hunch about the age of the vessel held at least some truth; this had been here untouched for a long time. Maybe that was why they had not received a call? This ship had been missing for decades at least, and in the vastness of space even the largest ship was easily lost into the infinite vacuum.

Dezza remembered to take out his scanner and get a reading. Zoë's helmet lamp continued to stab through the gloom, picking out the dust-dulled passageway of the airlock level.

"Air is stale. High CO2 and some carbon monoxide too."

There was an atmosphere, of sorts, but it was more than likely that the air re-circulation system had been offline for a long time. They were going to have to keep the suits on, for now.

"What now?" Zoë's voice echoed in his helmet.

"We explore, obviously."

*   *   *   *   *

A layer of dust blanketed the floor and dulled the walls and fittings to a matt finish. More fluttered gently in the breeze from the airlock before it settled back down with a slow laziness that gave the illusion they were underwater exploring a wreck. Even in the bright glare of the helmet lights, the colours seemed muted to greys and browns.

"Gravity is lower than it should be," said Zoë, "But there seems to be enough to stop us floating off the deck."

In the ghostly glow of their helmet lights they saw tired decorations and wall paintings showing scenes from Greek mythology and exotic landscapes. There was furniture, all antique and made of solid wood. Everything was dulled and wrapped in a blanket of dust. Dezza put his gloved finger to a painting of Neptune and rubbed it across. In the light of the lights the colours became brighter and more lucid as the dirt peeled away to reveal the image underneath that might have waited decades to be seen again by a person.

"This is one hell of a cleaning job."

She ignored him. "Let's try the next deck and see what we can find. Sooner or later we should find some kind of deck plan."

They reached a set of lifts and tried the call button. Nothing happened. Retracing their steps they found a stairwell and took them down one flight. At the bottom they stopped and instinctively switched off their helmet lights. Light seeped out from around the edges of the door.

"Tubs, are you getting this?" asked Zoë.

"Yeah. I see it all right," came the hissing voice on the radio transmission. "The reactor core is throwing out some power. If the riding lights were still working, then it stands to reason that something on the inside might still work too."

Dezza looked at Zoë. "Okay, let's go."

She pushed open the door gently, and light flooded into the stairwell. It took their eyes a moment to adjust to the glare, helped by their tinted visors.

Once their eyes had adjusted, they saw that this corridor was similar to the one above. Lights burned brightly in wall mountings, though stretching away to their left they could see that not all were functioning and intermittent chunks of the corridor were still dark.

To their right the corridor opened out into the top balcony of some kind of atrium. Here the lights were dimmed and allowed a view out through the arched clear roof of the starscape that embraced the silent Starliner. Hampered by their helmets they could only lean back and catch small glimpses, but it was enough to tell them that it must have once been spectacular.

Tiny lights marked the walkway around the atrium. Over the safety rail they could see at least a dozen similar such balconies running around from each of the decks that intersected here. At the bottom stretched out a series of features that looked as if they may have once contained exotic plants and trees. Now in the stale air of the Starliner they were little more than husks, long since dead.

Finding a grand staircase, they descended slowly step by step. There was more debris here, with the floor covered in piles of dirt that may have once been rotting vegetation. Fittings were tinged black with a kind of powdery mildew, as if damp had once been thick in the air.

"This is weird."

At the sound of Zoë's voice, Dezza looked around. She stood in the middle of the grand staircase checking her scanner.

"What?"

"Air levels. Oxygen levels are up and carbon monoxide is well down. There must be local pockets on the ship of good and bad air. Maybe because the air isn't circulating?"

He looked over the scanner too, checking its readings.

"You're right. Breathable. No toxic stuff either."

It was strange. Usually over time the air inside any abandoned vessel would even out. Of course, seeing was believing and the scanner was telling them the air in here was different to the air at the airlock level.

She looked up at him. "Want to give it a go?"

He could almost imagine her grin behind the mirror of her visor.

"Yeah, why not?"

Taking a deep breath he shut off the re-circulation of his suit on his wrist pad then reached up and unlocked his visor. He heard the hiss as air equalised and felt the cold tinge of the Starliner's atmosphere on his naked face for the first time.

"Are you mad?!" hissed Tubs' voice over the radio.

He ignored him. He had done this a hundred times before aboard derelicts, but they had always been those recently adrift with known systems failures. This was almost an alien vessel.

Exhaling slowly, he saw his breath curl in vapour into the air. He had not realised quite how cold it was on board. Then the moment of truth. Breathing through his nose he inhaled slowly. The air smelt musty and sharp. There were some harsh chemical traces, but the scanner had shown all of these to be benign.

"Well?" asked Zoë at last.

He realised he had been concentrating on the smell and taste of the air for more than a few seconds. He contorted his face up and opened his eyes wide.

"I can't breathe!" he gasped.

Zoë rushed forward, and he heard Tubs cursing on the radio before his face creased into a grin. He laughed.

"Got you going for a moment! No, the air's okay if a little old."

"Shit. Don't do that!" said Tubs.

"Just winding you up," he replied with a grin. Maybe it was about time that one of them brought some humour to this vessel.

Gingerly, Zoë shut off her suit re-circulation and cranked up her visor to test the air. She seemed happy with it, and her breath curled into the frigid air. "We'll have to keep a good eye on the scanners for now but this should let us explore for a lot longer."

They resumed their descent, heading for the lowest level and the floor of the atrium.

*   *   *   *   *

The deck plan had been found quite by chance. At the base of the staircase was a covered hall with wooden panelling and antique mahogany sofas with stuffing that had long since perished in the formerly humid atmosphere. Several lift doors lined up, shut, with the elevator indicators showing them on other floors. In the centre was a mahogany lectern on top of which was laid out an enamel stylised map of the decks.

Zoë cleaned the dirt from the display, rubbing hard until the black tarnish flaked off. The scanners had shown inconclusive readings on this muck, but it did not flag it as harmful. Whatever it was, it had certainly colonised the Starliner. Underneath, the enamel fascia was yellowed with age, but still perfectly readable.

"Result! Deck plan."

She hunched over it as Dezza stood by her side.

"We're here," she pointed, "slap bang in the middle of the passenger areas it seems. There's a shopping mall stretching off behind us, and decks below with gyms and cinemas, and passenger cabins under that."

"What about engineering?"

They scanned the bottom of the panel, rubbing off thick black muck to reveal the enamel underneath.

"Level underneath that is marked 'crew only'. I guess that's the best place to start. Once we get to the engineering levels we need to trace back and find the main reactor room. The Tug's scanners showed at least one still online, so we might be able to juice up some of the other systems and make this crate a little more spaceworthy for the voyage home."

"I hate to rain on your party," came Tubs' sulky voice, "But with a misaligned drive core, we are presently going nowhere."

Zoë and Dezza looked at each other. They had forgotten this in their haste to explore.

"How long will it take to fix so we can tow?"

"Twelve hours," Tubs replied after a pause.

"Let us know when you're done, and keep a radio link handy just in case."

She knew that Tubs would seize the opportunity to get away from watching their progress through the Starliner, and go and hide in the Tug's engine room where he felt happiest. She waited until he had cleared the line then flicked off the send unit of her radio. Dezza followed her lead.

"What's up?" he asked as soon as his radio was off.

"There's something I noticed that I didn't want Tubs to know."

She rubbed at the top of the enamel panel. Layers of muck flaked off, and some more writing came clear in ornate gold leaf copperplate.

"It tells us what this hulk is called."

He leant closer, trying to make out the words that were stylised within scrolls and artwork. Finally it was clear and they both stepped back.

"*Cerberus*," she muttered.

"Do you think it is just coincidence?"

"I hope so. If it's anything like other stories Astros tell each other they get more bizarre every time they are told. I don't like to believe in Tubs' hocus-pocus, but for now let's just keep this to ourselves."

"Agreed."

It was still hard to shelve the idea that Tubs had guessed the name correct first time. What grains of truth might there really be hidden away deep within the urban myth?

*   *   *   *   *

To reach the engineering spaces, they had to go down to below the passenger decks; of which there were at least half a dozen.

The grand staircase went no lower, so they turned their attention to the lifts.

"Maybe we can get down the shafts? There must be a maintenance access point," suggested Zoë.

Dezza jabbed a call button with a finger. He had not expected it to work, but was surprised when a light flickered on around the button and a whine of machinery somewhere kicked in.

"What did you do?" she asked.

"I pressed the button. It seems the power is still on."

She looked at the dim lights.

"Well, I suppose some things still have to work if the reactor is churning some power out. At least we can ride it down as far as it goes."

The lift did not take long to arrive. The indicator above showed it rising only a few floors to reach their level before the motor whine cut out. There was a moment's pause as the carriage levelled out before the doors vibrated, and stopped.

"Something must have jammed."

He tried the doors. They were unlocked but seemed caught on something inside. He heaved and they moved a little.

"Might be seized. Lack of lubricant," he grunted.

With one final shove the door shuddered open. Zoë gasped and stepped back. Shielded by the door, Dezza did not see what she had seen. Before he could ask her, the scanner started blipping.

"Bad air!" he gasped, realising the significance. Whatever the atmosphere was like on lower decks, the lift had brought it up and it had flowed out as soon as the doors opened.

Fumbling for his helmet he locked the latches in place and turned the air re-circulation system back on. Though his visor he saw that Zoë had done the same.

"We're going to have to watch out for that," he said.

Zoë ignored him, staring into the lift.

"What is it?" he asked, sensing something was wrong.

Turning, he saw what she was staring at. He stepped back, feeling his heart pound in shock.

"Shit!"

The interior of the lift had been shredded. Panels hung from shattered wires and burn marks showed where shorted electrics had ignited. Two bodies lay amidst the debris, no more than skeletons with tattered remnants of clothes clinging to their mottled bones.

Recovering from his surprise he ventured forward and moved one of the bodies. Metal glinted beneath bone. He moved it aside to reveal a gun, its power pack long since discharged.

"They've been here a long time," he heard himself say slowly, sliding the gun back.

"Suddenly I'm left wondering about Tubs' story," said Zoë.

He turned to her and held out his hand. She took hold of it tightly.

"We've seen worse than eighty year old corpses. Is it going to make you want to leave this salvage behind?"

She thought for a moment. "No."

Resolved to bring the Starliner back onto the shipping routes and to claim it as salvage, they entered the devastated lift and prepared to ride it down to the lower decks, uncertain exactly of what they might find down there.

*   *   *   *   *

Tubs' afternoon had started straightforwardly.

Upon getting the nod to work on the drive core, he quickly left the bridge and headed along the service corridors to the place where he felt happier: in the machinery spaces. Heeding Zoë's advice, he flicked on a communications channel on the machinery console and tuned it to the frequencies they were using. Turning the volume down, he left it to run in the background then settled down by the open panel to inspect the damage.

It seemed worse than he feared. The core was severely misaligned and it was actually a surprise that it had not failed sooner. He cursed himself for not pushing harder at their stopover three months previously to stay a few days longer for engine repairs. But Zoë had been forceful; there were places she wanted to go and things she wanted to do in the name of the pursuit of money. That seemed to be all it ever was with her: lust for money. Dezza, of course, just went along with her. If there ever were a casting vote in his hands, then nine times out of ten it would be cast in Zoë's favour.

He sulked, throwing himself into the task. All he had to do was patch it up enough to make one final jump back onto the shipping lanes, then on to the nearest spaceport. Of course, she would insist on towing the massive derelict along. In theory it should not make much difference. Once the Rösenbridge was open, mass was not important - just drop in and ride the tube. It was just actuating an accurate Rösenbridge that was the problem. With a misaligned core they might be left drifting light years from anywhere with nothing but an ion drive that would take generations to take them anywhere meaningful.

Buzzers wailed on the panel above him. He banged his head extricating himself from within the open panel. Cursing, he scanned across the controls. Several LEDs blipped in time to the buzzers showing energy fluctuations in the inlet manifolds for the core.

At first he thought it might be a glitch in the electronics, possibly disturbed when he had dug about behind the panel, but a diagnostic routine showed him that the faults were real this time. Even as he watched gauges swung drunkenly back and forth as power levels spiked.

Working quickly, he set up a containment field around the core but he knew it would not hold for more than eight hours. The rogue interference was persistent.

He traced the energy flows back along the panels and tried to work out where the power spike was coming from. Readouts showed it was not the secondary reactor; that was running on minimal standby power and its gauges read normal. One by one he worked through each system until he found the culprit. On the final console panel he saw a schematic that showed that power was spiking through the docking link. For a moment he refused to believe it. Hadn't Zoë said the Starliner's power was offline?

He checked the panel again. Diagnostics showed the docking link that had been inert when the tug had shouldered up to the airlock was now fluctuating power wildly. The only way to stop it would be to disconnect from the hatch and push off a little into space. That would fix the fluctuations, but it would also leave his two shipmates stranded on the derelict.

27

He cursed and reached for the radio. He had to call them back – only then could they break free and sever the errant connection.

Turning up the volume, he realised with a start that they had been trying to raise him for some time. A voice, earnest and increasingly desperate, was trying to call him.

"Tubs! Are you there? Please respond, over."

He recognised it as Zoë's businesslike voice. But what was that coming through around the edges? Her voice wavered; it almost seemed to Tubs as if she was scared.

"What is it?" he responded at last and instantly heard the relief evident in her voice.

"Tubs. Am I glad to hear your voice. We need you down here, now."

He felt the fingers of fear creeping over his body, and the sweat began to prickle on his back. Where was Dezza's voice? All over again he felt the rising wall of fear that he had felt the moment they had found the Starliner adrift, and his mind cast back to the stories he had heard in more than a dozen space ports. No! It could not have been real; he kept trying to assure himself. But they felt so much like false assurances.

"What's up?" he ventured, trying to hide the unease he felt.

"The structure, down just above the engineering spaces, it's failed. We didn't know it was unsound to this extent. Dezza went through. I can get him on a local low power band but it seems that most of the communications on his suit are damaged and he can only just talk with me. I'm going to need some help to get him out of here."

The reality hit Tubs, and nursed the fears that had made him more than willing to stay behind on the Tug in the first place.

"You want me to go out there? Into that, *thing*?"

"Come on Tubs. We need you. Dezza's hurt. I can't get him out on my own."

Caught between the rock and a hard place. He thought about the spiking power link. He had to get them back as fast as possible. Until they were aboard, there was no way he could get the Tug disconnected to stop that stress on the core.

"There is one thing you should know," he said, "The docking link went live and started spiking the systems. It's putting the core into a state of flux and setting up a resonance pattern. We have to detach or it will fail the drive core."

He knew Zoë would have to consider the news. There were many things that she would find a habit of brushing aside when it suited. But this? Even she knew the implications.

Set up a resonant frequency on a damaged and misaligned drive core and the damage gets worse quicker and quicker until the core fails. If they lost the core, there was no way back to the shipping lanes. Worse still, if it suffered integrity failure of its quo-field then it could destroy the Tug in the process.

"How long have we got?" she asked.

"Eight hours at the absolute most. In truth I'd rather detach within a safety margin of six."

"Then we have to get Dezza out now. I'll give you directions to get down here while you're suiting up. It isn't far."

He felt himself feel numb at the thought; he had been left with no choice but to confront his fears and venture out into the Starliner.

*   *   *   *   *

Zoë and Dezza took the lift down as far as it would go, ignoring the skeletons at their feet. Perhaps there had been a mass panic? With only so many lifepods available and maybe with life support going offline, the darkest of human nature may have kicked in. There was likely a reasonable explanation for the bodies. It was hard to ignore though that the pattern of damage suggested it had happened from outside.

With shredded panels on three sides, the inside of the doors were strangely undamaged, indicating that they had been open at the time whatever had killed those two on the floor and trashed the interior had occurred.

When the lift reached the bottom floor there was a moment's pause before the doors rumbled open. They strained to see through the darkness.

Dezza looked down at the blipping lights on his scanner. "The atmosphere isn't looking too good. High carbon monoxide, and a few other nasties. They may be coolant gases leached up from engineering; I'm not entirely sure. The scan is showing compounds I've never heard of before."

He flicked on his helmet light, and the beam stabbed out into the darkness. Bulkheads and decks showed in the beam, but fittings and panels hung loose, battered and distorted by ancient gunfire. Debris lay thick on the floor, with evidence of intense fires and burning. There had been intense fighting here; with small arms damage in evidence, but it had been a long time ago. Dust had settled over everything in a thin undisturbed layer that muted the destruction.

"Explosives and gunfire," said Zoë.

Dezza nodded. "Looks like fires too, probably cooked off from grenades. We're going to have to go carefully."

Zoë gingerly stepped over the bodies and out of the lift, flicking on her helmet beam.

"I think we can say we've found where those two came from," she said, looking back at the skeletons.

Dezza followed slowly but said nothing. He wondered whether the decks above might have been the scene of similar fights. What could have been the reason?

Broken and bent metal crunched underfoot. In some places, explosive rounds had eaten deep into plating and ripped holes through into adjacent rooms, even to the deck below. They stopped and shone a light down through one hole in the floor. The beam disappeared into a hazy mist. Ghostly shapes of machinery and equipment coalesced only faintly beyond broken walkways. The scanner showed that there was moisture in the air, as well as a cocktail of other chemicals.

"That's certainly where we need to head," said Zoë, "It looks like the first level of the engineering spaces."

"There must be an access staircase somewhere."

"It could be hard to find in all this mess."

"We'll manage."

It happened so fast; neither realised before it was too late. The deck shuddered beneath them, throwing them both to one side.

Scrabbling for handholds, Zoë's gloved hand found a twisted plate that held. Dezza's hands grasped frantically at material that held briefly before breaking apart, annihilated by a firefight in the distant past.

They felt the vibrations of rending steel as much as they heard the dull bass rumble. The floor sagged, then fell through. Dezza slid with it. From her suit radio she heard a cry, then a thump and a staccato of static as he hit the deck somewhere in the gloom below.

"Dezza! Are you okay?" she heard herself gasp into the radio as she worked to haul herself back onto firm deck plates.

"Dezza?" she asked again.

She turned and surveyed the corridor. Some of the deck was much weaker than it had looked. Damaged by small arms fire, it had given up under their combined weight and fallen through. She cursed herself for not being more careful. With nearly a decade of deep space salvage experience behind her, she should have known better. It seemed the excitement of a big pay day coupled with Tubs' unsettling fears had got to them a little and made them careless.

Bracing herself in case the metalwork gave further, she crept along the floor to the broken edge and peered over. Turning her helmet beam to full she studied the ghostly shapes of machinery through the humid mist that swirled now in the turbulence that had been set up.

It took her only a moment to see where Dezza had landed. His white suit shone against the grey backdrop.

"Dezza!"

Relief washed over her as she saw him move and sit upright. He was lucky to have not landed square on something too sharp.

Static hissed on the radio in several bursts. Dezza was waving to her. Was there a problem with his suit? Finally, a weak voice came across over the static.

"Zoë, copy?"

"Dezza!" she called back, relief awash in her voice.

"That was close, but the suit communicator is broken. All that seems to work is the short band. As long as I have line of sight I can talk to you. All the other systems appear to be working okay;

I can still breath," he said, surprisingly cool and calm considering his near miss.

"It's going to be tough getting you out of there. I'm going to call Tubs down here to help."

"He won't like that."

"Blast his superstitious mumbo-jumbo. He's going to have to get down here if he ever wants us off this hulk."

* * * * *

Tubs muttered expletives as he waited for the airlock to cycle. There was an atmosphere on the Starliner he knew, but Zoë had warned that for some as yet unknown reason it was variable and they did not want to contaminate the Tug's environment.

Lights pinged to green and he shouldered aside the hatch and switched on his helmet lamp. His heart rate notched up as the beam stabbed into the darkness, picking out the dusty corridor. Zoë had been pretty precise with her instructions, but he could see their footprints left in the accumulated dust. All he had to do was follow the trail.

The light at the bottom of the stairwell was unnerving. It was not right, he thought, for a derelict to still have lights working like this. It gave him a funny feeling that the original occupants had not quite left yet. He felt his heart in his throat as he glanced nervously around, half expecting to see people flitting at the periphery of his vision, but there were none. What was worse? Imagining people or there actually being people? He tried not to think about it.

The atrium felt odd when he reached it. So much open space with stars visible through the canopy above. He did not like it. Following the trail, he hurried down the grand staircase. It was easy enough to move around in the suit and it was a great help that the Starliner's gravity field generators still seemed to be working. He wondered how long could a fusion reactor continue running at minimal power with no overseeing? They usually required round the clock supervision, but it was conceivable that if no faults occurred, and with a plentiful supply of fuel, they could keep running unhindered for decades.

He pressed the elevator call button and felt the sweat in his suit as the elevator indicator began moving. Again he heard the little voice in his mind telling him this was not right. What would be in the lift when it arrived?

As it turned out, absolutely nothing. The car that arrived was not the one the others had used. He could tell by the tracks. Inside, its lights were on. He reeled back in fear as he caught sight of movement, then cursed himself when he realised that it was just his own reflection in the mirrored wall at the rear. With his visor down and his oversized helmet, he looked almost like an alien.

He jabbed the button. It took a moment for the doors to close. Not liking the idea of having his back to the door, he moved to the back, and waited.

As the doors slid shut his heart leapt in fear. He thought he saw something move, over there in the shadows behind the husks of long gone vegetation on the ground level of the atrium. It was just a quick glance and one that left him uncertain that he really saw it at all. Too late now as the lift doors sealed themselves shut.

A rasping noise filled him with even more dread until he realised it was only the sound of his own breathing echoing within the helmet. He chastised himself again for letting his fears get the better of him. He tried to think that Zoë and Dezza's scoffing at his tale had been with reason, and that he was working himself up over nothing. But it was hard to shake the subconscious fears running amok through his mind.

The lights in the elevator flickered as it juddered to a halt. A loose connection somewhere, he thought, trying to reassure himself. The derelict Starliner must be riddled with loose connections and blown circuits. It was still unnerving to him though in his present state.

Strangely, the corridor he emerged on was well lit. This was not how Zoë had described it. The floor was dusty, and when he looked along the line of elevator doors he saw that there were no footprints.

"Shit!" he exclaimed under his breath, "Wrong deck."

Shuffling back inside the elevator car, the flickering was getting worse. He fancied he could almost hear the sound of circuits shorting under the strain of their first use in almost a century. He jabbed at a button, expecting the doors to close and the car to ride down one more level.

Nothing happened.

He jabbed again, this time a little harder. The lights on the panel flickered once, then died. The carriage lights came back on, somewhat brighter but it was clear that something in the old electronics had finally expired.

Getting back out of the car he tried the call button in the corridor, hoping that another car would come and he could use that. Nothing happened. With a sinking feeling, he realised the controls on this deck had shorted out. The elevators were useless; he would have to find another way.

Trying to calm his fear, he began searching the corridor. There had to be a staircase somewhere close by. There usually was one near elevators in case of emergencies.

The corridor was well lit for maybe twenty metres. After that the lights had failed for another twenty before coming back on again. He could see the corridor going on and on into the distance. Looking in the other direction more of the lights were out in the same way.

"Try and keep to the light, for now," he muttered to himself, and headed out, checking doorhandles as he went.

Most were locked, and he guessed from their brass panels that they were most likely passenger cabins. The electronic locks were all latched into the secure position. Probably it was another circuit that had failed at some time. They were of no concern now. If Zoë's scheme to salvage the Starliner worked, then some-one else at a space port could go through them.

One door opened into a linen closet with shelves of sheets and towels piled high dulled by dust. How strange it felt to be exploring this place. It felt more like any hotel on Earth than a floating derelict in deep space.

All the other doors as far as the dark patch were locked. He plucked up the courage to move on and reached for his helmet light. Its beam flickered a moment then grew a little brighter. He tapped its controls and saw with a sinking feeling that battery power was low. Had he forgotten to charge it after last time he used it? He didn't tend to go outside so often and it was a while since he could remember using it. He turned it off, mindful that he would need what was left of the charge to get him back to the Tug. This was only twenty metres of darkness; he was sure he could cope with that.

It was strange just how quickly the darkness enveloped the walls and the floor. He could see the lights ahead of him, and if he looked over his shoulder the lights behind him too. But here without the aid of his helmet light it was hard to see much. There would be doors, somewhere, but he did not feel like groping in the dark.

He could feel the fear rising in him, like a panic attack about to happen. He could not go on. Fumbling for his suit radio he called through to Zoë.

"I've got out on the wrong deck. The elevator panel failed. Can you send a car up for me?"

He was relieved to hear Zoë's voice come over the static.

"Tubs? You sound awful. Where are you?"

"Deck above you I think."

Static hissed loudly in his ear and he grimaced. He could hear her voice, but it was faint and he could not make it out.

"Say again? You're breaking up," he interrupted.

Her voice came again, but it was even more muffled by static and sounded squelchy. He checked the radio power, thinking he might have forgotten to charge that too, but the meter showed it was nearly full.

In the darkness, a light flickered and from the corner of his eye he saw something moving. Wheeling around, something tapped against him. He screamed as his fear overwhelmed him.

*   *   *   *   *

Zoë heard the scream through the static.

"Tubs! Answer me!"

The scream had ended as fast as it had begun. Now there was nothing. She tried again but there was only static.

"What's happened?" asked Dezza on the short-range channel.

"Something's up with Tubs. I heard a scream on the radio and now he's not answering."

"He's been jumpy since we talked about boarding this thing. Probably scared himself with his own shadow."

"I ought to go find him. He sounded serious. Can you hold on?"

"Sure. I'll bide my time exploring down here. I'll just follow the conduit towards the reactor and see what's cooking in there. Scanner readings show that from the radiation it can't be too far from here."

"Okay. Just stay close to here so I can get you out as soon as I've got Tubs."

Tubs had said that he thought he was on the deck above. Moving back to the elevators she looked up at the indicators. Sure enough, one of the cars was showing where he had reckoned he was.

She used the car that she and Dezza had ridden down in. If Tubs' comments on electrical faults were true, then at least she knew that this one worked.

It took only a few seconds for the car to reach the next floor. She ignored the two skeletons at her feet; she would have to figure out a way to get Tubs past them. As the doors slid open she saw the lights were on here. She flicked off her helmet light and stepped out.

She could not see him, but a trail of footsteps in the dust told her where he had been. Glancing into his open elevator, she saw that the electronics were fried.

She tried calling him on the radio, but there was nothing but background static. Did he have a radio problem? His footsteps led towards a patch corridor where the lights were out. From the look of the trail he had been trying the doors on the way.

A light flickered momentarily and she thought she saw him.

"Tubs?"

The radio channel remained silent. The light flickered again and she saw him stood motionless, shoulders hunched.

"Tubs, don't screw around with me."

She flicked on her helmet light and the beam stabbed out. It was Tubs. She walked the last few metres, muttering to herself, and grabbed his arm.

His arm twisted and he floated round, rising a little off the floor. She gasped before she realised that she too was rising off the floor. Something moved at the edge of the beam. She looked over so the beam picked it out. A small, carved wooden ornament hung in the air, rotating in the patch of zero gravity; the gravity generators must have failed in this section of corridor.

"Tubs?" she repeated again in earnest. She felt her heart rate notch up and knew something was wrong. Fear clawed her mind.

Checking Tubs' suit readouts, she realised that he must have blundered into the floating ornament in the dark, and died of a heart attack. He had never had time to realise that it was nothing more than another failed circuit on the Starliner. She refused to believe he could be dead and tried the readings all over again. Maybe the suit was malfunctioning? She felt for a pulse, but the suits fabric made it almost impossible.

"Shit, Tubs, how could you be so spooked?" she muttered, and batted the ornament away.

It floated on eerily until it passed into the light and fell like a stone to the dusty carpet. How long had it hovered because of failed circuits before Tubs had arrived? No-one would know.

She tried the radio again before realising that Dezza could not answer. "Calm down, Zoë," she told herself trying to regulate her breathing, "Think logically."

Clinging on to the hope that Tubs might be merely unconscious she knew she had to get him back to the lift, and find Dezza for his help. It proved difficult to get Tubs to the lift. As soon as she reached the working gravity field his body fell like a stone and she had to drag him the rest of the way. It took longer than she thought, but finally they made it and she rode the elevator back down.

The doors clattered open and she recoiled in shock. The beam from Dezza's helmet light stabbed into the lift as he pushed in.

"Jesus! You scared me," she said angrily.

"We have to go," he said over the static of the short range link.

He punched the button for the atrium level and the doors slid shut behind him. For the first time he saw Tubs' body on the floor and looked taken aback.

"What happened?"

"He freaked out because of a gravity failure. His suit readouts are dead; we need to get him back for medical aid."

He knelt at Tubs' side as the elevator began to rock on the climb to the upper decks. Gingerly checking the readouts he reset the suit's controls, but each time Zoë saw the readouts flatline. Finally he shook his head and stood up.

"There's nothing we can do."

"Of course there is," she pleaded, "We can't just leave him."

"We can come back."

"Back?" she said, taken aback, "What do you mean? Why do we have to leave?"

"Problems in the engine spaces."

"What do you mean?"

"I think I found the reason the *Cerberus* is lying here derelict. We have to leave *now*."

She stood her ground. "I'm not leaving Tubs. He comes with us."

Dezza held her suit with a tightness that almost began to scare her. She made to protest, but his voice was calm on the radio channel. "Look, we can't help Tubs but we can help ourselves. There's something on this ship."

She laughed, but he continued stubbornly.

If I'm wrong – and I hope I am – we can come back for Tubs. But we have to move fast, and without a stretcher we are going to struggle bringing him along. Trust me – I don't want to leave a member of the crew any more than you do."

She looked at his helmet. All she could see was the mirror reflection of herself. But she knew from his tone of voice that he was serious. She sighed and her shoulders drooped. "Okay. But we *are* coming back for Tubs."

*   *   *   *   *

In the deck below Dezza had decided to use the time to look around. There was no sense in wasting any just because Tubs had got scared.

Through the mist in the engineering spaces he watched as Zoë's helmet light dipped then disappeared. Damn that Tubs! Well, he had a little time to explore at least, and that was something they were going to have to do anyway.

The scanner showed him that the levels and spread of radiation were consistent with the running fusion reactor core being at most fifty metres away. That wasn't far. Getting his bearings, he used his light to cut a beam along the walkway. Looking over the edge, he saw that the space went down a whole lot further than his helmet light could penetrate; he was lucky the deck had given way only where it had.

The mist was thick down here. From the scanner's readouts it was high in moisture and a whole lot of other weird chemistry. He suspected that some of it could have been a coolant leak from the reactor that had built up over time, but the radiation levels did not particularly support that theory.

The walkway came to a bulkhead. There was a hatch through which was shut, and the panel at the side glowed dimly. It rolled upwards effortlessly at the touch of a button and he stepped though into the light of the next compartment.

Blinking in the sudden brightness he flicked off the helmet light and waited for his eyes to adjust. There was no misting in this compartment, and it felt somewhat warmer. He could feel the air temperature change through the material of his suit. The scanner showed that the air in here was breathable again, free of any of the toxic compounds that had saturated the last deck. Carefully he turned off the re-circulation system in his suit and popped open the visor for a sniff.

It smelt a little sweet; there were traces of machine oil, and a little ozone – he hated that smell. Nothing to worry about. At least this would save suit power whilst he was investigating. He wished that he could talk to Zoë, but the suit communications were still down.

In the centre of the compartment were three huge toroidal structures: the fusion reactor cores that would provide the power for the Starliner. Two were dark and inactive, but the third glowed a deep shade of purple.

The panels told him there was systematic damage to several systems. Some-one had tried to smash up the controls. Why would anyone want to do that, he wondered?

The computer terminal showed blank; the main system was offline. He noticed the panels alongside had been damaged, gouged by a blunt instrument – maybe an axe. Wires hung in a shorn loom, though on closer inspection the loom had pulled apart at a connector instead of shearing through. Whoever had tried to disable it had been in too much of a hurry to do a thorough job.

Leaning down he tested the connections with the probe from his scanner. There was still live power on the line. A thought occurred to him, and he grinned. What if he just connected it back up? It was worth a try. Lining up the connectors, he blew off the dirt and pushed them together.

Nothing happened.

"Damn. Something else must be wrong," he muttered.

He wondered what it could be before noticing the screen had a blinking cursor at the top.

"Crashed out." He scanned along the panel.

Here the axe had been at work gouging into the fascia, but the damage seemed superficial. He found the switches he needed and flicked them one by one. The screen lit up and various logos appeared for a shipping line he had never heard of. He felt a rise of excitement; the system was booting.

Whilst he waited he looked over some of the other panels. Some were so badly damaged that he could not even tell what they were for, whilst others seemed to have been simply switched off. Finding the controls for the Starliner's power grid, he flicked open the relays and noted as lights blipped on across a schematic board. A red warning light told him there was an overload on the available power and he fiddled with the adjacent console for the one still running reactor.

He smiled – he was enjoying this. Maybe they could start up enough systems that they wouldn't need to tow. Maybe the Starliner could make the jump herself.

Upping the power transfer, he heard the steady throb as the reactor stepped up from minimal power after decades of running almost on standby. It was working!

"System ready," said a stilted feminine voice.

He spun around in shock at the sound of the woman's voice. Adrenaline pumped. For a moment he could not place where it might have come from, then he realised it was the computer's voice unit and breathed a sigh of relief.

"Hey, HAL, how's it going?" he said.

"Unknown order, repeat," replied the computer in an accent that sounded old and archaic.

He ignored the voice and typed quickly on the keyboard. It was easier than trying to hold down a conversation that seemed so eerie on a floating derelict.

Bringing up the log, he saw that the last official entry was nearly ninety years ago. So Tubs had guessed right on the timeline. Mostly it was mundane, but as he read he noticed that there were other entries, made both by the crew and by the computer's automated recording system. File after file rolled onto the screen. The more he read, the more concerned he grew.

The crew had sabotaged the ship before they had tried to make a break in the lifepods, but it had not quite been an act of madness. The logs talked about a Stellar fog that the Starliner had passed through no more than twelve hours previous. It seemed to have knocked them from the Rösenbridge. Before they could re-attempt the jump, the crew had become convinced that the fog had contaminated the electrical systems with *something*.

He read the description, then reread it. It almost didn't make sense, but the patterns of damage on the Starliner told him that the crew had certainly believed it.

They had encountered some kind of entity. It had entered the systems and begun somehow killing the passengers.

"Oh shit," he whispered.

The myth was true.

At the reactor panel he tried to shut down the systems he had started up. The crew had almost succeeded. Turn off all the systems and the entity would die, the logs said. They had almost managed it. Forced into some kind of hibernation, the Starliner had drifted for nearly ninety years with *something* sleeping within it.

They had to get away now.

The panel would not respond. No matter what he pressed, the reactor kept on running. Lights flickered across other consoles as system after system began to wake up. How was the Starliner suddenly able to power up things that had been off-line for decades? Then it hit him: the computer!

He returned to the computer panel. How did it all switch off? He remembered the connector he had pressed home and leant underneath to pull it apart.

"Intruder's detected. Despatch security to engineering to apprehend."

He reeled back before he could pull the plug with the words spoken with absolute calm by the female voice. It filled him with a feeling of unease, and he panicked.

"Oh shit!" he hissed, and ran.

He found a stairwell and used it. He knew he had to get up to meet Zoë, and fast. The stairs were well lit and the first doorway brought him out into the corridor in which the floor had given way. The lights were still out, but his helmet light illuminated the way. He almost forgot about the foul air until his scanner started blipping in warning. Stopping only to slam shut the visor; he powered up the suit's re-circulation system as he ran.

At the elevators, all doors were shut but one showed as starting to descend from the floor above. Was this Zoë? It had to be; though he wondered about how much substance there was in the computer's threats. He knew he had no time to hesitate, and must take a risk. He waited for the doors to open then piled into the car.

*   *   *   *   *

Lights were on all over the ship as they hurried back up the grand staircase in the atrium. Through the canopy above they could see more running and navigation lights blinking on. The ship was powering up. They paused only a moment as the sound of klaxons began to wail.

What the hell is that?" demanded Zoë.

Before Dezza could say anything a calm female voice began calling out in a pre-recorded loop.   "Intruder alert. Despatch security to decks C to G."

"Security?"

Dezza pushed her on. "I don't think we should wait to find out."

The airlock corridor was bright with lights when they arrived and the airlock door stood ajar. They paused in the corridor, uncertain of what to expect inside.

"Tubs when he came to find us?" asked Zoë.

"I'd like to think so," Dezza replied.

They slipped through the opening and pulled it shut behind them, sealing the levers as quickly as they could. In the brilliant whiteness of the airlock, lights were flashing. Impatiently they waited for the air to cycle, then stripped off their helmets.

"What's going on?"

"The core," replied Zoë after thinking a moment, "Tubs said it was heading out of alignment because of a power spike on the docking link."

The colour drained from their faces as they realised the significance. Hurrying through the Tug, they headed straight to the bridge, still in their suits; there was no time to change. They leapt behind the consoles and Zoë keyed on the computer.

"Power spiking – Tubs was right."

"Detaching now."

The Tug rocked and more warning lights blipped across consoles.

"Clamps won't let go."

Dezza punched up the ion drive.

"They will with a bit of brute force."

"That could compromise the hull!" wailed Zoë.

"Would you rather just sit here and wait for the core to fail?" asked Dezza in a cool and calm voice.

She gave it a moment's thought. "Do it."

The Tug shuddered as the drive power built up. On monitors, the view of the airlock showed up as glowing orange as the ion particle stream from the exhaust cones bounced off the Starliner's hull.

Then, with a rending of metal, the stanchions broke free and the Tug jerked out into space.

Warning lights and buzzers wound down, one by one. Checking off on the readouts it was clear that the core was stabilising now.

They both watched the receding bulk of the Starliner through the screen.

"What now?" asked Zoë.

Before he could answer, the Starliner appeared to flicker for a moment, then disappear in a bright flash. Gauges on consoles blipped and buzzers squawked again briefly before returning to normal.

"Rösenbridge jump," said Dezza slowly, almost unable to believe the readouts on his screen.

"You mean the Starliner just made a jump on its own? Where to?"

"I don't know."

"What about Tubs? We never went back for Tubs."

"We did all we could."

"But Tubs...?" she stammered. A tear rolled from the corner of her eye. "No-one is ever going to believe this happened. They're going to blame us for not going back for him."

"That is, if we can get back to civilisation any time this month," said Dezza, "We still have a drive core to realign or we are going nowhere. We just lost Tubs and the biggest pay-day we could have ever had."

Without waiting for her answer he slipped from his chair and walked off the bridge.

"I'm going to change," he called back, "This suit still stinks of that Starliner."

"What do you think that was?" asked Zoë tearfully.

Dezza thought for a moment.

"I think," he said at last, "We don't ever want to know."

*   *   *   *   *

It was a slow and painful limp to get the Tug back to the shipping lanes. Repairing the core was not easy; much damage had been done. Even then, it had survived one more jump before failing once more, leaving them ten days' journey short of the closest base even if they pushed the ion drive to its maximum.

When they returned, no-one would believe their story. For the most part, people seemed more concerned with the disappearance of Tubs. What had they done with him? The awkward questions kept coming, and none would listen to the answers they were given.

There was an inquiry, of course. But inquiries are vague bureaucratic entities that boast much and achieve very little. Of evidence, there was not a lot. In the end they were acquitted because of lack of anything substantial the inquiry could use, but the stigma remained. In many peoples' eyes, acquittal through lack of evidence counted almost as badly as guilt.

With the help of media's sensationalising, it no longer mattered what truth there was, but rather what spin the news feeds could put on it to sell more copy.

All eyes in the bar swivelled to watch as Dezza entered. It happened every time; he had almost become used to it.

A snigger went up from one corner. A group of Astros pointed and whispered amongst themselves. He chose to ignore them, and bought his drink in silence before finding an empty table in the corner.

It had been over a year since he had last dared tell anyone his story. It was a regret that he had ever mentioned what he had seen out in deep space; he should have known that no-one would have believed him. Ridiculed and ostracised as a fantasist, the story he had told in good faith when he had returned from deep space had haunted him like a bad penny.

"Hey, ghost boy!" came a shout from somewhere in the bar. A roar of laughter followed it.

He ignored it. In time they would grow bored and move on to other things, he thought.

"Hey, what's the matter? Did the monsters make you deaf too?" came the call again, this time closer.

He gripped his glass lightly, sipping from the foam of the beer as he tried to soothe the rage he felt inside.

"Strong silent type?" came the voice, this time from right behind him. He heard the sneer in the tone. Big man on the block, trying to play it up and look macho in front of his friends.

"Piss off," Dezza mumbled into his glass, loud enough for the man to hear.

"They say you make things up. The story is that you murdered your partner and made up ghost stories to excuse yourself."

The comment struck a nerve; it was too much for him to ignore. He whipped around and punched the man square in the face. He felt the sharp pain on his knuckles, but had the satisfaction of seeing the man fall like a stone.

The bar went silent. Take out the leader of the bullies, and the others all fall into line.

"Anyone else want to try and insult me?" growled Dezza, "Because if you do you had better be liking medical-bay food for the next week."

Without waiting for any reply – and there was none – he kicked the groaning man in the ribs and calmly returned to his drink. He heard the man's friends pick him up and drag him away, but no more insults were spoken.

He finished his beer, and left.

*　　　*　　　*　　　*　　　*

"Mr Booth? Mr Desmond Booth?"

The voice was official sounding and authoritarian. It sounded like trouble ready to happen. Dezza finished a mouthful of beer and placed his glass carefully to the bar counter without looking around.

"Who wants to know?" he replied carefully, never looking up.

This seemed to be enough for the man to satisfy him. Dezza heard him take up a seat beside him on one of the barstools. He risked a glance as the newcomer ordered a drink – a cup of tea. The man was dressed in a sharp-cut suit. Official business did not allow alcohol, Dezza surmised. Either that or he was not used to the hard life working off world.

"I'm from the Administration. Jonathon West is my name," the man said at last. He held out a hand to shake, but it was refused.

"I file my tax returns just like anyone else," said Dezza slowly.

West chuckled.

"No. It isn't about anything like that, though I happen to know that you haven't had a job to file a return from for quite some time."

"Then why are you here taking up my valuable time?" demanded Dezza curtly. "I already told the investigation everything."

"It's not that."

The man seemed to consider the words to use before he spoke again, slower this time. "What would you say if I were to tell you that the *Cerberus* came back?"

Dezza looked West up and down critically. His body language and face suggested that this was the truth; he was not fishing for a reaction but merely stating fact. Dezza felt the shiver of fear run through his body that he had not known since that day in space, five years previously. *Cerberus* was a name that could inspire fear to the very depths of his soul.

"Came back?" he said slowly, feeling the colour draining from his face.

West nodded. "Mr Booth. I really need to ask you a few things and this bar does not seem to be the best place for it. May we go and talk about this somewhere more private?"

He thought for a moment. That Starliner had been nothing but bad news since he and the rest of the crew run into it. No-one had truly believed his and Zoë's stories about losing Tubs. It had been the beginning of the end of a career that had promised so much.

If the *Cerberus* was back then it had come like a bad penny to ruin his life a second time. He did not want that. But it also sparked a thought that there could be a glimmer of hope of salvaging a reputation and clearing his name.

He downed the last of the beer in one and slammed the glass to the bar counter. He smirked as West jumped.

What harm could a few minutes of his time being taken up do? At any rate, a part of him felt attracted to knowing. As much as what had happened on the *Cerberus* had destroyed his life, its mention now was drawing him back. It felt like looking at a bad autoroute accident.

"Let's go," he said, rising from the stool.

*　　　*　　　*　　　*　　　*

The projector hummed in the centre of the room, making the dusty air above it shimmer with images. West droned on in the gloom along side as Dezza listened with only half an ear. The rest of his thoughts meandered through his memories, trying to decide whether he might really want to go back.

"The Starliner turned up about a month ago just beyond the way-point of the outer asteroid belts," West was saying, "We don't know exactly how long it was out there for. It might have made the jump recently, or it may have been there since you reported it dropping into the Rösenbridge after your encounter. In truth we have no way to tell."

The projector image changed with gut-wrenching speed, focussing from the trajectories of planets and stations in the system down to a long distance image of a ship.

Dezza leant forward to get a closer look, a shiver running down his spine. It was almost the same image he remembered from the Tug looking over the ship for the first time with Tubs and Zoë. He remembered how Tubs had not wanted to go. Then he had rubbished the man's fears. If only he had listened to him things would have been so much better. Hindsight was a powerful thing that only brought regrets.

"She was picked up by a salvage survey craft out on charter looking for mineral-rich asteroids for the deep space mining company. They took this image, which they sent back with a report. We asked them to go and investigate. At the time we did not realise it was the *Cerberus*. Navigation beacons were, by all accounts, non functional so we weren't to know."

"Just as it was for us," murmured Dezza.

"They went in shortly afterwards. We assume that they docked okay," West continued, ignoring the comment.

"Assumed?"

West avoided his critical gaze.

"We don't know exactly what happened. The last call we got was that they were moving in fine. Then after that the only other contact was about eighteen hours of their ship's automated distress beacon some time later. We couldn't raise them, and after those eighteen hours the beacon just cut out. We don't know why."

Dezza thought for a moment, then stood up.

"Well, my condolences to their families. Tough break." He turned to leave.

"Hey! Hey! Where are you going?" asked West frantically. Finally there was some emotion other than business-like authority.

"Me? I'm going home. It's been a long day, so save it for some-one that gives a damn."

"But don't you want the gig? You're one of only two people who have stepped foot on that Starliner in over eighty years and come back to tell about it. We need your knowledge to go out there and find out what is really happening."

Dezza chose his words carefully; trying to ignore the emotions he felt at the memories the briefing had provoked. "I already went there once and was lucky to get off that hulk. I *don't* want to go back."

"Don't you want to clear your name? You could do that."

Dezza stopped, halfway to the door. West smiled. Dezza silently cursed the way he had him on the hook.

"You've not worked properly since what was left of your team was disbanded. You crawled into the bottom of a bottle, and from the look of it were still there when we found you. No-one believed your stories and the inquiries were inconclusive."

"The logs were wiped on the Tug by the power spikes from the *Cerberus*."

"The Inquiry committee took the view that that was a little 'convenient'."

"They dismissed the case," snapped back Dezza.

"Only because they could not get together enough evidence to convict," retorted West, pushing dangerously at him. "The both of you got off on a technicality."

For a moment it seemed West was wondering whether Dezza would try to lash out. They stood in tense silence with only the background noise of the humming projector.

"Get some-one else," said Dezza bluntly, and turned to go.

"We already did."

Dezza stopped in his tracks, hackles raised.

"Zoë Armstrong was on the salvage mining vessel. It was a chance in a million and we thought that would give them the edge. She never returned."

"Zoë went back?" he asked, uncertain he could believe exactly what he had heard.

"Yes."

He contemplated for a moment, remembering the woman with whom he had worked so long ago. They had had a promising career and the *Cerberus* had destroyed it all. Maybe she had figured it was a chance to clear her name as well.

"I'll do it," he said at last. It wasn't something he wanted to do, but somehow he felt he owed Zoë as much.

West smiled. He had him hooked. From here it would be just a case of the long jag in the quo-field booths to the outer asteroid belts.

*   *   *   *   *

Alarms were already wailing as he shook the groggy hung-over feeling on exiting the quo-field booth. It had been a long, long time since he had travelled this way and it would take a while to get used to it.

Instinctively he reached to the side of the booth before he could stop himself, his hand searching on autopilot for the bottle of flat beer that for so long had waited at the side of his cot for the morning after the night before. Nothing shifted a hangover better, in the mind of an alcoholic, than another swig of Old Jim's gut rot.

He shook his head slowly. He would have to get used to going tea-total again overnight. As much as he had tried to plead, the salvage crew had firmly barred any alcohol on board. Spoil sports, though he knew deep down that their reasoning was sound.

Despite several months frozen in the quo-field, his body still acted like it was just the day after they had shut the lid on him.

"Glad you decided to join us!" came a voice.

It sounded loud and harsh in his ears and his face scrunched up.

"Not so loud. The sirens are enough already without you adding to them."

The burly newcomer laughed at Dezza's delicate nature.

"Give it a few days and you'll ease right in to the action lifestyle. We're on final approach so we started waking up the crew."

It was standard practice on high trajectory Rösenbridge jumps to ease out a little short and have just the main command crew check things out before moving the ship in for final approach and getting the rest of the crew from the quo-fields. Not every jump was so precise, and an error of only a tiny rounding inaccuracy on the computer programme could mean the difference between jumping into the centre of a star and jumping into clear space.

"Get yourself up to the command deck as soon as you can. We'll be going in as soon as we get close enough."

Dezza waved the man away.

"Yeah, yeah. Sure. Just as soon as I've got myself together."

Finding himself alone on the accommodation deck, he wobbled around until he found a galley area and raided its storage bins, looking for anything useful. He found orange juice from frozen concentrate in a fridge. Sniffing its open lid, he pulled a face. It wasn't what he would have liked, but he knew it was pointless hunting for alcohol because there would be none. If any of the crew had smuggled some aboard they would certainly not keep it here. It was even less likely that they would tell a man they considered at best an outsider where they had hidden any secret stash.

Holding his nose he downed the juice in one. At least it might do something for his headache. He wished that the sirens would stop.

* * * * *

There were four people on the command deck when he clambered in. The sirens had been silenced, but the glare from computer screens and consoles still hurt his delicate eyes.

Only one person looked up as he came in then quickly returned to their task. It was almost like Dezza was invisible.

He was a civilian on a military flight coming in hot. He was only here because fate had put him on the *Cerberus* once before, and they needed some-one with the inside knowledge. That was all he was to them, he realised. He was just a memory: a bit of information to make their job a little easier.

Through the screen he saw the endless blanket of stars rolling on and on. He had forgotten just how pretty and peaceful that scene looked. It had been a long time since he had been free to look at it without the fuzzy screen of pollution that surrounded space stations and planetary atmospheres. With a start he realised it had indeed been a long time since he had been in space. How the time flew by at the bottom of a bottle.

"No-one ever gets bored of looking at the stars."

The voice startled Dezza and he looked round. Behind him sat a clean-shaven man with military issue crew cut and dog tags; the man from the sleeping quarters.

The man smiled. "Tracker is what everyone calls me."

He extended a hand. Dezza took it and shook.

"Dezza."

"I hear you're our guide for the trip?" said Tracker.

Dezza looked back out of the screen. Somewhere out there the past was readying itself to come back to haunt him. He said nothing.

Tracker shrugged. "I read the report. No need to go over bad ground."

"So who is on this trip?" asked Dezza, desperate to change the subject. He had shipped in at last minute and barely had time before they froze him in stasis in the quo-field to see much of the ship let alone the crew he would be working with. West had been keen for them to move fast.

"Toze there is the Commander of the crew," said tracker pointing out a clean-cut thin man whose face was soft-skinned and lacked the scars of heavy tours in the thick of the action. "Top of his class, so they say."

Dezza saw in him the academy education that he had learnt to despise. Why did those in charge think that textbooks could replace hard-nose experience?

Tracker seemed to ignore his obvious lack of enthusiasm and pointed out the other two one after the other.

"Spanners is our resident mechanical genius, and Exbo is the last of the team. We call him 'cannon fodder'."

Exbo swung round angrily, his ears seeming to burn from the comment.

"Shut it, Tracker!"

Tracker laughed and took out a strip of gum that he folded deftly into his mouth and began to chew.

"Why do they call you Tracker?" asked Dezza, trying to smooth the air.

Spanners looked up from his panel and shouted across the command deck. "Tell him, Tracker!"

Tracker smiled. "They say I'm good at my job."

"Good at tracking stuff?"

"You could say that."

Obviously Tracker was a man of few words, though his smile betrayed a little pride.

Spanners slid from his chair and swaggered across the deck.

"They say you're so good you can track a turd through a space station sewer," he said with a grin that implied that this was a well-rehearsed exchange.

Tracker shrugged. "People talk."

Toze looked up from his panel.

"Easy, boys. We have a job to do. Get back to station, and stand by for engaging the ion drive as soon as we have a locational lock."

With a laugh, Spanners and Exbo detached from the group and went back to their stations. Tracker just sat calmly at his post, continuing as if there had never been an exchange.

Cool, calm, and whilst he was accepted by the others, Dezza got the impression that the man always considered himself operating on his own and in a group only by association.

He found himself moving across the bridge, not really knowing what he was to do.

Toze saw that he was feeling out of place.

"Pull up a seat," said the officer with a smile, and swivelled a vacant seat at the adjacent console.

Gratefully Dezza sat down, feeling more at home with a console in front of him even though he had little idea what it was for.

A holographic display unit hummed and flickered, and a floating starscape appeared in the centre of the command deck amid the faint aroma of ozone. Dezza's nose wrinkled; he had forgotten until now how much he hated that smell.

"Listen up people!" commanded Toze; "This is the sector we're in."

He tapped some buttons on his console and red and black routing lines appeared charting elliptical orbits and trajectories.

"We're here, at the outer markers. The *Cerberus* is over here, about four hours jag on the ion drive."

Keys tapped again, and the display revolved to reveal a flashing cross which joined back to their own position in the simulation by a dashed red line on a parabolic curve. With another tap of keystrokes, the image folded in on itself with nauseating speed, and the area of the cross grew until a long cigar shaped object hung translucent in the gloom.

Dezza leant forward, as the slowly revolving image seemed to draw him in. Toze was talking, droning on and on about mission technical data, but Dezza was not listening.

The image was small, but a lot of the detail he remembered was there. He saw the twisted bow that they had flown by looking without success for a name to appease Tubs' fears. He saw the canopied atrium that they had struggled through past the husks of dead vegetation to the lifts that had taken them down to the engineering spaces, and that had taken Tubs to his final resting place. He shuddered at the thoughts that came with them; of the logs on the computer console and the thought of what might actually be aboard that vessel.

He had refused to believe at the time. Even at the enquiry the words of the story had seemed almost unreal as he had recounted them. What he had said had happened, but to his own ears as he spoke it seemed like a tall story.

Zoë's story had sounded the same to him, even though he knew it too was true.

They hadn't been believed. In the light of the evidence, or lack of it, the enquiry had been forced to return a verdict that it could not be proven that he and Zoë had murdered Tubs.

So, innocent only on a technicality and that had been the millstone that had dragged him into the bottom of a bottle, to be taunted by those around him who believed only what they read in news reports, and what the journalists found it convenient to make their readership believe.

"Hey man, are you with us?"

The voice cut into his thoughts and brought him back to the world around him with a jolt.

"What?"

He looked around him, becoming quickly aware that other conversation had stopped and now the others were sat looking to him with varied amounts of concern.

"You okay?" asked Toze softly.

Dezza shook the last of the bad thoughts from his mind. "Yeah. I'm good. Just a few memories coming back."

Toze nodded. "Good. We'll need your memories when we get in close. I'll need to know what we're expecting in there and the layout of the decks."

*   *   *   *   *

The four-hour jag in the dropship was conducted without Dezza uttering a word. The ion drive rumbled on powering the ship through the vacuum of space, ever closer to the derelict, and the memories it held. Sure, the others talked a lot amongst themselves, but he was left alone by them to look inward into his thoughts and confront some of the demons that had haunted him over the last few years.

The bottom of many bottles had repressed the thoughts. Now the bulk of the Starliner was rolling past the command deck's screens, and the memories had become very real again.

He suspected Toze and the others were of the opinion that he would not hold up on the mission. In truth, he had become to wonder about himself too in the time he had had to reflect since sobering off the booze that had fogged his mind for so long.

He shook the thoughts from his mind. Well, let them think whatever they wanted. It did not change the truth about what had happened.

Outside, the grey bulk of the vessel rolled in closer as the dropship turned to run alongside. Navigation lights blinked. Just ass before, lights showed at random portholes. It was impossible to tell if the pattern of lights had changed since he was last here, even though it seemed to him that day had been only yesterday.

A beam of light cut out from the search lights at the prow of the dropship and began to play back and forth over the plating of the Starliner. In its powerful glare, the dust-slicked plating looked almost white. As it passed over portholes, the thick Perspex covers flashed in dazzling reflection. It was as if the *Cerberus* was signalling them in Morse, though it was only a quirk of the physics. There was no way to see into the cabins as they passed.

"Your testimony showed that you gained entry through the main airlock level," came Toze's voice, cutting through the reverie and making Dezza jump.

He looked around and saw the Commander hunched over a holographic projection that showed reams of notes and diagrams shimmering in the air. The man didn't look up, but it felt like there was a vacuum hanging in the air, trying to pull an answer from Dezza.

"All the lifepods were gone so we shouldered the Tug up to the main airlock and attached. I'm not sure if it will still be useable now. We had to burn off with force when the docking clamps wouldn't let go."

"There is a second airlock alongside. Scans are showing that the other salvage team docked and their ship is still attached. If the airlock is too toasted to use then we have to try the bays further back."

The thought of Zoë's ship left derelict attached to the *Cerberus* filled Dezza with a strange feeling of dread as the dropship crawled slowly alongside the dusty plating. If her ship had gone - if it had managed to detach and disappear into deep space, he could have kidded himself that Zoë was all right. But the scans showed the ship inert and dead stuck like a leach to the grey side of the Starliner.

He shook the thoughts from his mind, preferring to ignore them than follow the train of thought any further.

"Airlock bays coming up on the port side now," called out Exbo, "We'll have visual in just a few moments."

Heads turned to the view of the hulk scrolling by the screens. Searchlights continued to play over the plating, but now the flat sides studded by portholes gave way to a series of bays where lifepods had once been.

Dezza remembered these; it was the view they had had when they had come into dock on the Tug.

"Visual on the *Magellan* coming up."

The *Magellan* was Zoë's ship. To hear the name made it real. He felt the shiver run down his spine like a river of ice.

The *Magellan* appeared into view, coming ever so slowly into view as the dropship edged on slower and slower. Its plating was much cleaner than the *Cerberus* and the space dock-applied anti-magnetic paint, to stop interstellar dust from sticking, was still satin shiny in the glow of the searchlight.

But there were no navigation lights and nothing showed at the deck screens. For a moment Dezza wondered if the tinted anti-glare coating would stop them being able to see into the *Magellan*'s command deck, but Exbo's voice ended that thought.

"*Magellan* is dead. No electrical signals and no radio signals."

"Switched off or just damaged?" asked Toze.

"Hard to tell, sir. Looks to me like they must have shut her right down. Even the reactor core is showing as dormant."

"What about the emergency beacon?"

"Dead. Just like it was when initial transmission terminated. Control has been sweeping this area for a repeat signal and confirmed that they never heard anything more."

"So some-one turned it off?" asked Dezza. He heard the tremor in his voice.

"Cannot say until we go in and take a peek."

Tracker looked up from his console. "Well, we'll have to find another way in. That ship is blocking the one workable airlock."

Through the screen they saw the charring of the hull and twisted remains of docking clamps on the second airlock where the Tug had blasted free. Muted with a light dusting of space fines, the damage still showed fresh against the ninety year covering of dirt from space.

"With a salvage kit we can try and get in through the *Magellan*'s airlock," suggested Dezza.

He was trying to be helpful, to be part of the crew. Up until now he still felt like an outsider. He hoped they might let him be part of their team, but his hopes were quickly dashed.

"We don't have that kind of time, and there's no saying what we'll find inside that might stop us getting access into the *Cerberus*," said Toze calmly. "We find a clear lock at the rear bays and dock with that."

He didn't leave any opening for debate.

Dezza got the impression again that he was here because West had wanted some-one with any experience of the *Cerberus*, and not because the actual crew of the dropship wanted any help.

The last time Dezza had been this close to the Starliner it had flickered and vanished into the Rösenbridge on its own. According to West's story, the ship had done this at least once more to end up here. Where it had been in the intervening time was anyone's guess; there were no logs.

"What if the *Cerberus* drops into the Rösenbridge?" he asked.

Tracker shrugged. "If we're not docked, she'll just leave. If we're attached we just ride the tube like we're a part of her. Either way we aren't at risk."

He said it nonchalantly, but Dezza knew there would still be some risk. Without protection of a quo-field, riding the Rösenbridge would give each of them a pounding, if it came to that.

The dropship revolved on her axis and began feeling her way back along the bulk of the Starliner to where there was another set of airlocks at the rear decks.

*   *   *   *   *

Dezza never liked docking. It had been something he tolerated in his salvage days, but he hated those moments of uncertainty as the ships felt closer together. In the vacuum of space it took only one mistake to pierce a hull and jeopardise a crew.

Out here there was no-one you could call if something went wrong. Or at least, he thought as his mind turned to the eighteen hour emergency beacon that had brought them here, no-one you could call who would arrive in time to be of any real help. It would take weeks at the soonest for another ship to arrive if they received a signal. Out here you were on your own.

Zoë had always piloted the Tug. She had taken great pride in her skills, and he began to realise that it had been his trust of her that had made bearable those minutes of coming in to a dead ship on manoeuvring thrusters alone.

What made it worse was not having anything to do. Here he was little more than a passenger at the mercy of what an unknown crew could do. Not for the first time on the trip he felt the craving for alcohol return to haunt him, and he fought to repress the feeling. The bottom of a bottle had allowed him to cope for these last few years of failure, but it had never been an answer. Besides, he knew there was nowhere he could get any even if he wanted to. He looked from face to face of the dropship's four man crew and realised that this was a crew that worked together well even if there was no love lost between them.

A metallic grating reverberated through the dropship's hull and for a moment buzzers bleeped and lights flashed before a Christmas tree of green lit up on the master console.

Spanners let out a whoop. "And we're in."

Tracker flicked at a bank of panels, setting switches for systems as the main thrusters wound down. Soon the hiss of their jets would be replaced by the gentle ticking of metal cooling in the vacuum outside. That was one thing about all spacecraft: sound travelled well through their structure and no noise was truly private.

Toze stood up from his station and made to leave the command deck. "Spanners stays here and watches the screens. Everyone else suits up. We're going in."

*   *   *   *   *

Dezza had thought that they would use full body suits, just like he had done back when he had ventured onto the *Cerberus* for the first time. It was standard practice in salvage teams to tool up for the worst case scenario. What if a compartment was compromised and they had to face a vacuum?

But the military crew took a different approach. The *Cerberus* had an atmosphere, so why get tied down with cumbersome space suits? Instead, every man had donned nothing more than gloves and a breathing mask connected to a recirculation pack that sat snugly on their back. Scrubbing the air from the

Starliner's atmosphere, they could last far longer than a sealed system and allowed a much greater freedom of movement.

It made Dezza feel almost nakéd. He had grown used to the salvager's approach and it felt wrong to be able to be immersed into the derelict so closely. At least with a full suit there was some degree of protection from the cold and the dirt. You could kid yourself into thinking that you were not quite there. But with nothing but a flimsy breathing mask and gloves, there was no way of escaping the reality.

In the supply bay the others had taken an assault rifle as if it were the most normal thing in the world to do. He had hesitated; this wasn't part of the brief that he had been given back on the space.

Toze had seen him hesitate, and had signalled for him to take one; there were plenty – the crew had come prepared almost for a war. He had seen the look of resentment from Exbo as he had gingerly picked up the lightweight firearm; he knew the man trusted him less with a gun.

"You know how to use one of these?" asked Toze, his voice slightly muffled by the breathing mask on his face.

"Point and click interface," Dezza replied, trying to lighten the mood.

"Yeah. Something like that."

The joke fell on deaf ears and only served to strengthen Exbo's scowl.

Dezza followed the other three into the harsh brightness of the airlock and waited in the corner as the doors slid shut and the computer checked the seals.

Tracker slid open a panel and typed quickly at the controls.

"Equalising pressure now."

Dezza felt the knot of fear turn in his stomach.

"I thought the Starliner had an atmosphere? We can't decompress without suits?!"

Even as he said it he realised his fears had got the better of him. Exbo looked at him like some-one would look at a fool. The other two just chuckled.

"Atmosphere, yes. We're just making sure our ears don't pop and bleed when we open the door," replied Tracker before turning his attention back to the panel.

Dezza wished the corner would open up and swallow him. It was bad enough to have to go back inside the *Cerberus*. But to have to do it with people whom he knew at best did not fully trust him and at worst wanted him anywhere but here. Not for the first time he felt that this was going to be a bad day.

The airlock finished cycling and a tree of lights flickered one by one to green.

"Pressure equalised," said Tracker at last.

Toze nodded. "Everyone ready?"

They all nodded in turn. Dezza found himself looking at three expectant faces. "Ready," he said, uncertainly.

This seemed to satisfy the three military men and he found himself left alone again.

"Pop the hatch," ordered Toze.

Three guns clicked ready. Dezza wondered what they were expecting to find on the other side of the airlock. When he and Zoë had ventured in there all those years before there had been nothing more than dust and dirt. Did they really think there would be something they could kill?

The hatchway jarred open a fraction and air moaned briefly with a puff of dust making him jump. He cursed; he should have been ready for that.

Tracker reached through the gap and opened a dusty panel on the hull of the Starliner.

"Controls offline," he announced after jabbing at the dead buttons.

"We found the same," offered Dezza, "But the power rail is still live. You can jump the controls with a probe."

Tracker said nothing, but slipped out a toolkit. Prodding the probe into the controls there was a moment's pause before something sparked, and both doors rolled back.

For a moment no-one said anything. There was nothing to say. Beyond where the airlock door had provided a wall of safety separating them from the inside of the Starliner there was now nothing but darkness, yawning deep into a void. Dezza could feel the chill leaching into the airlock and with a shudder he remembered this cold. It was the cold that had played across his face when he had opened his visor in the atrium and played the joke on Tubs and Zoë.

If he had known then what he knew now, he would have sided with Tubs and they would have never set foot onboard.

But hindsight was a wonderful tool. If he had the power to know the future he would have picked the winning lottery numbers every time and never needed to go into the salvage corps.

Tracker was the first to switch on his shoulder mounted torch. It sent a narrow beam slicing into the darkness and picked out shapes in the gloom. Exbo did the same, then Toze and finally Dezza so that four beams flitted their way over the dirt and débris in the Starliner's airlock corridor.

There was dirt thick on everything, just as it had been when Dezza had gone aboard last. The corridor was different, but the muting of nearly a century of neglect remained the same.

Tracker held up a scanner and checked its readings whilst the others seemed wary to set foot beyond the clinical white decking of the dropship.

"Air is clean, nothing toxic."

"So we can dispense with the masks for now?" asked Dezza warily.

Tracker shook his head as Exbo sniggered behind him.

"The mask filters air from the atmosphere and makes it breathable. We wear them all the time; the scrubbers on your back just have to work less hard when the air is like this."

"Quit it Exbo," snapped Toze.

The sniggering stopped, but the hateful looks did not.

Toze led the way inside. Dezza found himself bringing up the rear.

For a moment he hesitated at the demarcation of clean clinical whiteness of the dropship and filthy grey dirt of the *Cerberus*. Not wanting to attract any more comments from Exbo he plucked up the courage, and made the final step of faith into the cold interior.

He was back after all this time. He had thought he would never see this ghost ship again, but it had returned like the bad penny he suspected it was. It had drawn Zoë here too for a second time and he was acutely aware that she had never left. He tried to shut the thoughts from his mind.

"Which way do we go?"

"What?"

Exbo scowled.

Toze ignored the private. "Which way?" he repeated, his voice stifled a little by his breathing mask.

For a moment Dezza felt lost, still disorientated by the thoughts that had rushed his mind on stepping out of the airlock. Why were they asking him, he thought? He had not been in this section of the Starliner. Surely they already knew this?

"We docked further along. We never came this far aft," he said. He realised his words sounded rather lame, though they were not meant to be.

"So what the hell are you along for the ride for?" spat Exbo, the malice clear despite the distortion of his voice by his breathing mask, "We bring this civilian all this way just to tell us he actually never came here before?"

"I thought we were going in where my team did," he protested.

"What a waste of good space."

Toze put out a hand to calm the private. "Stand down, private."

"Sir," he replied sulkily after a moment's pause.

"We were told that you had prior experience of this derelict and were hoping you could give us a heads up on what we were going to find."

"Only once we're back where the tug docked. I thought that was where we were going."

"The airlock being scorched and damaged put an end to that," he sighed. "I guess we're in virgin territory then until we can work through to where you can pick up the trail."

"There should be a way through to the atrium area that Zoë and I found. Find that and I can get you straight to the *Magellan*."

"Just a pleasant march for the morning," smiled Tracker.

"This place looks rough. Hard to believe that it was ever a hotel," said Exbo, glancing at the dirt encrusted furniture and décor.

"I've seen worse. It isn't a good military hostel until you see the roaches climb the walls."

64

The three laughed. Dezza felt left out again. He ran a gloved finger over the grime and it came away laden in a black filth that felt fibrous and slightly gritty.

A torch light played over his shoulder at the finger.

"What's that?" asked Toze.

"The muck that's covering everything. There seems way too much crap to have settled here regardless of the time this hulk has spent adrift in deep space."

"Things get dirty over time," offered Toze.

But Dezza shook his head. "Not this dirty. Any space ship is a closed system. All the muck here has to have been aboard before it was abandoned. It doesn't add up. I've been on five, even ten-year-old derelicts before, and there was never more than a fine dust. Here it's different."

He looked over the walls and to the silent grated panels where once air would have circulated from the scrubbing plant in the ship. Now the louvres were draped with straggly lengths of the fibrous filth that looked like weeds in a choked river.

"There would be some muck accumulated in the ventilation system over time that with no-one to dust would build back up over time, but not to this level even in a ship this large."

"Dezza's bogey men again," Exbo sniggered.

Dezza ignored the needling and malice that was laced within the comment.

"So where does all this shit come from then?" asked Toze, playing his torch over the walls of the corridor. Everything was covered in black filth. It was an even layer that seemed to have penetrated and tarnished everything.

"Could it be soot from fires elsewhere?" asked Tracker.

Dezza shook his head. "I don't think so."

"It looks organic to me," said Toze.

The comment prompted Tracker to take out his scanner and play it over the walls and the filth. Expectantly they all waited for it to churn out its results.

"Hard to tell exactly," he said at last consulting the screen, "It may have once been living, but it is completely dead now."

"Sterile?" asked Toze.

Tracker looked up. "That's the weird thing. There's just nothing here. No fungi, mould or bacteria cultures. This place is a tomb."

Exbo laughed. "Maybe Dezza knifed them too when he was last here."

It was as much as Dezza could do to fight back the urge to lash out at the man. Toze saw what was coming and stepped in to separate them.

"Hey, that's enough. We're here to get a job done and I don't want childish school yard shit getting in the way."

"Sorry Sir," apologised Exbo without much sincerity, "I just don't feel comfortable spending time close by a man who used a bogey man story to explain why one of his crew went missing in deep space."

"The tribunal cleared us."

"The tribunal didn't prove anything."

"*I* know what happened," snapped Dezza coldly.

"Not proven is different to not guilty. They just did not have the evidence to pin you down."

"Save it for some-one who gives a shit." He turned and would have lost it and lashed out if the officer had not intervened and pushed them apart.

"That's it - enough. Wind it down Exbo, or I'll personally bust your arse so hard you will be on shit-detail for the rest of your career."

The two men glared at each other, but nothing else was spoken.

"We have to find a way through. It seems none of you were here last time," he continued, ignoring the unspoken tension that persisted.

"That's not exactly true."

It took Tracker's voice to break the moment in a way the officer never could. Three faces swivelled around to where the man was hunched with his back to them on the dusty deck. He had grown bored with the bickering and had moved off to look at something that had caught his eye.

"What do you mean?" asked Exbo with uncertainty.

Tracker looked round to them and smiled. His gloved hand pointed to the dust laden carpet.

"Some-one definitely came through here recently."

At his finger tips, illuminated as he turned back to let his lamp play over them were a clear trail of footprints leading along the corridor.

"They came in up there." He pointed to where the lamp faded out into the gloom and could penetrate no further. "And then they went up there," he continued, turning to point past the three. "One person leaving one trail."

Dezza studied the prints in the light of the beam.

"Not one of my crew," he said slowly.

"My guess is some-one from the *Magellan*," offered Tracker.

Toze activated his radio.

"Spanners. Are you seeing what we are seeing?"

Static buzzed a moment then Spanners' voice came through clearly.

"Roger that. I see footprints. Nothing more than some-one's dainty size thirteens passing by for a stroll."

He ignored the sarcasm. "Can you double check the scans of the *Cerberus*? There are definitely no readings?"

"Way ahead of you. Already checked and triple checked. There is nothing showing up. Whoever it was, they aren't there now. But the steel deck plates are engineered heavy and it's impossible to get a reliable deep reading. If there is anyone still around then they certainly aren't local to you."

"Where did they go?" whispered Exbo.

"Wherever it was, they didn't come back," replied Spanners.

"At least, not this way," said Tracker gruffly. He did not wait for a reply as he stood up and wiped the dust from his gloves. "They could have made their way back on another corridor. What now, Sir?"

"Okay. Split into teams. They came from somewhere and went somewhere. It can't be too hard to follow a trail as clean as that."

Exbo raised his hand and his mouth creased into a grin of malice.

"What is it, Exbo?" sighed the officer.

"Permission to not go with the crew killer."

Dezza turned to lash out, but the officer stepped in and stopped them, pushing them apart.

"Permission denied. That's enough. Now I want two teams to follow this trail each way."

He looked to Tracker. "You're with me. As for you two lovebirds, you had better kiss and make up because you are working together."

Exbo made to protest but the officer cut him off.

"No more lip. That's an order. As Dezza is more familiar with where the *Magellan* is docked, you're going to follow the trail back that way. We'll assume that's where they came from. We'll find out where they went. Now move out and stay in radio contact if you find anything."

*   *   *   *   *

Spanners might not have been the loudest of characters, but what he lacked in volume he more than made up for in shrewd observation. He had made it through the academy with average grades on average marks, and had never sought to draw attention to himself. There was a personal motto, if he had ever been pushed on the subject to give one: keep your head down, keep out of trouble and you will go far.

In a way he had not particularly chosen the military as a career; it had chosen him by virtue of his Father and Grandfather. It had been their livelihood, and it was easier to go with the flow and follow in their footsteps than to carve out a new path in uncharted territory. It was just an easy pay cheque.

On the radio chatter he had heard all and had for the most part listened quietly with interest at the exchange between Exbo and Dezza. He knew Exbo reasonably well; they had been on two other missions together now. The man was a loud mouth with an overly inflated self-opinion, but in reality was all talk and no substance. 'A fool' would have been Spanners' short description of him. He got off on other people's misery and in truth Spanners did not like him. He reminded him of the loud mouth jocks that he had had to endure bullying from throughout his school career.

Exbo did not ever seem to realise that Spanners could listen in at any time. Every muttered insult and every dark comment that the private thought were only to himself were there to be heard by Spanners if he chose. But then, Exbo had not caught on to a lot of things. He still did not know what his nickname really meant; that was one that the others found amusing. Just to watch the little prick strut like a peacock thinking he was the It Man whilst all the time he was considered little more than expendable cannon fodder was fun in itself. Spanners doubted that the idiot would ever find out.

He had listened to the exchange between the private and Dezza and could tell there was much friction between the two. Some of the comments made by Exbo actually surprised him. He did not know that the objectionable little shit was this well read and actually knew something about a tribunal that had happened years before. Of course it had been big news, for a while. Then the gloss had worn thin and the media had grown bored and had moved on to peddle some other crap to blow out of all proportion.

The media had been against Dezza and Zoë from the start, Spanners remembered. They had been vilified even though they were never officially found guilty of what they were accused of. A media stigma is a hard one to shift. Throw enough mud and some will stick; the media did not care so long as they were selling the news for a profit.

If he were truthful to himself, Spanners would admit that he had honestly not made up his mind. Dezza's story had seemed incredible at the time, and few had believed him. Yet, after all these years, here they were and at least one part of Dezza's story – the *Cerberus* – had turned out to be real. A shudder ran down his spine at the thought of what else might be true.

Toze had asked for a sweep for life on the Starliner. Spanners had already anticipated this, but not out of forethought for what those on the away team might need. Instead it was to allay fears born from the other cryptic stories Dezza and Zoë had given in their testimonial.

He only vaguely listened to the team arguing over who was going with who as he ran the scans for a third time, tweaking the controls and looking for a way to penetrate deeper into the Starliner. But every scan showed up completely clean.

He wished he could cast loose in the dropship from the airlock and make an external pass over the entire Starliner. Metal deck plates and other structural components tended to screen scans, and they were only effective at short range. Against the massive bulk of this vessel there was no way he could do reliably more than a fraction from here. But he knew that Toze would never sanction the dropship detaching whilst the team were aboard the *Cerberus*; he would not want the risk of being left marooned.

There was little more he could do other than to analyse the readings fed through automatically from the team.

*   *   *   *   *

Dezza could not help but feel a sense of superiority over the smug private he had been forced to team up with. The man was so detestable and blatant in the way he showed his distaste for people. Yet, when Dezza had checked that Exbo was out of earshot before leaning closer to Tracker before the groups had finally parted on their separate routes, he had found that life was not all bad.

"Tell me; why do you call him 'Exbo'?" he had whispered.

Tracker had looked up. "You really want to know?"

Dezza had shrugged as Tracker continued.

"It's short for 'expendable'."

Dezza had wondered for a moment, spelling out letters in his head. "Shouldn't that be with a 'p' instead of a 'b'?"

Tracker had glanced to where Exbo was checking his gun.

"Yeah, but we didn't want to make it too obvious because he might have got disheartened if he knew he was only here to run at bullets."

Right now Dezza felt buoyed along by knowing this little fact. A little piece of one-upmanship that he would keep to himself, for now.

He didn't say much; there was nothing to say. Exbo kept one step ahead of him, keeping up a pace that suggested he was taking great delight in trying to lose Dezza. But Dezza could keep up with the best of them and kept on right behind.

The footsteps were easy to follow and it didn't take a great tracker to see where they came from. Decades of accumulated dirt had settled across all surfaces of the Starliner. There really

70

had been no-one here for a long time, and it showed; the footsteps stood out clearly.

Why had they not immediately seen them when they had entered through the airlock, Dezza wondered? Though sometimes it was the things that stared you in the face that hid the best.

The trail became more smudged the further they followed. Dezza nearly walked into the back of Exbo before he realised that the private had stopped and was crouching down on the floor to take a closer look.

"What do you make of these?" he asked. For a moment rivalry and distrust was lost as training took over where there was a job to do.

Dezza leant in close and crouched by his side. Gently he leant his firearm on the deck beside them to have both hands free. The steps were smudged and the edges scraped. He wondered if they had been deliberately defaced.

Exbo produced a pack of gum and took out one strip. He lifted the breathing mask for a moment and folded it into his mouth. Then he put the pack away without ever a suggestion of offering anything across.

"Looks to me like they were in a hurry over something," he said as his jaws clamped down on the gum.

Dezza tried not to breathe. The breathing mask filtered most smells, but the harsh tang of spearmint still made it through. It was a smell he despised. From an early age it had been the smell of the gum the jocks at school had chewed. The unmistakable smell of being bullied, along with cheap aerosol deodorant. He hated the smell – the smell of teenage desperation. How apt it came now from another bully just like those almost forgotten in the past.

"Running away. Yeah, could be."

They looked up and two beams of light from their torches followed the tracks to a bend in the corridor where they disappeared to one side into the shadows.

The Starliner had been built with kinks in the corridors. In the dark they were not noticeable until they loomed out of the gloom, but Dezza guessed that once upon a time when the lighting worked, the idea of staring into infinity down a corridor over several miles long could have been disorientating to passengers. One dogleg cured all that.

"How do you want to go from here?"

Exbo looked at him with scorn as his jaws chewed away relentlessly.

"Are you afraid that your bogey man is going to jump us or something? We keep on following. Looks like we're coming to something interesting."

The man laughed and slung his gun with a finger on the trigger before marching confidently to the kink.

Bottling the urge to fight back or to say something, Dezza found himself following silently behind. Beyond the corner the torch lights picked out smashed panelling and an accumulation of débris that filled the corridor to half its height. They stopped in their tracks as the two beams picked their way over it.

Exbo reached for his scanner. "What the hell is this?"

Dezza slung his gun tightly over a shoulder out of the way and stepped up to the blockage. It did not reach quite to the ceiling. There was a gap big enough to climb through.

"Some kind of barricade," said Dezza at last.

Exbo snorted, not looking up from the scanner. "Why the hell would anyone want to do that?"

Dezza tested the strength of the piled débris. It had been wedged in tight and well. It seemed more than able to hold his weight. "You tell me."

"Scanner says there's nothing more than inert crap here. Wood, steel and lots of your 'sinister slime'."

He looked up at the sound of Dezza hauling himself up.

"Where the hell do you think you're going?"

Dezza paused to glance back. "Over it, of course. Or had you forgotten we're supposed to be following these tracks? They came over so we go over too."

He did not wait for a reply. As he crouched through the narrow space between the barricade and the ceiling he heard Exbo muttering and struggling to climb behind him.

The barricade didn't stretch far and he soon found himself climbing down over shredded timber. His brow furrowed in concern and he bent down to take a closer look.

"Hurry up with that scanner!" he called out to the still struggling private. He got a grunt in acknowledgement.

But he did not need a scanner to see that the damage here was fresh and new. Char marks showed on the wood where something had gouged into it, taking away chunks. The filth had not had time to recover the exposed edges and he saw the glint of gold paint shimmering on the mouldings.

He felt something metallic roll under his foot. Bending down, he fumbled in the dirt and pulled out first one then another half a dozen spent bullet cartridges.

He looked around as Exbo finally jumped down from the opening at the ceiling to his side.

"Do these look fresh to you?" he asked, passing the cartridges across to an outstretched hand.

Exbo took them and rolled one between a finger and thumb. Finally he held it close to the breathing mask and took a sniff.

"I can still smell the faintest trace of the charge. These weren't fired that long ago."

"Days? Weeks? Months?"

Exbo shrugged. "Hard to tell, but certainly not more than several weeks or the scent would have faded too much to smell them through the mask."

"I found signs of something else too," said Dezza. He indicated to the gouged wood.

Exbo slung all but one of the spent cartridges to the ground and knelt by Dezza's side. He fingered the scorch marks.

"Fresh gun shots. Probably the same age as these cartridges."

He flashed his torch beam around the corridor. Other gouge marks showed in the walls and ceiling. On the floor the muck was heavily disturbed.

"Some-one made some kind of stand here by the look of it," said Dezza.

"Maybe. I'm calling in."

He pressed the send button on the radio.

"Spanners, you there?"

There was a moment's hiss of static than the tinny voice of Spanners came back to them, distorted and strange in the silent depths of the Starliner.

"I'm always here. What do you want?"

"Are you getting the video feed? We've got evidence of gunplay down here."

There was a pause before Spanners voice sounded again. Dezza imagined the man taking a moment to view a screen that he probably had not been paying as much attention to as he should have.

"Looks like bullet traces. I'll run an analysis."

Exbo held the spent cartridge up to the camera lens alongside the lamp on his shoulder and played it over in the bright light.

"We got these too – should give you the data you need to run a diagnostic. They're fairly recent issue. Look like mercenary stock from the outer colonies to me."

"Give me one moment and I'll be right back to you."

The line clicked dead with static. Back on the dropship he would be running the video feed through the computer. Using various programs he would be able to project the likely trajectories of the bullets and distances from which they were fired.

In the gloom of the corridor the pair waited. Apart from the quiet hiss of their breathing the only other sound was the steady chewing of Exbo's jaws on the gum.

Dezza wished the man would just spit it out.

Finally the radio buzzed again with static and Spanners' voice came across.

"Got the info. Looks like there were two sources of gunfire somewhere up the corridor. It's difficult to see exactly because light is an issue, but the computer reckons no more than thirty metres."

"Copy that."

"There's one other thing though."

Exbo stopped in his tracks. "Oh?"

Analysis picked up gunfire going back the other way. Same issue cartridges too. Looks like they were fighting each other."

"But there's still only one set of tracks," whispered Dezza.

"Actually," replied Exbo slowly, "There were two."

He scanned the floor. Sure enough in the jumbled pattern in the dirt two different sized boot impressions could be made out. The indent from the soles showed they were the same make and model of boot. The only logical conclusion would be crew from the *Magellan*.

But why would they be fighting each other, Dezza mused. Then the thought occurred to him from a memory that had lain in the back of his mind since he was last here. There were things in the ship's log that had suggested the *Cerberus*' crew had fought with *something* on the decks of the Starliner.

He looked back to the barricade. Yes, that was old. The material had been piled here long ago - time enough for the coating of filth and tarnish to be thick and penetrating. But the material certainly wasn't the result of collapse of the structure. In the gap through which they had crawled he could see the ceiling was still intact. This stuff had been hastily dragged and dumped here by the *Cerberus*' crew.

Exbo was still crouched on the ground, looking over the tracks when Dezza came back to him.

"I'm calling the commander," Exbo announced and reached for the radio.

Through the static they heard Toze's voice.

"What is it."

"We got a second trail, and evidence of gunplay."

There was a moment's pause before the reply came through.

"Any sign of life?"

"Just footprints; nothing more."

*   *   *   *   *

In truth, the *Cerberus* was turning into an anti climax for Toze. He had read and reread the reports. Based on the testimonials given at the tribunal, Dezza had babbled on about some kind of evil entity that had possessed the ship.

It had been considered a tall story then, and the only thing that had saved him and his crewmate Zoë was that no other evidence could be found to contradict them. In Toze's opinion the tribunal had demanded a massive proof from the prosecution that they simply could not give without access to a Starliner that had conveniently disappeared. A military tribunal, he knew, would have been much less forgiving on the salvage tug's crew.

His briefing had also contained some information on the *Cerberus*. Despite being little more than a *Mary Celeste* myth to most people, West had managed to dig up material in the archives. The *Cerberus* was real – although Toze knew that by being stood on it. Deep within vaults at the Central Records Bureau he had found the computer slug that had given them a vague idea of the original story. It had been before the third great stellar war, when mining companies had fought for control of the mineral wealth of the stars. In the process records were lost and destroyed as companies rose and crumbled on the political winds.

The shipping line that the *Cerberus* had belonged to had been one such casualty. They had become nothing more than just a footnote to the history of interstellar luxury travel. When she had gone missing, it had been assumed she was victim to raiders from a company battle. It was not until one of the lifepods turned up empty years later that a different story had emerged.

But it was a story that was sketchy to say the least. So much so that in the absence of any real evidence, it had become the seeds of the myth that had become whispered by the Astros in every bar across the system and in the process had become distorted beyond any true meaning.

He suspected that the others doubted Dezza's story too. It wasn't that they had taken a dislike to Dezza – though it was clear Exbo was the exception to this. It was just that the story the tribunal had been asked to believe was a tall one to say the least.

They stopped again for Tracker to go through his ritual of crouching down and inspecting the tracks. The officer waited impatiently. They had been doing this every hundred yards, and it was beginning to grate.

"What is there left to see? Tracks are tracks," he said impatiently.

Tracker held up a finger. "Not entirely. That's where I guess I am different in my outlook than you."

Toze put his gun to one side and knelt down.

"Okay then. What have you got?"

There was a tense moment's pause, as if there was something meaningful to be said. Then Tracker looked around with a smile at the officer.

"Okay, you got me. There isn't anything different to find." He stood up, dusting the muck from his gloves. "I just do it sometimes for effect."

They moved off, following the trail. They seemed to go on and on without ever letting up. How far could one person wander aimlessly around a derelict? More to the point, what would they find when they reached the end of the trail?

"Do you really think that Dezza's story is true?" asked Toze at last, looking for a way to break the monotony of their task.

Tracker shrugged. "You have to admit, that his story is checking out good so far."

"Unless it is all just a lucky coincidence and he is seizing upon the opportunity in a last ditch effort to clear his name."

"Then where did the crew of the *Magellan* go?"

It was a reasonable enough question. If Dezza was hitching a ride on a lucky coincidence, then there were far too many coincidences going his way. Sometimes a grain of truth lurked inside every web of suspicion.

"I don't know," he conceded.

He suspected that Tracker too was feeling the disappointment of the mission so far. It had sounded so good, to be walking into the unknown checking out monsters in space, but all there seemed to be was a floating derelict filled with nothing more than junk.

*   *   *   *   *

"I see light ahead!"

Exbo's muted hiss startled Dezza, though the glimmer of light from behind the next turn did not bother him. "I've heard of kids being afraid of the dark, but the light was never that scary last time I checked."

Exbo ignored his snide comment. "What do you think?"

"I think some-one left a light on," replied Dezza dryly.

Exbo scowled, reaching for the radio. "Spanners, come in. We've got lights on down here."

"There's lights on all over the Starliner," came the reply through the static, "It all seems to be hit and miss as to what circuits work and what don't."

Exbo switched off the radio without reply.

Dezza knew all this had been in the brief, but he doubted more and more that Exbo had not read it and was relying on other people to fill him in as he went along.

"Let's move in," hissed Exbo, slinging his gun at the ready and moving off without waiting for Dezza.

Dezza followed, a smile on his face.

They reached the light and slowly stepped into the glare that seemed so bright after the enforced darkness of the rest of the *Cerberus*. First Exbo then Dezza switched off the torches; there was no need for them here.

In front of them a vast open area opened out. Chandeliers hung from above glowed brightly despite decades of being left on. Their crystal decorations were dulled by dust, but still bright.

The room had once been used as a venue for balls and parties. There were upper levels that looked out over the main area from balconies, and tables and chairs stretched across the main floor in neat rows laid out for an event that would never come.

"It looks like it was just left yesterday," whispered Exbo.

"In that case the maid must have walked out a few years before," retorted Dezza, running his gloved finger over the nearest chair. It came away coated in the same grey filth that had been elsewhere.

"Some kind of function room."

"No shit."

They stepped gingerly further into the room. So far the ship had proven empty, but on the floor the trail of footprints still wound between the tables showing that at least recently the Starliner had been host to other guests.

Dezza suddenly felt himself grabbed and thrown to the floor. Wriggling around he realised he was pinned down by a rigidly still Exbo. He made to protest and fight back, assuming that the private had flipped. But he saw the look on the man's face, and he too froze.

Exbo was watching, still and motionless. What was it that had caught his attention? Dezza turned his head to look, but from the floor could not see anything that did not seem out of place. He even scanned the front edges of the balconies for signs of something, but they were all empty.

"What is it?" he whispered at last, careful to keep his voice down.

"I thought I saw movement," said Exbo almost inaudibly.

"Where?"

Slowly Exbo stretched out a free hand and pointed. "Over there."

Dezza looked. He saw nothing but bright lights, rows of potted plastic plants with leaves dulled from green to grey by dirt and neglect. Behind them he saw the end of the bar which ran along one full side of the room.

"I don't see anything at all," he replied. Then a thought struck him and he twisted free of Exbo and stood up.

He looked in the direction that Exbo had indicated. At first he saw nothing, then he too saw movement. He made to duck back down before realising what it was, and smiled that they had both been taken in. "I think it's just the mirrors."

Exbo crouched beside him and his face creased into a grin.

"Goddam it!" he whooped in a voice so unexpectedly loud that it sent a shiver running down Dezza's spine.

Before Dezza could reply, the private had leapt up from the floor and bounded across to the bar. Sure enough, in the ornate and angled glass hidden behind row after row of bottles, his own distorted reflection stared back like a sick joke from the hall of mirrors at a funfair.

"Rattled by my own pearly whites in the mirror," the private muttered through a smile.

He unslung his gun and placed it on the bar top and then in one leap vaulted to the other side. He scanned the optics reading the age-browned labels with interest. After all this time the contents had either leaked away or had congealed into syrupy residues.

"Shit. That is the perfect crime."

He tutted and took a bottle gingerly off its mounting. As he turned it over the thick brown sludge oozed down the inside of the glass in sticky lumps. He wiped the dust from the label.

"Thirty year old oak aged." He did a mental calculation. "That makes it over a hundred and twenty now."

Dezza leant over the bar to see. "Not quite. They only age in the cask. As soon as it goes in the bottle it doesn't age any more."

"Looks like it kept ageing anyway."

"Air must have got in. The seal on the optic can't be perfect, especially after nine decades."

Dezza tried to suppress the alcoholic feelings inside him. One look at the familiar shaped bottles and he could feel the cravings return. At least the syrup that was left was not drinkable.

"It's just junk," snapped Exbo and tossed the bottle over his shoulder before Dezza could stop him.

It bounced with a loud thud on the bar and kept rolling drunkenly along the dust. There must have been a slight slope to the counter. It picked up speed before veering off to smash on the floor.

The echo sounded loud in what had been until now so quiet. Dezza found he could hear the noise reverberating up through the room and ringing from the chandeliers. Without people in it, the room's acoustics served to amplify loud noises rather than subdue them.

"What the hell are you doing?" he hissed angrily.

The private seemed pleased that he had riled the civilian. The energy of Dezza's discomfort with the noise seemed only to make him keener to keep trying.

He picked another bottle from the optics and heaved it with all his strength over the bar and across the room. It bounced with a loud thud on a wall and smashed somewhere in the shadows. The tinkle of glass echoed.

"Finished?" asked Dezza angrily.

Exbo leered, the leer he had used back on the dropship when he knew he was getting to Dezza. It only served to stoke the fires of hatred that Dezza felt deep down inside himself.

"Hey, I don't see any of this crap belonging to anyone any more. I'll do what I like."

He wrenched another bottle from the optics and hurled it to the same fate.

"What's the matter," he taunted, "Scared that the noise might bring your ghosts?"

"We're wasting time," said Dezza, refusing to be drawn in by Exbo's taunts.

He turned his back on the private and made a point of walking off across the room. A bottle whizzed by his head but he refused to flinch; that would only give Exbo some of what he wanted. He could feel his heart racing. He wanted to turn around and leap over the bar and throttle the private. But he knew he could not give the man that satisfaction. Instead all he could do was leave.

He saw Exbo's reflection in the dusty mirrors behind the bar and realised that the man was following him. He heard the rattle of another bottle being pulled down and expected it to come flying past, but it never did. Instead he heard the private whoop with joy.

"Oh yes! Jackpot!"

He turned as the private thumped the empty bottle down on its side on the bar and bent down out of sight. A syrupy mess dripped from the open neck, soaking into the layer of dust on the wooden bar top. He heard the sound of Exbo grunting, along with something heavy being dragged. What had he found?

"Stop wasting time," Dezza called out with some uncertainty.

Exbo ignored him, and reappeared with a grin and a sealed bottle of liquor in each hand. The liquid inside was still all right, sealed from the deterioration that had ruined all the bottles on the optics.

"Ever wondered what a hundred and twenty year old booze tastes like," he taunted. Without waiting for a reply he banged the bottles down onto the bar top and levered the top off one.

Even before he caught a whiff of the whiskey, Dezza felt the twisted knot of craving rising inside the pit of his stomach. It was even worse when he did finally catch a tang of the crisp fresh alcohol.

It seemed that Exbo knew just how to push his buttons. Looking Dezza in the eye he wiped the rim of the bottle and slipped up his breathing mask. He took a stiff swig, gulping the liquid down.

Then he put the bottle back on the bar and gasped in satisfaction before wiping his mouth with the sleeve of his jacket and pulled the mask back down.

"Want to try some?" he leered.

Dezza stood motionless, looking at the bottle. It had to be worth more than a year's pay. Hell, it was worth more than a year's pay even when he had a good job and income. He knew it would be the best drink he had ever had. But that was why with an aching heart he knew he could not. One drink would lead to another and another and before he knew it he would be right back at the bottom of a bottle pissing his life away.

He shook his head and stepped back.

"No."

Exbo sensed the inner turmoil. He picked up the unopened bottle and tossed it to Dezza. He only just caught it. A shiver ran the length of his spine as he turned the dusty bottle over in his hands. The private knew how to yank his chain, and right now that chain was rapidly running out of slack.

"Plenty more down here," said Exbo as he leant down. There was a chink of glass on glass and first one then another bottle were brought up and placed on the bar.

With an aching heart and much difficulty Dezza walked forward and put the bottle carefully on the bar next to the others. He took a step back, just to be certain that he could not just reach forward and rip the top off the bottle in a moment of weakness to his cravings.

Exbo slipped his breathing mask aside and took another long gulp. The golden liquid sloshed invitingly in the bottle before he let out a contented sigh.

Dezza shook his head. "Stop messing about. You'll get pissed sloshing that stuff back like water."

"I'll do what I like," snarled Exbo menacingly. He had not even bothered to put his breathing mask back. The scanners had shown the air as breathable here, but it was still a risk they had been told not to take.

"I'll go on without you if I have to," said Dezza defiantly.

Exbo laughed, and took another deep swig from the bottle. He picked up one of the full bottles and tossed it across the room.

Like the empties before, it bounced off a wall and smashed somewhere out of sight. Liquid gurgled from where the broken bottle had come to rest.

"One for your ghosts," Exbo sneered.

Partly in anger, partly in disgust Dezza turned on his heels and began to walk without looking back. He could hear the gurgle of whiskey again as Exbo took another drink. Trying to shake the thoughts from his mind, he picked up the footsteps in the dirt on the floor and followed them on his own leaving Exbo behind.

*   *   *   *   *

The corridors in front of Toze and Tracker went on and on, and with them went the trail. At times the footsteps would become confused and fill one side of the corridor, as if the person making them had stopped for a rest before carrying on.

"How much further are we going to have to follow this shit?" complained Toze.

Tracker played the scanner over the walls and floor as they stopped to take stock.

"Until we find where they go."

"Shit, I know that!"

"Yeah."

"Don't Nixon me," snapped Toze, becoming irritated at Tracker's short answers.

Tracker looked up and smiled. "That is, unless they just get up off the deck and fly away."

Toze looked at him quizzically. "You aren't buying into the civilian's ghost story are you?"

The words hung in the dank air a moment.

"Are you?" replied Tracker after a moment's thought.

Toze laughed, trying to break the mood. It seemed almost impossible to him to work out Tracker's mind and what he really meant. It had always been like this, in the three missions they had run together as a team.

Tracker had joined them with good references, the officer remembered. He had been transferred in because he was the best, and the reports said just that. But what they didn't give was any clues to his background above and beyond what was absolutely necessary.

Toze mused that he was a private man, all things told. He had turned up with a military issue kit bag slung over his shoulder and that was all. Most men have a few personal items that serve to remind them of home or loved ones. This man arrived with nothing. He was a one man fighting force who never let emotion betray anything about his past or what he was thinking.

"You have to admit that the more we find the more his story still fits," he found himself saying.

Tracker returned his attention to the readouts on the scanner. It was infuriating, thought Toze, the way he always did that. Look busy whilst you think so no-one can tell what you're thinking of from the look on your face.

"Still getting nothing out of the normal. Air compounds are good; the air recirculation system must still be working somewhere close by for it to be this clean after ninety years."

"Usually after five any bacteria in the air clears it out if it isn't"

Tracker looked up. "Now, that's something the scanner keeps picking up."

"What?"

"Bacteria. Or at least, a lack of it. There just isn't any."

"Ninety years is enough time for solar radiation to sterilise this place."

"The original filth, maybe. But we're well out into deep space, and the *Cerberus* was when the civilian's first crew found it too. Where it has been in between is anyone's guess, but they would have brought *something* with them."

"You saying that we should be able to pick up the germs that Dezza brought last time?"

"And the crew of the *Magellan*. One of them came through here, and the scanner isn't picking up even a background trace of anything organic."

Toze nodded. He knew that the military scanners were extremely sensitive at close range. Tracker had a point. "Could the recirculation system have scrubbed them out in just a few weeks?"

Tracker looked to the silent vents on the wall draped in tentacles of filth.

"Not here. The vents haven't been working on this deck for a very long time."

He took off a glove and held an exposed finger up in the air.

"No breeze either. Seems odd to me."

Toze thought for a moment. Was this bringing the conversation full circle back around to the question of what Dezza's tribunal report had said? He wasn't sure that he wanted to discuss that.

"Let's move on," he snapped, gesturing to where the footsteps continued out of sight beyond where the torch beams could penetrate, "This trail isn't going to follow itself."

*   *   *   *   *

The stairwell showed a flicker of light long before they reached it. In the darkness of the corridor, it had been Tracker who had noticed it first. With one hand he tapped the officer on the shoulder and pointed wordlessly.

Toze had thought that it could have been a reflection from their own torches, but it remained even when they switched them off. They moved on slowly, taking generous moments to run the scanner for clues, but there were none.

The light was coming from around a door set into a large recess to one side of the corridor. There were elevators here too, but their panels were dark and showed no power.

"What do you want to do?" asked Toze uncertainly.

"You're in charge. You're the one who tells me."

He nodded. "Fine. We move on. The footsteps go that way, so we do too. The civilian's report said that not all the Starliner was completely dead, and we did see a lot of lights still on during the fly-by."

He flicked on the radio link. Static buzzed in his ear for a moment and he winced, fumbling for the volume control.

"Spanners! Are you getting this."

The radio buzzed loudly then a distorted voice came through the noise. It was difficult to make out.

"Say again?"

The noises pulsed, sounding like a human voice, but they could not be made out as distinct sounds or words. Toze looked to Tracker who checked his radio receiver too. Nothing but noise came from his too.

"Radio signal is distorted, Commander," he said, "We must have too much structure in the way to get a good signal."

"Damn!"

He looked to the door again. The scanner was showing as clear. He shrugged, and with his gun slung at the ready, eased it open and slid on through.

Beyond the door was a large room that stretched off in parallel to the corridor. It was airy and light and it took a few moments for their eyes to adjust. The walls, ceiling and floor were pristine white, a clear marked contrast from the rest of the Starliner. It was laid out as a well-equipped gym with weight machines, treadmills and an assortment of white and chrome devices. Mirrors ran the length of the opposite wall, reflecting an eerie image of the two men in their fatigues.

Dirt-streaked men in military camouflage gear holding rifles and with faces obscured behind breathing masks did not really fit all of a sudden.

"This doesn't look right," said Toze slowly.

"Well, if it is any consolation, I'm seeing it too."

Toze reached out and hesitantly touched the nearest exercise machine, as if it might dissolve at his touch. It didn't; it was real all right. He felt its cold metal frame clearly through his glove.

"We found the gym deck then. But why is it so clean? The rest of the ship looks like my old student digs, but this looks like we missed the maid by only a few minutes."

Tracker nodded. Bending down to scrutinise the metalwork of the exercise machine he saw that it had no tarnish and no coating of the dirt that had plagued the rest of the Starliner that they had seen. He flicked open his scanner and waited patiently for the machine to come back with a reading.

"Air's clean."

"The air was clean almost everywhere else. The air recirculation system is online – Dezza's report said much the same thing too."

"No," repeated Tracker firmly as he passed across the scanner for the officer to take a look, "The air is so clean we might as well be in a computer technology lab. There's not a shred of dust or contamination in here except us."

Toze checked the screen. The man was right. The readout showed nothing in the air. He waved a dirty gloved hand in front of the sensor for a moment in case the machine was somehow damaged, but it faithfully detected the dirt on his glove. It was not the machine that was at fault. "This is so weird."

"We ought to try to call this in."

Toze nodded in agreement and switched on the radio before remembering that it had been jammed by static just a few moments before. However now the channel hissed with only background noise, so he tried anyway.

"Spanners? Are you receiving?"

Spanners' voice came back so clear and loud that for a moment the officer seemed surprised. But he recovered and panned the camera on his shoulder around the room.

"Check the screens and tell me what you think."

For a moment there was silence on the channel. But just as he was beginning to wonder whether it was still connected Spanners' voice came back clearly.

"You boys found the maid's closet and thought you'd make your Mothers proud?"

"Can the bullshit. This is serious."

"Okay. I see a gym. It looks like it's come straight off the set of a period drama on the entertainment system. That wouldn't be weird except I know you're on a creepy haunted derelict at least four light years from any civilisation."

"That's kind of what we thought," muttered Tracker. He peeled away from the officer and began to carefully walk between the aisles of equipment getting readings with his scanner.

*   *   *   *   *

The equipment was old, but recognisable. Gym leisure equipment changed every few years with the whims of whatever fad took hold. Some things just dated fast, and no-one had thought chrome and white was a clever combination for a very long time. He had seen stuff like this rotting in junk shops before now back on Earth, but never looking like they had just come out of the fitness studio showroom.

Looking closer at the saddle of a rowing machine he saw slight signs of wear. They had been used, but not much. Whoever had used them though had not been back for a long time. Except, that by rights they should be covered in filth like the rest of the ship.

Ignoring the officer babbling across the radio, he looked for the vents that showed where the air would be circulating through. Elsewhere in the Starliner these had been partially choked with what looked like black water weed. He found it and stepped up to the wall where it was. Pristine white just like the rest of the room he stood on tiptoes to get a closer look.

He frowned. Something was not quite right here. Taking out the scanner he held it close to the slatted vent to get a reading.

"Everything okay?" called out Toze as he looked up from his radio conversation.

"I guess so, except this panel is clean. But there's a flow of air coming through; I can feel it."

Toze shuffled his way over through the gym equipment.

"Separate system from the rest of the ship?"

He checked the readout of the scanner and his brow wrinkled into a frown at the readings. "Apparently not."

"What?"

The scanner was passed across and the officer took a look. The readings showed that there was dirt here; the air ducts were filthy just like the rest of the ship.

"That doesn't make sense. Then the vent and the whole room should have become as filthy as the rest of the ship."

Tracker ignored him. He had taken a small toolkit from his belt and took out a small screwdriver. Poking it between the slats of the vent, he scraped it along then carefully drew it out. The tip was black and furry, covered in the same instantly recognisable muck that they had seen elsewhere.

Toze leant forward to take a closer look. The scanner confirmed it.

"So, some-one did clean this place recently?"

Tracker scraped the muck off the screwdriver and carefully replaced it into the toolkit. "It would look that way."

"The crew of the *Magellan*?"

"Not unless they really wanted to pump some iron in between exploring."

"Then what then?"

"You tell me."

"You're supposed to be the tracker in the group. Hell, that's why we call you Tracker."

Tracker sighed. "I'm a tracker not a psychic."

"I've run a scan on the different wavebands from the video feed," Spanners' tinny voice interrupted from the radio.

"Anything fun?" asked Toze.

Spanners chuckled. "The conspiracy theorists amongst you are going to love this. Evidence of molecular disturbance in rigid geometric patterns. They're on the mirrors, the walls and the floor. Hell, even the ceiling's been done."

Toze looked blankly at Tracker, who shrugged. "You might want to try English?" he sighed into the radio.

"It means that something gave this place a rub down with a cloth and cleaning fluid and was really anal about it. Every wipe of the cloth was the same as the last. I mean, *exactly* the same as the last. I'd say maybe a cleaning mech. Or a real neat poltergeist."

"Can the spooky shit. I don't think any of us really fully believe the civilian's ghost stories," snapped Toze.

"You have to admit his story hasn't been contradicted yet," said Spanners, "It still could be one possible explanation that fits."

"I'll believe it when I see it," rebuked the officer.

Tracker rested his hand on the officer's radio, attracting his attention. "This isn't necessarily a closed channel, Sir."

Toze thought for a moment then nodded. Perhaps it wasn't such a good idea to criticise and ridicule their companion when he could be listening.

"Okay, let's keep the channel closed unless we have anything meaningful to say."

Tracker nodded, satisfied. "Then I suggest we have a look and see how far the maid service goes. If we find a bot then we know it isn't ghosts."

*　　　　*　　　　*　　　　*　　　　*

Dezza had not wanted to leave, but he had not wanted to stay either. To watch a man – no, a fool – gorge himself in that way was sickening and filled him with disgust. He also felt the pangs of envy. The alcoholic in him was still there, fresh into rehab crying out for one last fix to ease the passage through the dry desert of recovery.

But he could not let himself fall back to that path. He turned and walked away without looking back. In truth he saw in Exbo greedily gulping the alcohol as a mirror image of himself. It was an image he hated himself for seeing. It still haunted him as he walked on into the darkened depths of the *Cerberus*.

He made much better progress without the private needling him all the time and it helped him to forget the booze and the cravings it had roused. The footprint trail turned into an open area where lights showed a set of elevators. On the floor the footsteps suggested that the people who had been here had stopped to try and get the lifts working. A panel stood open at the side of the lifts and tools littered the floor.

A shiver ran down Dezza's spine; it was as if whoever had tried to repair the wiring here had only just left. He nudged a screwdriver with a boot and saw that there was no dirt on it whatsoever. How creepy that felt. It made him feel like at any moment a person would come down the corridor to pick up their work where they had left off.

But the scans performed by Spanners had not shown anything living, and that included *Magellan*'s crew. It had made the others doubt. Of course, even a haunted house looks like a house when viewed by those who do not want to believe.

He knelt in front of the panel and took a closer look. A multimeter sat still connected by a pair of probes to various circuit boards. He recognised their design and knew that whoever had worked here tried to wire across the power to the rest of the controls. He had done something similar himself when the Tug had docked all those years ago.

He felt a pang of regret of the loss of Tubs and Zoë, but forced the feelings from his mind. It would not do to be lost into demons from the past right now.

The multimeter's screen was blank, but when he prodded the keypad it lit up again. Probably it had gone into power saving when the last user had left it. Looking at the tracks in the dirt, it looked as if they had been called away in a hurry. That, and they had left their tools behind.

It was a familiar model. Spinning the dial he chose a range and tested the lines that the probes were still attached to. A needle flickered and rose; there was power, though it was not crossing over to the main circuit. Gingerly he removed the clips of the probes and replaced them on another set of circuits. Before he placed them, he noted that the contacts on the wire were unmarked; the last user had been disturbed early in their task for whatever reason.

A cold shiver ran down his spine and he turned nervously to glance up and down the darkened corridor. For a moment it had felt as if some-one, or *something* was watching him.

But his shoulder light picked up nothing but the shadows of fittings and furniture that had long ago succumbed to the settling of filth and dirt upon them. He shook his head, shamed a little at the thoughts that had passed through him.

"Shit. Don't start up with the bogeyman crap now of all times."

His eyes felt dry and dusty. Some of the débris that had been stirred up by his feet must have got into them. He blinked a few times to clear the feeling and returned his attention to the panel. As much as he tried though, he could not remove from his mind completely the feeling of not quite being alone.

The contact points were dirty. There had been no engineer to use them in over ninety years, so he found an emery pen from the adjacent toolkit and gave them a rub until they shined with the dullness of pitted bare metal.

With the probes attached he found the main circuit was dead. Hardly surprising given the lifts were not working. He traced the circuits' power diagrams until he found the culprit. At the back of the panel a bundle of wires had melted through. Looking closer, something had dripped onto them causing the plastic shielding to deteriorate and fail until they had shorted. He ran a gloved finger over them and a crusty black deposit crumbled away. Whatever it had been it was inert now.

In the toolbox he found spare wire. Cutting a piece to length he carefully attached one end then held the other at arm's length as he scraped it over the next contact.

It sparked, and for a moment the entire corridor around him flickered brightly. Something moved in his peripheral vision and he turned instinctively to look, nearly wishing he had not. It was as if something was moving in the air before the wire in his hand shorted again. Then there was darkness and nothing but the shaking beam of his shoulder light. Breathing heavily, he looked along the corridor, but the feeble beam picked out nothing but what had been there before.

"Shit!" he exclaimed breathlessly.

His heart was racing with the fright. It had seemed almost as if there was a hazy face hovering in the air. Try as he might, he could not recall the vision properly. The more he tried to concentrate on the memory so the more the image in his mind seemed to taunt him and fade.

"Get a grip of yourself," he hissed out loud. His voice seemed unexpectedly loud and tense in the air.

The shorting wire had at least flickered the corridor's lights. Maybe that had triggered hallucinations? He looked closely into the panel and tried to steady the torch's beam so that he could see clearly. Yes, there were other circuits in here. When the power feed had shorted out it had isolated more than just the lift.

Screwing his eyes shut to stop himself seeing any more, he said a silent prayer to a God he did not believe in and thrust the wires together and twisted them tight.

They fizzled, and he smelt ionised air briefly through his mask. And then, there was nothing. He waited a moment, then opened one eye slowly, then the other. No monsters and no faces hanging as a haze in the air.

The lights in the corridor had reactivated. Glancing left and right he saw that all lights glowed as far as the kinks in the walls.

Compared to his shoulder light, the light was terrific. He reached up and flicked the puny light off.

"Looks like I won't be needing that."

The lift control panel glowed operational now. It had all been down to one shorted power feed. He looked to the toolbox on the floor that now looked so much less strange for being there despite the dirt. Had the original owner known how simple the repair job would be?

Looking around the deserted corridor, there was a lectern against the wall opposite the lifts and it stirred a thought in his memory. Remembering the one that Zoë had found in the atrium, could this give him a clear guide to a way through? Probably, he thought.

He stepped over and wiped the filth from its surface. Enamel showed underneath. It seemed unaffected by the tarnish and soon glowed back brightly as clean as the day it had been installed.

It was marked in the middle with a red arrow so he knew exactly where he was. Tracing down and across the surface with a finger he found the open space of the atrium with ease. So it was not that far away! It was still a number of floors above, but he glanced over his shoulder at the lifts and wondered whether they really would still work and make it easier to get to the right level.

He moved back over and outstretched a finger to the panel, then hesitated. He remembered the one that had come for them when he had explored the *Cerberus* the first time. What other horrors were waiting to be found in the depths of the Starliner? He put those thoughts aside, gritted his teeth, and stabbed the button and heard the motor whine kick in.

The car seemed to Dezza to take an unusually long time to arrive. Glancing up at the indicator above the closed doors he saw that it stuttered and slowed. He wondered if this was just the result of years of neglect on the fascia, but the motor whine became increasingly more laboured.

Looking to the still open service panel he expected any moment for all the circuits to die in a puff of shorting electronics. But it did not happen. The whine came to an end as the car reached his floor. Mechanics grated beyond the wall and the doors shuddered, then stopped only an inch apart.

"What now?" he muttered impatiently and reached forward to try and part the doors with a little brute force.

They were jammed. He could feel them slide a fraction of an inch further then something metallic stopped them. Bracing himself against the edge of the doorway recess, he managed to get the fingers of one gloved hand into the crack between the doors for better purchase and pulled with all his strength.

Something grated and groaned and the doors shuddered open a couple more inches. It had been more of an exertion than he had expected and he stopped to catch his breath. He had not remembered being this out of shape. Maybe the breathing mask was restricting him? He pulled out his scanner and took a reading of the air in the corridor. It checked in within all acceptable parameters; it was safe to breathe.

Gingerly he unhooked the mask and slid it to one side. Without its heating element the air seemed frigid, but only smelt stale.

He glanced through the gap; the inside of the lift car was completely dark. Another fused circuit perhaps? Something banged just above and he heard the sound of a cable whipping backwards and forwards under tension. It made him jump and he reached for the shoulder torch and flicked it on. He pushed it to the gap and peered through.

The lift car was there, of sorts. The back and one side appeared missing and he could see through into the structure of the lift shaft. Angling the torch beam to show more, he saw that the floor was there, but bent at a ninety-degree angle. Beneath it several cables dangled which had formed part of the hoisting mechanism. He could see that some cables were still intact and able to draw the car up, but others had been partially detached in whatever incident had ripped the car in two. Stretched out they were taunt and rigid, snagged on something. That was what had caused the strain on the motor and the indicator's erratic progress.

Something pinged loudly and the car shook violently. Dezza realised the cables must be under terrific tension; this was not a car to ride to another level. Getting his torch to illuminate as far

94

as it could into the lift shaft structure he could see that cables in the adjacent shafts looked as if they too may have suffered damage. It was not worth the risk.

There was a loud whipping noise, and out of the corner of his eye he saw one of the cables was no longer stretched tight. Something in the dark shaft made a noise like an approaching tornado, and instinct made Dezza drop back like a stone from the door.

The metal of the door reverberated to a massive blow and they puckered into the corridor. He thought he saw a hint of steel whipping by the crack between them. The booming noise of the impact echoed eerily, slowly fading until the only sound left was the gentle creak of metalwork from within the shaft.

He debated for a moment whether it might be safe to take a look. He guessed that the jammed cables had broken causing them to whip back up the shaft. He had been lucky that the still-closed lift doors had taken the hit. If they had opened first time he would have got a steel cable in the face; a sobering thought.

Another twang and a roar signalled the remains of the lift car breaking free to drop back down the shaft. He could hear it rumbling unchecked on its rails for a good while, gradually getting fainter, until finally a crunch echoed back up as it impacted at the bottom.

His thoughts jumped for a moment as he realised that the lift shafts might go all the way to the Starliner's outer hull. What if the impact caused a breach? On a fully functional ship there were safety systems to shut down adjacent compartments to a hull breach and stop explosive decompression. But the *Cerberus* was not exactly fully functional.

But the rumbling did not expand to anything more sinister, and quickly died away. The hull had not been compromised.

"I guess the lift's out then," he chuckled to himself, almost surprised at his capacity for humour so soon after such a close experience with danger.

He peered gingerly back into the lift shaft and played the torch beam across the space that was now empty. Looking up he saw the gently swinging frayed remains of the steel cables. They had sheared through just above the remains of the car. The structure of the shafts showed fresh angry metallic gouges where the steel ropes from below had whipped through.

He shuddered at memories of using the elevator on the *Cerberus* before. The thought had never crossed his or Zoë's minds when they had stepped into that car. It had worked just fine though, but they had never thought to check further. Sometimes salvage was about an element of blind faith and foolhardiness.

He tried the doors alongside the lifts and found one that led into a small office. He wouldn't have given it more than a second glance, but it did not seem quite so dirty in here though the dust was thick. There was a desk with a white computer terminal set against the wall. He tried the keypad, but the system was completely dead.

Looking over the walls he saw they were covered with framed notices that still seemed legible behind their glass. They listed ship's regulations and duty cycles. He read a few, but they seemed so old fashioned. He stopped and laughed – that was because they were. Sometimes it was hard to believe that a ship could float this long untouched in space as a time capsule to another century.

Under the desk was a wooden stool with a leather cushion. The leather was cracked and in need of some care that it would never get. He wagered that if anyone tried to sit on it then it might just split apart and disgorge its stuffing onto the floor. The desk drawers were not locked, and curiosity got the better of him and he slid them open one after another.

In the main they held stationary supplies. Even in the age of computers, sometimes a piece of paper did certain jobs better. Most of the pads contained pre-printed forms. The paper was aged brown and cracked apart when he tried to turn the pages. Some discarded used forms, lay in the bottom with curly copperplate handwriting, but it was too faded to read more than a few words.

Another drawer held nothing but a cracked glass tumbler and a small bottle whose label said it was some kind of Vodka, though the seal was broken and it was empty. They had once been hidden under some paperwork, but that had cracked and disintegrated over time to leave the secret contents exposed.

He slid it back and shut the drawer. So hidden alcoholism was nothing new.

*   *   *   *   *

Exbo had not meant to get drunk, but sometimes one drink turns into another and another so quickly that it is easy to go unnoticed. Back at the space station on leave he had spent much of his time in bars drinking himself under the table and getting into minor trouble with the shore patrol.

He thought of himself as having a tolerance to booze, but it was conveniently forgotten that deep space missions were always conducted dry and that those first few trips to the bar after return always turned hazier quicker than the trips the following day.

He knew that Dezza was getting over a drink problem. It filled him with glee on the sight of that first full bottle of sealed alcohol that here was a way to get the man he hated in the most effective psychological way.

It had disappointed him when Dezza had turned and just left; it wasn't the reaction he had hoped for. Even when he had slung a bottle it had been ignored, and Dezza had gone.

He had not meant to stay in the bar, but the liquor was the finest he had ever tasted, and it's hard to say 'no' to just one more when you have spent your life deluding yourself that you aren't a slave to the bottle. So he had downed huge mouthfuls of the sweet-tasting liquor and felt that familiar comforting fire of Dutch courage rising up from his belly. It was certainly the finest he had ever tasted; usually he drank the cheapest, most revolting mass-marketed filth that a bar had to offer. When you drank to oblivion, you might as well do it on a tight budget. But the alcohol was strong and was in a stomach that had been away from the drink longer than he had thought. The booth that had held him in stasis on the journey to the *Cerberus* had destroyed perception of time between end of leave and start of mission. It was easy to forget that a month in stasis was one hell of a detoxification for the body.

97

The bottle gurgled empty and he dribbled more than a mouthful down his front. The bar's surface was swimming with spilt drink, though he hardly noticed. Greedy hands fumbled for another bottle as the first flicked from his grip and rolled off over the edge of the bar to thump to the floor. It did not break; he did not care.

He found another bottle. But it seemed now to him that there was two bottles, each slightly hazy and moving nauseatingly from side to side. Actually, through the funk of his mind he realised that the whole room was doing much the same. He was very drunk.

The mind sobers up quickly when presented with the surprise of the unexpected. Exbo would never be certain what it was that had attracted his attention, but he felt the adrenaline pulse through his body and the hairs go up on the back of his neck.

The bottle was pushed away, forgotten and he slipped the gun to the ready and looked down only to check that the safety was off.

"Dezza?" he called out, though with uncertainty.

There had been a noise. But he could not quite recall what it had been and even now as the seconds ticked by he began to wonder whether he had heard anything at all. Had it been the sound of himself rifling the bottles?

He shook his head and grasped the gun tighter. Damn that Dezza! Maybe he had come slinking back? Toze would not approve if he knew they had split apart. Well, it was on Dezza's head; he had been the one to skulk off.

He heard something again. It was nondescript, at the edge of hearing but he was more certain this time he heard it even though if asked he would have been unable to place exactly what it was a noise of.

"Dezza! Quit messing around and get in here where I can see you," he called out.

No! It was not good to show an element of fear in front of the civilian. But such thoughts did not subdue the rising feeling of fear he felt.

"Okay, that's good now. You've had your fun and your own back now stop this fooling and let's get back on with following the trail."

There was no answer. For a moment he listened, straining his ears until he could hear nothing but the hiss of the blood coursing through his veins.

Something tinkled on the floor beside him, a soft crack of broken glass breaking apart further. He spun around expecting to see a grinning Dezza by his side, but instead saw nothing but fragments of booze-streaked glass that had already been crunched underfoot. He had probably done it himself when he had eagerly rifled the bottles and smashed some of the empties off the optics.

He knelt down and prodded the fragment with a gloved finger. It rocked on the floor and the private smiled.

"Scared by a broken bottle. Shit! What would the others have said."

Something appeared to move in the reflection of the mirror above him behind the optics. It was distorted, and from his crouched angle he could not really see. At any rate it stopped when he looked directly at it.

Dezza creeping up on him? He smiled; he would get him this time. Picking his moment he cradled the gun ready, then jumped up planning to give Dezza a taste of his own medicine and a scare he would not forget.

Instead, he screamed. In a panic he pulled the trigger on his gun and with a roar it began discharging a hail of bullets. Glass smashed and pucker marks marched up the wall.

The gun didn't stop firing until its magazine clicked empty, and the weapon thudded to the floor amongst still-hot spent cartridges.

*   *   *   *   *

Spanners analysed the video footage from the cameras attached to Toze and Tracker in the gym. It had bothered him that a cleaning robot might have settled only to clean one area of the Starliner continuously for over ninety years, though he supposed it was possible.

The screams and the harsh cracks of the gun were muted with the volume being down but they still drew that first pulse of adrenaline. Surprised, he glanced over the monitoring screens, and scanned along to find Exbo's.

It was streaked by static and snow, intermingled with occasional flashes.

"Don't do this to me!" he exclaimed. He banged the screen with the flat of a fist, as if this might somehow improve the signal. It didn't.

"Spanners, what the hell is going on?" came Toze's voice from the headset.

"Exbo, Sir. But the video link is down."

"What about Dezza's feed?"

He had not thought of that. He checked across to the adjacent screen, but it was fuzzy and showed a picture that looked badly tuned. Frantically he fiddled with the controls on the console trying to enhance the picture and cut out whatever was causing the interference, though he suspected it was the structure of the Starliner.

"Speak to me Spanners!" Toze's irate voice buzzed from the speaker.

"Can't tell, Sir. Must be something structural in the way blocking any feed. I can't see a thing!"

"Then we have to get through to them and find out what's happening."

Spanners saw the two clear video feeds on his console lurch and begin to jog. Tracker and Toze were already running to retrace their steps through the Starliner.

From the speakers Exbo's screams reached a crescendo and then stopped abruptly. The gunfire, however, continued in sporadic bursts.

"Exbo! Answer me!" he barked angrily, but there was no response and no sign that the private had even heard him.

"Shit."

"What's going on?" hissed a familiar voice from the console.

It was Dezza! Spanners grabbed the headset and pressed them close to one ear.

"Where the hell have you been?"

"Long story."

"Save the fairytale. What the hell is happening down there? I've got Toze screaming in my ear for answers and all I'm getting from the video feeds are static."

"I can't help you. Who's firing?"

"You mean you don't know?! It's Exbo," answered Spanners, the uncertainty creeping into his voice as he felt a sinking feeling, "But I thought he was with you?"

"We separated. It's a long story."

"Well you had better get that story good because Toze will unscrew your head and poke shit down the hole if he thinks you are messing him around."

The sporadic gunfire came to an end and nothing but hissing static followed it from Exbo's channel. Distracted, Spanners jabbed at buttons but nothing brought it back.

"Gunfire has stopped," panted Dezza's breathless voice. It sounded as if he was running to retrace his steps, though his video feed still showed fuzz.

"I know. Everything is dead from Exbo's feed."

"Well, I'm nearly there."

One of the screens on Spanners' console began to clear, and static began to give way to hazy shapes of real things rather than electronic noise.

"I'm getting your feed back. Are you nearly there?"

"Just one minute."

The image vaulted drunkenly around discarded furniture that had been piled on one side of a corridor. It was making Spanners feel a little motion sick; he hated these feeds. He found he had to look away for a moment. Then the image fuzzed up again and Spanners reeled at the angry buzz of static on the headset.

"I'm losing feed again," he shouted.

"He's gone," came Dezza's disbelieving voice.

Spanners looked back at the screens. Exbo's feed was still fuzzed, but Dezza's showed clearly. He saw the bar and the bottles lined up against the mirror behind it. The lights were on, but it was clear something had happened; a pall of white smoke hung in the air. At first he had thought it might be interference, but then he realised it was from gunfire.

The image flitted from side to side as Dezza moved around. Something caught Spanners' attention, but it was gone from the screen before he could really look at it as Dezza moved on.

"Stop. Right there. Move back a little."

The image moved, but not back to where it had been.

"A little more. It was on the bar top; I saw it as you walked past."

The image moved, and finally the objects came back into view. Spanners leant closer to the screen to get a better look. Finally he leant back and massaged his eyes with the back of his hands.

"Well?" asked Dezza.

"That is just plain weird, man."

*   *   *   *   *

The doors at the end of the pristine gym led on into equally pristine locker rooms. It was as dated as the gym equipment had been, yet looked as if the last users had left only moments before they had entered.

"The maid has been busy," said Tracker.

Toze nodded. "I wish she would come do my apartment some time.

Lockers stood in parallel rows. Like the rest of this area they were painted in the same clean shade of white.

Tracker tried the doors of the first couple on the nearest row, but they were locked.

"You won't get anywhere without keys," said Toze.

Tracker took out a small pointed device that had been secreted on his belt. Without looking round he knelt down and worked it into the nearest locker's door lock. "Just depends on what type of key you mean," he said softly without looking up.

The lock soon clicked open to the work of the lock pick. Placing the tool back into his belt, Tracker swung the door open and peered inside.

Toze looked on critically. "You have skills that weren't in your file."

"My file doesn't mention a lot of interesting things, Sir."

He reached in and took out a pleated white wrap-over skirt and a pair of gym pumps.

102

"Very pretty," chuckled Toze, "But not your size."

Tracker ignored the comment. "The material is old and there's dust in here," he said, feeling the skirt through his gloves.

He carefully put them back into the locker and ran his finger around the edge of the metal door. "They've been in here untouched for a long time. The edge of the door shows signs where dirt has worked its way in, but it's been repeatedly cleaned off the outside of the door."

Toze leant closer. It was true that the inside of the locker looked far more tired than the outside, and there was a line of congealed dirt around the edge of the door that looked to have been forced in over time.

"Cleaning robot?"

Tracker shut the door carefully and stood back up. "I'd say that's looking more likely than any kind of spooky shit. Pre-programmed and just doing its job, it's never strayed beyond its patch when all the other robots have long since stopped working."

"Then where is it?" asked Toze.

"Could be anywhere." He moved into the next isle behind the lockers.

Toze hung back, trying the other locker doors.

Something moved in the corner of his eye and he swivelled round thinking it might be the cleaning robot. Instead to his surprise, he saw a woman standing there, just seeming to be looking at him. He felt a shiver run down his spine and levelled his gun.

"Zoë?" he asked, full of his uncertainty.

The woman winked, but did not reply.

"What did you say?" Toze's voice came from behind the lockers.

Tracker looked around. By the time he looked back, the woman was gone. He moved slowly to the end of the lockers, but the room beyond was empty. In his mind he tried to recall the woman. She had not looked anything like the pictures that had been in the files of Zoë. She had not seemed to look at him, but through him in a way that had made him feel exposed and odd. Come to think of it, her clothes had been clean and more like a uniform than the grubby work gear that a deep space salvager might wear. He began to wonder if he could have imagined it?

"Hey Tracker, what's up?"

He turned to see Toze stood behind him.

The officer never got an answer. Muted and tinny, they both heard the patter of gunfire across the radio, and looked at each other in surprise.

"Standard marine issue weaponry," said Tracker thoughtfully, the image of the girl put to the back of his mind, "That's one of our own."

Toze reached for the radio. "Spanners, what the hell is going on?"

"Exbo, Sir. But the video link is down," came Spanners' crackling response after a moment's pause.

"What about Dezza's feed?" he demanded

Nothing but static and muted sounds of Exbo's screaming and gunfire came across the channel.

"Speak to me Spanners!" Toze snarled.

"Can't tell, Sir. Must be something structural in the way blocking any feed. I can't see a thing!"

He looked to Tracker then barked into the radio. "Then we have to get through to them and find out what's happening."

They picked up their heels and ran, the gym and the locker room. They paused only a moment outside to turn on their shoulder lights before they pounded back following their own footsteps in the dirt.

*   *   *   *   *

Dezza was crouching in the centre of the room as the pair came hurtling in. He barely looked up to acknowledge them both.

For a moment they both looked around, taking in the bar and the débris that was strewn across it. A slight haze of smoke still lingered in the air, drifting ever so slowly towards still working air vents.

"What the hell happened," demanded Toze, "Where is Exbo."

"Gone," replied Dezza softly without looking up.

"Gone? What do you mean gone?"

The officer took a step closer and looked at what Dezza was doing. On the floor beside him lay a standard issue gun, but it was not his own; that was still slung over his shoulder. A wisp of smoke drifted lazily from the barrel of the discarded weapon and Toze could see the floor was scattered with spent cartridges.

Dezza looked round. "I mean he just isn't here." He stood up and ran his hand over a wall that was puckered with fresh bullet holes.

"I thought you two were together? You must have seen what happened?"

"I left him here whilst I went on ahead. I came back as soon as I heard the gunfire."

Toze must have been able to tell he was holding back on him. There was something the civilian was not telling him, and he was going to push to know.

"Why did you split up?" he asked in a dangerous calm voice.

"It isn't important," Dezza mumbled.

"Yes it is! One of my men disappears in a hail of bullets, and you think that the reason you decided to do your own thing and leave him here just isn't something I might like to know?"

Dezza thought for a moment, then his shoulders sagged.

"He found a few bottles of liquor that were still drinkable and went stupid with them. I guess he thought he could get to me by taunting me with the addiction I had to kick to come here. I turned and left."

"Let me try another story on you," said the officer darkly never taking his eye off the man, "You got pissed at the private and found the perfect opportunity to take him down."

"Like shit!" hissed Dezza, dangerously close to exploding with rage.

"I've not been blind to the way you two have been at each other since the moment you met. He didn't like you and you certainly did not like him."

"I wouldn't kill a man."

"What happened to Tubs?"

Dezza reeled back. The words cut with the icy pain that an assortment of Astros had managed over the years since the tribunal. It did not matter how much he protested his innocence or fought back or did nothing, they kept on coming at him.

"You read the report," was all he could find to say.

For a moment the two men glared at each other, the emotions running high before Tracker's voice cut through the tension.

"I think something odd happened here."

They looked over. He was stood by the bar running his fingers down a string of bullet holes. Alcohol still pulsed from broken bottles scattered on the bar top. He took one gingerly in a hand and held it up to his mask.

"Something odd?!" said Toze with incredulity in his voice, "That's the understatement of the damn century."

"Where's the body?" asked Tracker quietly, "Because I don't see it."

Toze looked around, suddenly seeming aware for the first time that the man was right. There was a gun on the floor but any other traces of the private were missing. He must have sensed that the tracker was hinting at something else; that was the man's style. He never told everything at once but instead liked to lead people to the answers. That was his way as if he just liked the idea of helping people find their own way to what he meant.

Dezza looked around too. Then it struck him.

"The tracks?" He looked at the floor behind him. Some of the spent cartridges had rolled into the dirt, but there were no other footprints beyond where they had followed the tracks across the room. "Yeah. No tracks. Exbo didn't leave."

"That makes no sense!" spluttered the officer, "Of course he left otherwise we'd be seeing a body."

"Unless our man here can hoist two hundred pounds of corpse on his back and walk away with perfect steps, then I'd say he's clean," offered Tracker with an annoying calm voice.

"That's bullshit."

Tracker took a closer look at Dezza's gun. "And Dezza didn't fire a single shot. You think Exbo squeezed off two hundred rounds and there isn't even a scratch on the civilian. I don't think so."

"So what the hell was he firing at?" demanded Toze.

Tracker ran his eyes warily over the expanse of the room, almost as if seeing it for the first time and sizing it up. "You tell me."

"You're the tracker."

"All I know is that all he hit was the scenery."

Toze grimaced and activated the radio. "Spanners, give me details on Exbo's vital signs."

"No signal," came the static riddled reply.

"Video feed?"

"Negative."

"What do you mean? It can't all be dead?"

"I've retraced the logs and everything just drops at the same time. I can't tell you any more than I know, and I know nothing. Even his homer comes back with no signal. Another thing: Dezza couldn't have done it. I saw him come back into that area just before you did."

"Shit!" Exclaimed Toze.

Dezza knew from picking up snippets of conversation back on the space stations that the military deep space crews wore electronic micro beacons that could be used to pinpoint them on a mission if need be. The squaddies he had overheard in bars seemed bizarrely smug that even if they died in action, their bodies could be found and shipped back for a funeral with honours. It was a morbid pride that he had never understood. But for Exbo it seemed the faith of the squaddies in their equipment had finally been misplaced.

"What now, Sir?" asked Tracker.

Toze thought for a moment. "He can't have got far. We look for a body."

* * * * *

Try as he might, Spanners could get nothing from running and re-running the feed that the computer had recorded from Exbo. He cursed himself for not paying the attention he should have. He should have been watching those screens like a hawk. But it was easy to get distracted.

The feed ran back to a point where he saw the bar and the expanse of the room. Mounted with the shoulder light, the camera saw whatever the light illuminated. With computer analysis, the operator could see far more than the people out there in the derelict ever could.

It seemed odd to see what he knew might be the final moments of Exbo. Watching closely the picture jerked, and static engulfed it. Not before he thought he had seen something. Typing quickly on the controls he rewound the feed a few seconds and played it again. Yes! There it was again, just as the feed faded into static leaving a burst of audio of nothing but screams and gunfire.

He found himself rewinding those seconds of recording and watching them over and over again, as if his brain could not quite get enough of those frames on the screen. Rubbing his eyes he wondered for a moment if it was just patterns in the static, like those people who claim to see figures and messages in the fuzz of de-tuned video screens. It did not matter how many ways he looked at the image and how many times he rubbed his eyes, that same image bothered him. Was it or wasn't it?

Finally he froze the frame on the screen and stared at it hard. There, melding with the first vestiges of static that would later obliterate any feed, he saw what looked to him to be the white ghostly image of a disembodied face lunging in the direction of the camera.

It sent an icy chill racing down his spine. He did not want to believe the ghost stories, but sometimes even the sceptic is faced with evidence he cannot find any reasonable explanation for.

He was just about to reach for the radio channel when a vibration through the dropship's hull startled him. Waiting and listening with the blood pumping in his ears, he ran the sound back over in his mind. What the hell was that? For a moment he began to wonder if he had imagined it, pumped up from the fear raised by the image.

Another thump made the blood run cold in his body. That was real; he was not imagining it. At first his thoughts were a débris strike from space: it could have been tiny rock fragments bouncing off the hull. But a nagging feeling told him that the noise had come from somewhere else.

To calm his fears he moved over to the navigation console and punched up the holographic display. An image of the dropship, stuck like a tiny bump on the side of the *Cerberus,* shimmered into view and he stared intently at the readouts that hovered by its side.

A frown crossed his face; there was nothing on the navigation sweep and the logs showed there never had been. For a moment he wondered again if he might have imagined it, but the doubts pulled at his mind; those sounds had been very real.

Another thump, and a vibration that was unmistakable made the beads of sweat break out across his forehead. There was no mistaking it that time: it was coming from the airlock. He swung himself back to the seat in front of the main console. Could it be Exbo? He checked all the telemetry again, but everything on Exbo's channel was still dead.

"Damn!"

He drummed his fingers on the panel in front of him, wanting to believe it could be Exbo. It was a glimmer of hope in an explanation that did not bring with it questions and fear. But he knew from the deep down feeling in the pit of his stomach that it could not be the private.

As another thump echoed through the ship he reached for the radio and put a call out to the three still aboard the Starliner.

"Guys, I hate to be the one to bring this up," he said in a wavering voice, "but I think we have a situation here."

*   *   *   *   *

The argument was in full swing when the call came through the radio. No-one was paying attention, but Spanners repeated himself louder and they had to listen.

"I said, we have a situation here."

In the background through the channel they could hear the rhythmic banging. There was also no mistaking the fear in Spanners' voice.

"What's going on?" Toze barked into the transmitter, but any response was lost to a sea of static and noise. "Say again?"

Still no reply. He hit the transmitter in disgust. "What the hell is wrong with this stuff."

Tracker held his hand up for quiet. "Can you hear that?"

They listened. At first it was difficult to hear anything, then the far away noises of metallic could just be made out in the distance.

"Shit," said Toze slowly, "It really is happening."

"What is that?" asked Dezza.

Tracker shrugged. "Sounds like some-one hammering on an airlock door with a hammer to me."

"We're all here."

"Except Exbo."

Tracker's comment silenced them. They could hear the sound clearer now.

"You saying he might not be dead?"

They looked at the gun, and each realised they were clinging to a false hope. But the sound was still real, whichever way they looked at it.

Toze tried the radio again and was rewarded with Spanners' voice across the static. Ominously the sound of the banging came loud and clear across the link.

"There's something out there," said Spanners. It was clear he was scared. "I need to check the video link and see what's out there."

Dezza felt a pang of fear run down his spine. It was happening all over again.

*   *   *   *   *

The communications console showed everything was working normally. Spanners glanced over the panel as the banging continued relentlessly. He had tried contacting Exbo on his radio link, but got nothing. He wondered if there could have been a systems malfunction, but that image from the video record still haunted the back of his mind.

All that was left was to try and make contact through the airlock's intercom. He paused with his finger hovering over the button. He told himself that there were no such things as ghosts and said a silent prayer before letting his finger drop.

The echo of steel reverberating rang loud through the headset and he had to turn the volume down to a manageable level.

"Exbo. Is that you?"

There was no pause in the banging and it continued without breaking stride.

"Exbo!" he shouted, even louder this time.

He got no response and threw the headset off his head in disgust. All he could do now was turn on the video link and take a look. Even though it would be just a picture on the screen, a part of him felt scared to look. If it wasn't Exbo, what would it be? He agonised for a few moments.

The buzz of static and a voice in the headset shocked him with a start.

"Spanners! What's going on?"

He recognised Toze's voice and breathed a sigh of relief. The apprehension was making him jumpy. "I'm going to check the video feed and see what the hell is out there," he replied.

Not waiting for a reply he took a deep breath and turned on the video circuits and peered at the screen as a picture flickered on. It was hard to see anything as it seemed so dark. He could just make out the innards of the Starliner as a series of shapes in the gloom of furniture and the outline of walls behind.

The banging continued unabated, but it was impossible to see the inside of the airlock from this angle. Something moved at the periphery of the screen then was gone. Manipulating the camera controls he panned the image and tried to focus on the inner airlock door that was shut. The picture moved with agonising slowness, then stopped just short as the very top of the airlock door came into view.

Something in the gloom caught his attention, and he leant forward until his nose nearly touched the screen, trying to make out what he saw. Then, in the moment it happened, he reeled back in shock and desperately pounded his hand across the console trying to shut off the image.

The cry of alarm faded out into the staccato of static across the radio. Toze tried to call Spanners but all he got was static. He was about to retry when Tracker put out a hand to stop him.

"Do you hear that?" he asked in a dark voice.

"Hear what?" asked Toze in confusion.

"There isn't anything," said Dezza.

He was right; the banging that they had heard faintly echoing down the corridors of the Starliner had stopped.

Tracker nodded, his eyes searching the edges of the room as if looking for some unseen enemy. "Yeah. That's what scares me."

Toze reached for the radio. "Spanners. What are you doing? What's happening? Speak to me!"

The radio buzzed and Spanners' voice came back through. Toze breathed a sigh of relief.

"Where the hell have you been?" he barked.

"I… I think there's something in here." Came the faltering reply.

"Something in there?" demanded Toze. "Did you open the airlock?"

"No."

"Then how the hell can there be something in there with you?"

"I'm telling you, I feel like there's something in here with me."

"Tell me Spanners: how could anything have got in there with you if you kept the dropship sealed down."

"I think it came through the electronics. One minute there was, well, *something* out there and the next thing I know the lights are starting to flicker on the command deck and it's just not there."

"What's not there?" demanded Toze, but there was no answer from Spanners.

He seemed somewhat distracted.

Tracker reached for his own radio. "Spanners, listen to me. Calm yourself down and sit and think this through. You are letting your fears get to you."

The radio buzzed with another burst of static, but Spanners did not answer.

Tracker looked to the officer. "What do we do?"

"We have to go back and see what he is doing. If he's going to freak out on us they he could jeopardise everything."

Tracker led the way out of the bar and back along the trail of footprints in the dirt. The Starliner had not seemed quite so menacing before, but what it had lacked when they had arrived, it had more than made up for now. They reached the barricade and began climbing up one by one.

From the direction of the dropship they heard the strains of a new noise, and they stopped on top of the mound of débris. Dezza recognised it immediately and the distant memories of days roaming the stars on salvage missions made it all flood back. It sounded like the hiss of jets, muted and dulled by the thickness of the Starliner's hull, and with a sinking feeling he knew the only ship it could be coming from was the dropship.

"Hurry up!" he yelled and began scrabbling ahead through the tight tunnel on top of the pile, "If that sound is what I think it is we have to stop Spanners some how. He's detaching the dropship from the airlock!"

On the other side of the obstruction he paused only to help the other two down, then they turned and ran.

As the corridor turned to open out at the airlocks, Tracker held them back and indicated they should wait a moment whilst he checked the way ahead. The sound of jets was louder here.

It seemed like an age before Tracker waved them on and they slipped out into the open area that had welcomed them onto the Starliner so innocently when they had arrived. The airlocks were already closed and sealed and all they could do was see through the observation windows the bulk of the dropship rotate away from them as it finished its undocking procedure.

"What is the idiot doing!" screamed Toze.

They were too late. There was nothing any of them could do to stop Spanners now.

*   *   *   *   *

He had felt the presence from the moment he had seen the image dissolve on the screen. Reeling back from the console he had felt the instinct to turn off the feed. Something told him that if

113

he could cut himself off from that image then everything would be all right. As the screen returned to blank though he was left with the queasy feeling that he had not quite been quick enough. In his mind he ran the image he had seen in that final second, over and over again. He had hardly believed it; maybe it was a product of the stress and fear?

He had seen a ghostly white phantom in the shape of a face seem to dissolve at him as if pouring itself into the camera and onwards to his screen.

The banging had stopped almost instantly, as if that phantom had been the cause. He looked around and realised that his clothes were sticking to him from the torrents of cold sweat. Wiping his face with the back of a hand, he felt the sting of the sweat in his eyes.

For a moment he sat and stared at the blank screen, running the thoughts through his mind that he was panicking over nothing. But it felt so false when his subconscious would not listen. Suddenly every tiny sound aboard the dropship's command deck made him gasp and his eyes darted furtively with each tiny noise that before had seemed like nothing to him.

"Pull yourself together," he muttered, but his voice sounded somehow empty and odd.

Something creaked behind him, and he spun rapidly in his chair. There was nothing there and his eyes darted backwards and forward looking for what might have caused the sound.

"Just the structure of the ship contracting like it always does," he tried to reassure himself.

It seemed like a good explanation and a *safe* explanation. He had not believed in ghost stories before, so why start now? Yes, he thought, that's a better way to think.

The headset buzzed with voices through the static making him jump until he realised it was the others. Gingerly he slipped the headset back on – he had not even realised in his shock that he had taken it off. He heard Toze demanding to know what was happening, and in a faltering voice he found himself telling him that he felt like he was not alone. The officer seemed sceptical, but it was the truth that he did feel like *something* had just poured itself in down the electronics as if it was nothing more than an open tube.

The lights seemed to flicker and he looked up to the panels above him. Did they do that before, he wondered? He certainly had not noticed it if they had. He let the headset slip off again; putting the clamouring voices to the desk. They could wait for now. Then he noticed that his breath was beginning to leave a trail in the air every time he breathed out, and his heart rate began to increase.

He pushed himself out of his seat and pulled himself to the adjacent console. Scanning his eyes down the screens he saw at first that everything looked normal on the atmosphere of the ship. So why was it so cold? Then he noticed the cabin temperature on the gauge visibly falling.

An odd feeling told him there was something behind him. At any other time he might have looked, but in that moment he was paralysed with fear. Every nightmare he had ever had came back all at once into his head and in that moment Spanners was the small child too frightened to look in the closet at night in case there were monsters. It was a feeling he had not felt since childhood.

"What do you want?" he stammered, shaking as the sweat rolled off him. He could almost feel the icy fingers clawing at his back.

He never got an answer. Summoning the last shreds of his courage, he counted to three and turned.

*   *   *   *   *

Toze hammered his fists on the airlock door as he saw the dropship hesitate and waver under its jets, but there was nothing he could do. With their noses pressed against the icy cold of the thick glass, they watched, as the ship wallowed then veered to the side.

"He's going to hit those aerials!" exclaimed Dezza.

To the side of the airlock level, an array of antennas pointed out into the starscape with several winking lights illuminating their vast length that must have been more than a hundred metres.

The central mass was a steel pole that stretched out but there was a forest of wires radiating out at all angles and tied back to the hull of the Starliner.

The dropship came closer and closer. For a moment it looked like it might correct and just miss the tip, but the manoeuvring jet that fired twisted the ship around and failed to stop. All they could do was watch in stunned disbelief as the dropship looped into an uncontrolled roll and sliced through the aerial array before grazing the Starliner across its upper superstructure.

They felt the vibration of the impact running through the floor beneath them before they heard the echo of steel grating against steel.

There was a flash of light as something exploded silently in the vacuum out on the dropship then a jet of vapour erupted from the stricken vessel's side propelling it in an arc back away from the Starliner.

With sinking hearts they could only watch in stunned silence as the dropship flashed again and pieces of the hull peeled off in the decompression before the spinning remains drifted away to be lost against the backdrop of stars.

The dropship was lost, and with it had gone Spanners and any explanation of what had really happened.

*   *   *   *   *

The interior of the *Cerberus* seemed far more foreboding and unfriendly than before. For Tracker and Toze, this was *real* now. Where they had been sceptical before they had entered the stasis for the Rösenbridge jump, now they were starting to believe.

Toze took it worst. Dezza had been here before and maybe he knew what to expect. He had already lost a crewmember to this ship and had had the time to learn to deal with it. For the others there was not that luxury; this was the here and now of it all.

If the officer had admitted the truth, he would probably have said it was the first time he had lost a man under his command, much less two. But he would never tell the others that even though it was likely the biggest thought on his mind weighing down his consciousness.

Tracker never showed what he thought. Behind those deep blue eyes there could be any manner of thoughts lurking, or none. No-one ever knew. But he had to have been rattled by the experience. No team ever lost first one then another man from right under their noses with nothing firm to account for it and walked away without some kind of psychological baggage. But on the outside Tracker was still the same old calm and reflective man that he had been from the first moment that Dezza had stepped out of stasis and met him.

"The only way off this hulk now is the *Magellan*," said Dezza.

Tracker nodded. "I go with the civilian's idea, Sir," he said to Toze.

Toze seemed to agree.

It was not hard to pick back up the trail of the footsteps that had taken them into the Starliner the first time. There had been no discussion as Dezza told them to follow his lead. They might have still harboured some doubts over whatever stalked the *Cerberus*, but at least the deserted *Magellan* provided a glimmer of hope. It was not part of the *Cerberus*, even though it sat silent and dead attached to an airlock. It had come from a known background and not straight out of the hazy past and an urban myth. It represented a lifeline back to the real world.

At the corridor with the lifts, Dezza sensed the pair behind him hesitate upon seeing the still open panel and tools ready by its side bathed in the unnatural glow of still working lights.

"It's just as I found it," he heard himself offer in explanation, "Some-one from the *Magellan* must have left them. I finished the job and got the circuits working."

Both said nothing; they had seen the puckered steel of the lift doors buckled and stung by fresh damage.

"What happened?" asked Tracker.

"The cable must have snagged then snapped. It whipped up the shaft and did that."

Tracker ran his hand over the door, as if feeling for the pulse on some dead or dying animal.

"Don't worry," said Dezza, "There's a deck plan behind and we can get down the stairwell to the level we need."

Toze went to look at the lectern, but a rumble echoed faintly from somewhere a long way away down the corridor that they had come making all of them look up. Dezza saw that there were beads of perspiration on the other two men's foreheads, and he could feel his own start to prickle too.

"What, may I ask, was that?" asked Tracker slowly.

The noise echoed again. It was indistinct, but ever so out of place on a floating derelict.

"The dropship hit the outer hull hard. It could be structural damage," offered Dezza, but the explanation did not seem to convince him let alone the others.

"I'd like to believe that," said Tracker softly, "But I'm beginning to think that a hull compromise could be the least of our worries."

"I suggest we get the hell out of here whatever that is," said Toze. Nobody argued. "Where's the stairwell?"

Dezza needed no further motivation as he led them through an adjacent doorway into the dirty stairwell behind.

They hammered down the stairs taking them three at a time. If that noise had been structural, then there might not be a lot of time and they each knew that, even if they did not particularly believe it. On a functioning Starliner there would be more than a hundred redundant systems in place to seal off compartments with hull damage. But there were no guaranties here that anything might still work as they should.

The levels were marked off with huge numbered panels. Most of the passengers on the Starliner would have used the lifts, so the these were far more utilitarian than the corridors they led off. At each level a door was set into the side just like the one they had entered through. It was easy to become disorientated, and it was only the tall numerals on the wall that stopped them losing their bearings.

At the bottom level Dezza made to shove his way through the door and into the corridor beyond, but at the very last moment Tracker reached forward and grabbed him, shoving him hard against the wall.

"What the hell?" Dezza stuttered, but Tracker put a finger to his mask and gestured him to be quiet.

Behind him he saw Toze's face wrinkle in confusion.

"What are you doing?" demanded the officer.

"Something's wrong," replied Tracker slowly. He let go of Dezza and dusted him down. "Sorry about that, but I just had this hunch."

"Hunch that I was going to run off?" snorted Dezza indignantly, "Come on. Drop the crap; I had enough of that from Exbo."

"God rest his soul," interrupted Tracker. He leant over and gave the door a push. It swung open at an angle. Behind it was nothing but inky blackness. Reaching up to his shoulder he switched on his light and played it through the opening.

"I don't think you would have liked it in there," he said as if this were an everyday occurrence.

Toze and Dezza looked through. The torch light stretched out into a void. At the edge of the door, deck plating stretched out for maybe a couple of feet with tattered remnants of carpet clutching on as strands, then the metalwork twisted down and disappeared into a hole that seemed to have been torn into the Starliner's innards.

The light from the torch penetrated the slightly dusty air as a beam that petered out after a few tens of metres without illuminating anything other than a few twisted stanchions that pointed up from the abyss like a petrified forest of decayed steel.

"It's a long way down into oblivion."

"How did you know?" asked Toze.

Tracker looked nonchalantly around the stairwell. "The dust patterns are all wrong. You can see from the airflow that what was beyond the door was nothing but empty space. Call it instinct, but instinct told me that dust should not look like it's drifting like sand in a summer breeze."

It was true; there was a pattern in the dirt around the edge of the doorframe. Decades of the passing of air patterns had forced the dust into furrows and grooves across the wall and over the remnants of the carpet. Undisturbed for nearly a century, it had given the man the clues he needed to the danger beyond.

"What could have caused that?" asked Dezza, still shaken from his near miss with death. If Tracker had not stopped him he would have certainly plunged into the void. There was no telling how far down the hole went.

Tracker shrugged. "Structure failure. Something ripped this deck apart and at least a couple below. Hard to tell."

"We have to find a way around," interrupted Toze.

Tracker nodded. The torch beam played upwards revealing a ceiling of the deck above. Twisted fragments showed the outline of where rooms and walls had been. Ornate ceiling plasterwork looked wholly out of place.

"Deck above still looks sound. Maybe we can make our way through up there and drop down the other side."

"And what if this damage stretches all the way?"

"It can't," he replied, "It must be localised or the Starliner's hull would just buckle outwards under the forces of the vacuum of space. Besides, this damage is old – see the dirt and tarnish over where the steel has failed. Whatever Dezza saw when he was on the ship last should still be there, just as he left it."

Dezza led the way back up the stairwell to the next deck. He stopped at the door and pushed it gingerly open in front of him this time, half expecting an extension of the void. But there was nothing but a corridor lit by still glowing light fittings and occasional patches of darkness where fittings had blown. He tested the deck carefully; fearing it might give way. But the structure was sound and easily held their weight.

"Is it safe?" Toze asked.

"Safe as it will ever be."

Another rumble echoed from above down the stairwell. It was fainter than it had been, seeming further away. None of the three needed any more encouragement to go on.

"Safer than I feel staying here," announced Dezza, and moved through quickly. The others followed.

*   *   *   *   *

The idea had been simple: find a way across the damaged areas then locate a stairwell to take them back to the level they needed. Sometimes things are never that simple. Instead, the corridor came to an end at a ninety-degree T-junction. They faltered, but Tracker made a decision and led them to the left. But presently this corridor came to an end too, facing them with having to double back and try the other way.

Another junction, then another left them disorientated and unsure of direction. Finally they came back to an intersection only to be presented with their own tracks disappearing from left to right.

"Face it: we're lost," sighed Dezza.

Tracker knelt down and examined the tracks. "Definitely made by us. I'd agree with the civilian."

"There's got to be a way out," cursed Toze, "They can't have made this maze to trap passengers. Can we find our way back to the main stairwell?"

The floor began to vibrate beneath them. An echo reverberated down the corridor like a dull moan of escaping air.

"Hull breach!" hissed Dezza, but Tracker shook his head.

"No air movement. I'd say that retracing our steps right now might not be the cleverest thing."

"Why so?"

"I think, we're being tracked," he said, weighing up each word carefully.

"Tracked!" snorted Toze.

It did sound incredible, but then the noise came again, a little louder and they all turned to look down the empty corridor.

"Then, you tell me what that noise is," said Tracker softly.

"The stairwell seems to have been the only way in though," protested Toze.

Dezza shook his head. "No. There will be other ways like fire escapes and service areas. There has to be more than one way in and out of each level.

Tracker nodded. "Look for a door that doesn't have an electronic lock on. Any of the others are likely to be passenger cabins. Find one without and we have a chance at the magic way out of here."

He pointed to the nearest door. It had a chunky box beneath the handle designed to take an old fashioned electronic card. These must be the passenger cabins, and the others nearly kicked themselves for not realising that any door without one must lead to something other than a cabin.

They fanned out down the corridor checking each door in turn. With so many lights not functioning, it was a matter of walking up to each door and feeling for the card reader. All the lock circuits were dead, and none of the doors yielded to a twist of the handles. They were just another failed circuit on the Starliner.

A handle yielded under his hand "Over here! I've got one!" hissed Dezza. Feeling below it there was no keycard box.

The door moved no more than a couple of inches then stopped. Something was jamming it at the bottom, but the gap was not big enough to feel through for what it was.

"I need some muscle here."

Toze and Tracker threw their weight behind it, and with a grating noise the door shuddered open some more.

"I think I can get my hand in now," said Dezza, and went to slide around the edge.

Tracker stopped him.

"What now? Another void?"

Tracker's smile was visible despite the mask. "No patterns of dust. I'm just not the one rushing to push my hand into a dark hole after all that we've seen so far." He leant forward and whispered, "I'd be more careful is all I'm saying."

When Tracker put it like that it made him a little nervous. There was something about the man that demanded to be listened to. He had an air of knowledgeable authority without ever seeming to usurp the officer. It suddenly struck Dezza that it was the attitude that had made him warm to Tracker more than he had to any of the others.

They took his advice and put their shoulders into the door. It moved a little more, but still refused to open easily. The gap was wide enough now to get a light through and Toze waved them to a stop and shone his light through. In its beam they saw the dusty remnants of a laundry room. Shelves of linen lined the walls, and there was some kind of chute structure in the wall at the back.

"Bingo. Looks like we could try the laundry chute to get out."

122

"Can you see what's blocking the door?"

The light angled round as far as it would go before it wedged against the frame.

"Not clear. Some kind of tangled mess of equipment."

"You want to try putting a hand in now?" Dezza asked Tracker.

The man nodded. "Seems okay."

He reached past the officer and fumbled behind the door.

"Well jammed. Something wedged this shut real good."

It gave a little and the door began to move.

"I think that should loosen it up enough. Give it another shove."

They moved back and gave the door another terrific push. There was the snapping of wood and the door yielded enough for them to start squeezing through.

Toze was the first to go. "I'll make sure we're clear," he called back. It was a tight fit and his belt caught in the frame.

"Shit. Give me a hand here."

Tracker felt around under his legs. "I got it."

Material ripped and the officer fell through into the room. A groan was jolted from him.

"You okay Sir?" asked Tracker.

"Fine. Just tripped on this crap and.... Oh."

His words faltered. Tracker and Dezza instinctively pressed to the gap.

"It's barricaded good from the inside," said Toze slowly, "And I found who did it. There's a body in here. Not much left of it but bones."

Dezza remembered the bodies in the lift that he had ridden with Zoë. He had not really thought about it much since; they had had to leave so quickly. With a knot in his stomach he realised that Tubs' body would still be in that lift where they had left it in their haste to leave. He did not relish the idea that they might find him again. What would just five years on a derelict in space do to a body that was still sealed inside a suit? He did not want to know.

The deck beneath their feet vibrated, cutting his thoughts mercilessly off short.

"What the hell was that?" came Toze's voice.

Tracker looked around. From the wall fittings down the length of the corridor dirt fluttered, dislodged by the vibration.

"Structure failure?" suggested Dezza.

Tracker shook his head. "I don't think so. More like some kind of impact."

Dezza opened his mouth to say something, but the words were forgotten as the deck shuddered again. This time a moaning rumble echoed in the corridor as more dirt fluttered to the floor.

"I think," suggested Toze from behind the door, "We should look at getting the hell out of here."

Dezza looked to Tracker.

"Unless you have something better to do, I suggest you press your pretty self through that gap."

He did not argue. Squeezing through, Tracker quickly followed. The rumbling was getting louder and more powerful; the corridor lights began to flicker.

Behind the door cleaning equipment had been used to barricade it shut. Bars had been forced through the hinges, and these had resisted their attempts to enter. Even now they were bent and buckled but largely held. If it were not for the tarnish and decay, it would not have opened at all.

Dezza hesitated at the body. It was difficult to tell gender after so long. Huddled against the wall nothing was left of it except a skeleton that was draped in remnants of cloth that had decayed with the body. He wondered how they had died. They might have huddled there in fear from something, barricaded in with nothing but faith to keep them going. It had been a faith that had faltered and let them down.

"Forget the stiff. Help me close this," grunted Tracker.

Dezza helped him push the door back shut and wedge the hinges. Just what exactly were they frightened of? He did not know but he felt the fear rising. There was something out there. The noise was getting louder as if warning of the approach of whatever had banged on the airlock of the dropship and spooked Spanners. It had certainly seemed real enough to him.

With the door wedged they turned their attention to the back of the room. It wasn't very big, and had most likely been used by staff changing bedding in the passenger cabins.

Toze popped open the hatch on the chute and peered in. "Tracker! Get over here and give me an opinion."

124

He glanced in and tested the air. "There's some airflow. Anyone got a flare?"

"I've got some." Toze flipped open a pouch in the belt and slid out a slender red candle-shaped cylinder.

Tracker took it and twisted the top. Immediately it spluttered and flared and a red glow bathed the whole room more powerful than their torch beams.

"Let's see just how low you go."

He held the flare into the chute and dropped it.

Three faces leant over the lip to watch it drop down ten feet of chute before metalwork ended at a twisted lip and the flare fluttered off into nothing getting smaller and smaller until it flicked off something and disappeared. It must have more than a dozen floors. It was a fall that would easily kill a man.

"Down is not an option."

Toze flashed his light up the chute. Dull steel reflected its glow maybe ten feet then an opening in the side showed where there had to be another linen room on the next deck up.

"That's where we want to be."

"Any ideas?"

The deck shook again more violently. A rain of dislodged dust fluttered down the chute from the vibration.

"We need a rope," said Toze.

Dezza looked around the room. There was nothing other than piles of neatly folded bed-sheets stacked on the shelves and shrouded with a layer of undisturbed filth. An idea struck him.

"Knot the sheets together. If we're lucky they'll hold. Get something weighty on the end and we can sling something up there to wedge in the hole. Lightest person goes first and secures it whilst the other two hold tight this end in case he slips and falls." He looked to Toze.

The officer nodded. "Let's do it."

Some of the sheets were so perished that the material ripped as they were tied. Others seemed to have been protected from the effects of ageing in the middle of the piles and held better. It was still hit and miss as to whether they might hold. The rope soon strung out across the floor, made from those sheets that seemed still strong after all the time undisturbed, though there were still doubts in Dezza's mind. You wouldn't trust your Grandmother's old sheets for climbing out the bedroom window he thought, and these were more than twice as old.

A broken off piece of metal from the shelving provided a heavy object that was knotted to the end of the rope by its centre. Its weight would provide a means to hook the rope through the opening of the deck above.

"Who thinks they can throw the best?" asked Toze.

The other two looked at each other. "I'll take the first go," said Tracker with a smile.

Toze handed him the bar and rope and he leant through the chute's opening. There was not much room and he had to twist himself onto his back and brace himself against the opening to get both hands free.

With the mound of sheets coiled onto his belly, he narrowed his eyes to judge the distance and threw it. His aim was good, and the metal clunk and thud that echoed back down the chute told the others that he had done it first time.

He tugged the rope gingerly. It gave a few inches then the bar lodged on something and it seemed to hold. He wriggled himself back out of the chute and looped the other end of the sheets to the bottom of the shelving.

"If it gives whilst the first of us is climbing up, I'd rather know the other end stood a better chance of holding me," he said, and winked.

It seemed that Tracker knew he would be the lightest without even asking. There are some people who grow old without ever putting on an ounce of fat, and he was one of them. Dezza could see in him a man who took a secret pride in his body. Five in the morning runs and a watchful diet; Dezza had seen the type before. He had once been the same, but years in the bottle had not been kind.

Tracker lay his gun against the wall by the chute and took off his belt. There was nothing to be gained by testing the sheets with any more weight than they had to. He put his upper body through the opening and tested the sheets with a last tug; they held.

"See you on the topside," he said and without waiting for an answer he launched himself through and was gone leaving only the bundle of sheets dangling that twitched as he climbed higher.

Dezza leant through the hole and looked up. He could see him working his way up bracing his weight against the structure as he clung to the home made rope. The man climbed like an eel and quickly reached the next level and vaulted through and was gone.

The sheets twitched a moment then his face reappeared. Under the mask there was clearly a grin.

"Okay, bring my stuff and get up here one at a time."

Toze pushed his head past Dezza's and looked up the chute.

"Is there a way out up there?" he hissed.

Tracker gave him a signal with his fingers that meant there was. "Sure. Laundry room. The corridor outside looks like a service level; easy way through without getting lost in a maze."

"Shit," said Toze, glancing to Dezza, "If we had known we could have gone straight onto that level from the main stairwell."

Dezza found himself glancing down the chute. His light picked out the jagged edges, then inky darkness.

A rumble echoed from the floor and the chute. Instinctively he looked up, expecting to see something falling, but there was nothing. Dust fluttered into his eyes and he cursed, pulling himself back into the laundry room.

"Shit!" he exclaimed, blinking the dirt from his eyes. They hurt like hell and streamed, but he could see.

He was surprised to see Toze white faced, looking at the barricaded door.

"What's up?" he asked, confused, before realising that the vibration was coming loudest from outside in the corridor. Then it stopped, like it had never been there.

"Ever get the impression," said Toze slowly without taking his eyes off the door, "That we're being followed."

"Followed?"

Before Toze could answer the door shook as if his from outside. Both men reeled in shock.

"What's going on down there?" hissed Tracker's voice from the chute.

The door shook again and a metallic vibration ran through its hinges.

Dezza took hold of the officer and pushed him towards the chute. "No time to argue! Get in there! I'll follow you out."

He nodded. Tying Tracker's belt around his own waist and slinging the gun over a shoulder with his own he swung out into the chute and climbed hastily upwards.

The door reverberated again, filling Dezza with the feeling of icy fear. What the hell was that? Backing to the chute he never kept his eye or the barrel of his gun from that door. It was well barricaded, probably better than when they had found the room. But with a sinking feeling he doubted it would hold whatever was outside for long.

He thought of the sounds they had heard before. When Spanners reported there being something outside the airlock of the dropship, they had all heard the faint noises. They had been sceptical, even when Spanners had seemed to find it real enough to detach from the Starliner and lose control. Now it seemed more real than anything else did.

"Hurry it up!" he called out to the chute.

"Nearly there; just one moment."

The door shuddered and the barricade began to crumble.

"No time!" Dezza yelled and in a moment of panic he realised just how Spanners must have felt. Slinging the gun in such a hurry over his shoulder that he nearly dropped it, he grabbed at the sheets and swung out into the chute.

He felt the material start to give under the combined weight of two men, but it just spurred him to climb faster ignoring the warnings from Toze. In the laundry room he heard the door withstand another blow, and it sent the adrenaline pumping hard in his body.

*   *   *   *   *

Toze had hardly got through the opening before Dezza appeared at speed and launched himself through onto the floor.

"What's going on down there?" asked Tracker.

"It's at the door," he spluttered breathlessly.

128

Without uttering a word, Tracker pulled a knife from the belt around Toze's waist and sliced through the sheets in one. Kicking them through the chute opening, he heaved the metal door shut and locked down a latch. The chute was sealed.

He looked at the two companions sprawled on the floor before calmly taking his belt and gun.

"I suggest we move on." He led the way out of the door onto a well-lit dirty corridor beyond.

They moved quickly, as there was no way of telling how close what had followed them and tried to trap them in the laundry room might be. Every corridor looked the same - just dirt and decay flitting by in the beams from their torches. But Tracker had a knack to knowing which way to turn. The others might be hopelessly lost, but he never faltered more than a moment at each junction.

Three times he stopped, urging the others to silence with a hand gesture. They would wait, the seconds ticking by with antagonising slowness as Tracker listened, always trying to sense the coming of the creature. But each time there was nothing; they never waited long.

They passed a huge room filled with the remnants of a party that had been over before it started long ago. Their lights glittered on shreds of tinsel and table decorations and a hundred tables were laid out for guests who had never come.

Tracker never stopped and as the other two faltered to take a look he warned them to keep on the move. There was no time left to explore, so they just headed on, relying on the skills of the tracker.

*   *   *   *   *

Even through the breathing masks that filtered out some of the smells, Dezza recognised the atrium. He had not realised it had a unique scent when he had been here last with the Tug crew. They had been so preoccupied that it had never occurred to them. Maybe it was the smell of what was left of the decayed plants. Perhaps it was ionisation from space through the material of the vast canopy above that afforded a view of the immensity of space. Some places just have their own unique sensory feelings.

That smell had meant nothing at the time, but sometimes in the years that had followed he would be woken up in a sweat after a nightmare and it had seemed almost as if that smell had lingered in his nostrils. Some people said you could not dream smells, but Dezza knew they were wrong because he had smelt the atrium of the *Cerberus* over and over again. It was a smell that had driven him further into the bottle.

Now was different. Perhaps there was something in experiencing a thing for real rather than a memory of it that could be warped in perception over time.

"I've been here before," was all he found he could say. In his chest he felt his heart beginning to pound as his memories asserted themselves in his mind.

He did not want to be here. Summoning up courage, he fought with his instincts and feelings that made him want to turn and run, and made himself take the final few steps to the end of the corridor. He moved into that open void that his memories had twisted in his nightmares to his own personal hell.

It was much as he remembered it. In part some of his fears had been that there would be something else here, waiting for him. But there was not. The husks of long dead plants still huddled across the main area bathed in the eerie glow of starlight and picked out in relief by the passing of three torch beams that played across the vast open area.

Toze rolled his head back and gazed up at the stars. Far away from the pollution of atmospheres this was a sight that only those who had deep space experience could ever truly appreciate.

"That is one hell of an amazing view."

Tracker pointed to one dot amongst others in constellations that seemed so far away. "As a hunch that one is Earth. I'd have a fifty-fifty chance of saying I could see your house from here."

"I live on Mars when I'm not at work," replied Toze.

"It was worth a guess."

The officer looked to Dezza. "You can guide us to the airlocks where the *Magellan* is from here?"

Dezza nodded. A part of him felt the rising fear of what might they find there. Zoë had been aboard that ship, and it was still here. That meant in his mind that she was still aboard the Starliner. Or at least, her body had to be. He did not want to see that; she had been a good friend, and he wanted to be able to tell himself there was still a chance for her, no matter how slim.

"Sure," he found himself saying.

The corridor had brought them out one level above the plaza area and on the opposite side from the grand staircase. Each level had a walkway that ran around the entire atrium and it was easy enough to follow it around.

As they neared the staircase Tracker put up his hand to call a halt and pointed to the floor.

"Tracks. Some-one's been here recently."

Leading around the wide walkway from the direction of the staircase a clear path in the dirt had been disturbed showing the bright crimson of the carpet underneath. It made for a striking contrast compared to the muted dark grey of the dirt of the floor from where the trio had come. There were a lot of footprints, and in places the dirt had been disturbed over and over again so that it was impossible to pick out individual boot indentations.

"Too many tracks to have been exploring," said Tracker, kneeling down to take a closer look at the edge of the tracks. "Looks like a lot of heavy equipment being dragged by. Difficult to tell if they were coming with it or going."

He pointed to the edge of the mess. Scrape marks showed that something heavy had been moved and the number of times the marks criss-crossed suggested that it had happened more than once.

Tracker looked up at Dezza. "Any ideas?"

"Not unless they found something to salvage here. They were a salvage crew, right?"

"If that's the way I read the brief, then yeah."

Somehow, Tracker did not seem convinced and to tell the truth, Dezza thought much the same.

"Whatever happened here we don't have time for it," interrupted Toze, "Let's get to the *Magellan* and see what it's going to take to dust off this crate. I don't know about you two, but I've got a pretty good idea that I don't want to be hanging around on board this hulk any longer than I absolutely have to."

Dezza led them around the last part of the walkway. Despite the clear path trodden through the dirt, he found himself walking along the edge making new tracks in the dirt. There was something about standing in dead men's footsteps that unnerved him.

At the grand staircase the trail led up. For one moment Dezza found himself looking back down the stairs towards the floor of the atrium and saw that in the dirt, faded and muted by the few years that had passed since, where his own footsteps along with those of Zoë and Tubs. It left him feeling cold and numb to be reunited with his past like this. For the first time in years he felt that moment when he had walked down these steps with clarity that had until faded over time. Then there had been no evidence of other human activity; the *Cerberus* had been dead.

Almost.

He remembered the computer system deep within the engineering spaces and the information it had given him before he had realised the truth behind the *Cerberus*. No-one had wanted to believe when he and Zoë had returned to the shipping lanes and civilisation. He looked to the other two and wondered whether they believed him now. After all they had been through he sensed that there was no longer a question over the story that had started a thousand fights in a hundred bars.

"Some-one else went this way recently," said Tracker pointing to the tracks.

Dezza saw that Tracker was pointing to a single set of boot marks that ran down the edge of the stairs.

"They didn't come back either," said Toze.

"Or at least, not this way."

Toze shrugged. "Whatever."

For a moment Dezza stared at his own boot marks, then turning up the stairs he led the way up to the top level. Here the trail was confused and obscured by the same trail they had found on the walkway. It at least allowed him to put from his mind the thoughts of what had happened here before.

At the top a shiver ran down his spine as he spied the lights still burning bright in the corridor. Follow it along, find the stairwell by the lifts that did not work and the airlock was by the painting of Neptune that would most likely have Dezza's glove prints across it. It was strange how the mind recalled such little details.

He had grown used to the lights sometimes being on aboard parts of the Starliner. When he had first come it had seemed so surreal. The trail led them along the way he remembered and out to the next final level. It was dark here, and they had to switch back on their lights. Three beams picked out the last corridor and he found himself shuddering not just from the cold, but from the nightmares that had haunted his sleep.

Neptune was there, with the clean stripe across just as it had been before, but he ignored it. At Tracker's silent instructions they hung back from the airlocks. One was shut tight showing where the Tug had once docked. The muted boot prints peeled away from the mess of other tracks and ended at its now closed steel bulk showing where the original Tug's crew had walked.

A second airlock door lay open revealing the black void of the *Magellan* beyond. The mass of tracks went in, and the beams of light picked out the ground in dirt across the floor of the airlock.

"We found the *Magellan*."

Tracker put his finger to his mask to indicate quiet. Unslinging his gun he checked the chamber was full before indicating the other two to keep him covered. "I'm going to check inside."

"What are you worried about?" whispered Dezza, "That ship is the only thing so far that we know exactly where it came from."

"That's what fills me with curiosity."

"Shit, Tracker," hissed Toze, "You aren't flipping out on me now when I need you most?"

"Easy, Sir. I just want to be clear. We have an entire salvage crew unaccounted for and I want to be certain. Call it erring on the side of caution."

"Ghosts?"

"No, but if there's anyone holed up in there then after what we've seen I'd not only expect them to be trigger happy when people come knocking, but positively disappointed if they didn't shoot first and ask questions later."

Toze nodded. "Okay. We'll keep you covered." He flicked the safety off on his gun and turned to Dezza. "Keep in close."

*   *   *   *   *

The airlock area was dark and Tracker could see nothing. Adjusting his shoulder light for maximum brightness he edged to the corner of the open door and eased himself around the edge.

The *Magellan*'s airlock stood open in front of him. He recognised it as standard commercial fleet equipment. To one side the light picked out a computer interface panel and controls. He glanced at it but the screen was inactive and there was no illumination of the panel. Probably dead, he surmised, and moved past it.

At the rear the inner door was shut and sealed. Running his glove around the edge he could feel it was fitting flush, which indicating the seals were pumped up and it was locked down.

"Found something?" asked a voice from the Starliner behind him.

He looked over his shoulder at the two faces peering round the edge of the door, and laughed. They looked like two kids afraid to step any further into an abandoned house they had been dared to enter. It was just like being at school.

"Inner door is sealed and the panel looks dead."

"Sealed from which side?" asked Dezza.

"What?"

"Which side has it been locked down from?" he asked again, "I mean, did the *Magellan*'s crew get back on board or did they lock it down when they left?"

He looked back at the sealed door in front of him. He had not thought of that. Quickly he ran through his mind specifications of commercial salvage craft airlocks. It had been a while since he had had to use them.

The computer panel would have told him, but that was dead. He moved back and took another look at it under the watchful eyes of his companions. Taking out a small tool from his belt he released the panel fronts and eased the access open into the connections underneath. A quick check with the scanner told him the line was dead; there was no power.

"Reactor core must be offline," he said grimly, "There's no way to tell unless we can get in and see who, if anyone, is there."

He saw Dezza shudder at the idea. There was every chance, Tracker knew, that if the crew of the *Magellan* had made it back then his former crewmate would be amongst them. Not for the first time it made him appreciate just why he never formed much attachment to anyone he was posted on a mission with.

Others had throughout his career misinterpreted it as him being a slightly eccentric reclusive loner who preferred his own company. In the military on deep space work risks were high and so could casualties be. Four light years from the nearest medical unit, even the most slight of injuries could prove fatal. In truth, he never wanted to have to lose anyone he had grown to care about.

"So how do we get into this crate?" asked Toze, breaking his thoughts.

He nodded to Dezza. "Talk to the salvo."

Dezza thought for a moment. "There's got to be an emergency release. Under the panel. When all the power is down it's a case of flipping three clamps and then pumping it open by hand."

A hollow howling like the moan of wind through trees echoed from the Starliner. Tracker felt his heart rate leap and he guessed the others felt the same as they turned and edged into the sanctity offered by the dead airlock.

"Our banshee is back. Dezza, get over here and get this door open." He un-strapped his belt and tossed it to the man as he knelt by the open panel where it was caught deftly. "Any tools you need, you'll find them in there."

He moved to the open part of the airlock and levelled his gun into the Starliner.

"Let's get this thing shut."

He pulled open a panel to reveal a locking lever. He pulled it to the unlocked position and then heaved his weight against the airlock door. Toze did the same. Amid much grunting the door began to slide and the opening back into the Starliner grew smaller and smaller. With a final heave they got the doors within inches. Tracker returned to the panel and began pumping on another lever to get enough hydraulic pressure to make the doors seal tight.

Vibrations rumbled through the structure and a dull moan echoed even louder from the dark corridors. Toze levelled his gun to the gap and played his light through. The corridor was empty, but the rivulets of dust fluttering from air vents dislodged by the vibration kept catching the light.

"I don't know what's real and what's not out there," he cursed. He called across to Tracker, "Are you any nearer to getting that thing shut?"

"Almost there."

The doors began to twitch as the hydraulic system reached pressure and slowly slid in agonising burst together closing the gap until the metal meshed with a dull thud. The locking lever thumped home and a breathless smiled.

"Done."

"Is it secure?" asked Toze.

"Totally."

He looked at the door and ran his eye around the seal. "Enough to stop whatever that thing is from getting in here?"

"It'll secure us from a vacuum. From ghosts though, your guess is as good as mine."

He ignored the jibe about ghosts and turned to where Dezza crouched on the floor, struggling under the main panel pulling out wire bundles and testing them with a probe.

Dezza barely looked up as he spoke. "This thing is a mess. It's going to take time to find the right lines and shock them with a power pack. Time we just don't have."

"What do you mean?" asked Toze, confused, "We've got the airlock battened down. We're safe in here, aren't we?"

Dezza chuckled. "Tell him, Tracker. You know what I'm talking about don't you?"

It was true that Tracker never missed anything. It was easier to let him do the talking whilst he carried on probing wires and cursing whoever wired this thing for their love of any colour as long as it was red.

The officer looked across. Tracker smiled under his mask.

136

"Air is going to be the limiting factor, not whatever is out there." He looked around the airlock slowly. It was not exactly cramped for three people, but it was not the biggest of spaces either.

"How do you mean?"

"Well, there's three of us in here, and I don't see any sign of power to run the air recirculation system. Do you?"

The officer seemed to realise the truth in what he was saying. In the confined space there was only so long that the breathing apparatus connected to their masks could function. Starved of the oxygen and swamped by the carbon dioxide being breathed out it would not be long before the air would become clammy and poisonous and they would slip into unconsciousness.

"How long have we got?" asked Toze tentatively, in a way that suggested he was not expecting to like the answer he would be given in any way.

Dezza shrugged. "A few minutes. Just breath slow and don't get panicked."

"Kind of hard not to feel a little unnerved."

All three jumped as the airlock door reverberated to three steady rhythmic thumps.

"What the hell was that?" whispered Toze.

No-one answered; all were straining their ears, listening. At first it was difficult to hear anything except the breathing of the three, but slowly other sounds were able to be made out: a slight grating noise from beyond the steel of the door and a shuffling noise.

Tracker gently put his ear to the door and listened, but it seemed he could hear no more than the others could.

"Anything?" hissed Toze.

He shook his head. For a moment it seemed that whatever was on the Starliner was gone. Then the door rumbled to a final impact sending Tracker back a step in surprise. He waited; watching the door as if the thing outside might rip it open at any moment, but no more bangs came and even the shuffling they had heard was no more.

"I guess it lost interest."

"Or went to find a can opener," muttered Dezza. He twisted the last of the wires together and used the power from the scanner to send a current into the dead wires.

The inner door slid back, and air eddied as pressures equalised. Dezza saw them both stand ready with their guns. What were they expecting, he wondered? How long had it been since the signal from the *Magellan* had faltered and disappeared? It had taken West and his department a while to put together this rescue mission of sorts, he knew. Could a member of the salvage crew survive holed up in a dead ship that long?

In truth, he knew that they could not. The power was offline and he had found not even a residual current in any of the wiring behind the panel in the airlock. The ship had to be dead. Whether they would find the crew in there would be another matter, and he did not relish the prospect of finding out.

"This ship ain't going to check itself out," said Tracker, and he stepped confidently into the airlock and into the unknown of the dark and dead ship beyond.

*   *   *   *   *

The air smelt stale and dank even through the screening of their masks, but the scanners showed it was clean with oxygen levels high enough to be good to breathe. The air recirculation system was offline though, and that meant it would only be a matter of time before the three of them would deplete the supplies that still lingered in the ship's atmosphere.

After so long on the *Cerberus* it came as a shock to see surfaces that were clean and tidy. There was no dust and dirt in here unlike the Starliner. But without power and lights the ship seemed every bit as unfriendly and foreboding as the derelict that it was docked to.

The *Magellan* was not a huge vessel, and it did not take them long to move through it. In the prep room beyond the airlock they found suits still hanging on the racks waiting to be put on by crewmembers who would never return like headless bodies that their imaginations went into overtime to fill with imaginary

138

creatures. Some of the hooks were empty, their suits taken and used and now wherever the fallen crew might be. From the smell of the air, Dezza guessed they could not be aboard the *Magellan* as even in this short space of time the bacteria that would inevitably live within the ship's recirculation would have begun decomposing the dead. They were not here. At any rate, the air would have been long since depleted of its oxygen if there had been anyone aboard.

A short access tube led through to the crew quarters. Around a central chamber there was laid out a small food preparation area were six cots and their accompanying stasis controls. All were empty, filled with dishevelled sheets that still lay where they had been thrown back as the crew had left.

On the kitchen counter a discarded meal half finished bristled with mould growth that seemed to shine in the glow of their lights. The controls for everything were dead and they were left to move on through into the next access tunnel that led to the command deck.

Inside the tunnel they stopped to check a hatch that stood propped open in the floor. Three shoulder lights trained through it and shone down illuminating a short ladder that led to the machinery spaces beneath.

"What do you think?" asked Toze, "Unusual to need access to the machinery deck."

It was true. Most of the equipment that would have powered the *Magellan* did not need permanent monitoring and adjustment. Unless there had been a problem, there would have been no need to go down into there.

"Could explain the power failure," offered Tracker.

Dezza nodded, remembering back to his time aboard the Tug with its ageing drive core. For a moment the sinking thought crossed his mind that if it had not been for a misaligned core, he Zoë and Tubs would never have run into the Starliner. "If their core misaligned, they would have had to go in there to sort it out. If they had problems fixing it, the safest option might have been to shut it down."

"Could you get it working?" asked Toze.

It had not occurred to Dezza, but he gave the idea some thought. "Yes," he said at last, "If the damage is not critical I could at least try and get the power back online."

"That would give us air recirculation," said Tracker.

"Okay, get on it," said the officer. He turned to Tracker and signalled for him to follow through into the command deck.

Checking that he still had Tracker's tools, he lowered himself carefully through the hatch and slid down the ladder. He was not made to fit these narrow access ways that expected a younger, lighter person, and the fit was a little tighter than he might have liked.

At the bottom he stopped a moment to listen and to play his light across the small room. It was low, with just enough room to crouch. He only barely recalled the similar spaces in the Tug. That had been Tubs' private domain and they had only entered it reluctantly after he had gone to nurse that old ship back to the shipping lanes.

Technology had not changed much over the years, and to his surprise he saw that the *Magellan*'s machinery spaces seemed disturbingly familiar to that day, years in the past.

He could hear the other two moving around on the deck above, and knew that they would be expecting results soon. There was no time to get his thoughts caught up in events of the past. Banging his head on pipework that was just below the line of sight for his shoulder light made him curse. Which idiot had decided that shoulder mounted was the way to go? Typical military equipment designed by committee locked away in their little rooms in a comfy air conditioned building somewhere in the manufacturing facilities on Mars.

At the back of the machinery spaces he found the drive core. It was weird to have to find the thing by trial and error. In a working ship it emitted plenty of light from the variety of access panels. Here it was completely dead. He glanced over the consoles at the side. All the gauges were black and the diagnostics screen showed nothing even after he found and tripped the reset switch. "No power anywhere," he muttered before catching himself with a thought: what about battery backup?

Of course, it might be long depleted, he thought, as he looked across the console panels looking for the circuits he needed. The curtailed distress signal would have been running on something and could conceivably have ended the moment the batteries finally died.

He found the panel he needed and flicked the switches. It was dead too. He was about to give up on it when the beam from his light picked out one access panel that was ajar.

Strange, he thought. Why would that be left open? He shone the light over it, and tried to remember from the Tug what it might be. He pulled the panel fully back. Inside were rows of cylinders in regimental rows pushed tightly into their clips. At one end empty slots showed where two more should go. For a moment he was stumped what they might be, then he realised they were just the circuit breakers.

His brow furrowed as he wondered why two might be missing and the panel be open. Perhaps they explained the power loss? He checked inside the bottom of the open panel in case the removed breakers might be there, but they were not. Looking around he tried to think where spares might be kept.

In the end he found one quite by accident by treading on it. Peering down he saw it had been discarded to the floor. Scooping it up he looked around and found the other close by. They had been pulled out and just thrown away. Try as he might, he could not come up with any reason in his mind as to why anyone would do that.

He toyed with just shoving them back in, but a nagging thought told him that there had to be a reason they had been pulled. At any rate, one had been damaged when he had trodden on it, and looking at it closely he saw the hairline crack across its crystal cylinder. If he put that in it would blow regardless of whether or not there was a fault on the relevant circuit.

"What's up?"

He turned with a start at the voice. He had not heard Tracker coming down the ladder.

"Shit. Don't do that after all we've been through all ready."

Tracker looked at the breakers in Dezza's hand. "Tripped out on the power?"

Was there no end to what this man knew about whatever was put in front of him? It seemed that he was familiar with just about anything. He pointed to the open panel.

"I found them already pulled. Some-one took them out long before we got here. One of them is broken. I didn't know whether to just try pushing them back in or not."

"The worst that can happen is they pop straight back out."

When it was said like that, it did not seem like such a stupid thing to have tried. Fitting the unbroken one up to the last slot in the panel he pushed it in, and waited.

Nothing happened. He tried the screens on the console but everything was dead. Still no power. Taking the breaker out he tried it in the other slot. This time there was a buzzing noise and lights flickered on across the console.

"Jackpot. We got battery power back."

He checked over the console and tapped the gauges that now showed a readout. "Over eighty-five percent power left in the cells."

"So some-one was still here all that time after the distress signal was begun and decided to pull the plug," said Tracker slowly, "Why?"

It was a thought that had not crossed Dezza's mind. What possible reason would a member of the crew had to pull the plug on the only possible means of raising help? It did not make sense.

"What did you do down there?" Toze's voice echoed down the hatchway.

"Just a circuit breaker out, that's all," called back Tracker.

"Okay. See what you can do with the air system."

Dezza scanned over the console. There were lights on now, but everything had tripped to standby. He would have to find the right controls and boot the systems back up one by one.

"See if you can find the lights."

Tracker nodded and fanned out into the gloom. It was hard to see when all they had were a couple of shaky shoulder lights that were already showing signs of fading from being on for too long.

The consoles were self-explanatory and each module was labelled. Dezza found lights already blinking showing standby power on the recirculation system and a cursor blinking on the screen. Within seconds he had it running and was rewarded with the cool tang of machine fresh air drifting from the vents.

"Air's on!"

There was no answer from Tracker. A gut feeling told Dezza that something was not right, and he turned to look. The man was standing by the casing of the ship's core, just staring in through an access plate. His bulk was between Dezza and the core and he could not see what it was he was looking at.

"What's up?"

"I think I found why the ship is powered down."

There was something in the tone of his voice that made the sweat prickle on Dezza's forehead. Even before he looked through the plating and saw what Tracker had seen, he knew it would not be good. For a moment the shock of the sight sent the icy shivers running down every inch of his body before he reeled in shock and felt the nausea rising and had to look away.

"That ain't something you see every day," said Tracker softly.

Dezza's mind raced. "What the hell?" He chanced another look, bracing himself for the image.

Through the slightly fogged clear screen within where there should be a glowing core, the chamber was empty and stripped bare. In its place, slumped in a foetal position, lay the body of a man, bloated in death but still recognisable.

"What is a man doing where the drive core should be?" It was all he could say.

"I guess he didn't go in there looking for somewhere warm to spend the night." Tracker bent down and shone his light over the entire interior. "The manifolds are gone too. All that's left is the sealed chamber. That's why the scanners didn't detect anything in the air when we came aboard. It's sealed from the outside. That means some-one put him in here."

There was no answer. Deep down Dezza was glad it was not Zoë. He had not wanted to find her like this, and that first pulse of shock had set his mind racing in case he recognised the face as hers. But this was a man not a woman, probably one of the other members of the salvage crew judging by the stained overalls.

He remembered the drag marks they had seen on the *Cerberus*; heavy equipment being moved.

"You think perhaps that the crew removed the cores themselves?"

Tracker nodded. "Yeah. Why though is anyone's guess. They must have had a reason."

"What about the secondary core?"

All ships carried a second, smaller core that allowed auxiliary systems to be run whilst the main core was offline. It did not have enough power to operate the drive machinery, but it could run environmental systems.

Behind the main casing, there was a second smaller cylinder. The inspection plates were dark and revealed that at least some of the machinery was intact inside. Where the toroid in the centre should have been though, the vital component was missing.

"They took the core from this one too," Dezza sighed.

"But they left the manifolds," said Tracker. He moved back to the ladder out of the crawl spaces and began to climb out. "I'll tell the Commander what we found."

*   *   *   *   *

Toze had said nothing on seeing the body in the chamber. There was, after all, not a lot that could be said. The chamber was little more than scrap without any of its important components anyway. Why pop the seal and risk contaminating the rest of the ship? So the dead salvager was to be left in his tomb for all eternity.

With battery power they estimated they could last in the *Magellan* for at least a week. After that the power would fail, long before any rescue could come. That, however, was the least of their worries.

In the glow of newly restored backup lighting the three sat in the central crew quarters. The ship's logs had revealed very little and seemed for the most part little more than a basic written log of legally mandated events. Salvage crews were not noted for their love of bureaucracy. Of the crewmember in the core chamber there was no explanation. At any rate, there had been no further manual entries after the *Magellan* had docked.

The *Magellan*'s escape pod was missing, with the only explanation being an automatic entry in the log. Chronometer entries indicated the power had ceased within seconds of the pod firing off into space.

In Dezza's mind he felt the secret hope that maybe it had been Zoë who had made it out alive. But lost in the vacuum of space, it would have been a leap from the frying pan into the fire. Protected by a quo-field, it was like hoping a message in a bottle might eventually be found. Still, it gave him hope.

The banging on the airlock had not happened again. As they had worked through the *Magellan* taking stock of equipment and supplies, they had taken it in turns to listen at the airlock, for any signs of life from the Starliner. But there had been nothing but unremitting silence. Whatever had followed them had gone.

From tools and supplies that were missing they concluded that the *Magellan*'s crew had taken the ship's drive materials back into the Starliner for some reason, still unknown. On the command deck, open panels had revealed that more than just the drive cores were missing. Modules had been unplugged from many of the systems rendering them useless and impossible to repair unless the missing pieces could be found. A search of the *Magellan* told them what they had feared: that the modules had gone and were not aboard. With falling hopes they realised that meant that there was no way of sending another distress signal; there could be no call for help.

Without information or clues they could only opt to finally take the cots that had been abandoned by the lost crew long before them and get some rest after a surreal meal of food packs they found vacuum packed and still edible. But it was a long night aboard the *Magellan* forever waking from the nightmares and listening for the return of the noises that never came. No-one spoke of it, but the thought of a dead man sealed in a drive chamber beneath their feet was a strange feeling to try to put to one side and ignore.

*   *   *   *   *

Tracker had made the plan in the cold frank hours of the early morning. Though in space, with no day or night, time had become arbitrary; a set of numbers kept by a computer and nothing more.

Without the cores the *Magellan* was nothing more than a floating hunk of dead metal. The salvage crew had stripped them out and taken them into the *Cerberus*. If they ever wanted to leave, they had to get power back, and that meant going for the cores and finding where they had been taken.

It would take two to follow the trail they had seen in the atrium. When the floors were so caked in dirt, everything left a mark. It was only a matter of following the trail to its end.

*   *   *   *   *

With power, the inner door of the airlock responded to the control panel and slid shut behind Toze and Tracker. For the first time since the day before they stood where they had found the *Magellan* with nervous apprehension of what they might find outside the airlock. Using the ship's scanners they had found nothing. The Starliner might as well have been completely derelict.

Toze felt his heart rate notch as he keyed the codes on the panel to cycle and open the final barrier to the derelict. He saw the other two tensing as the dial counted them down and the locking bars clicked gently to the open position. With fingers firmly resting on triggers they watched as the door eased back in its runners and the black void of the *Cerberus* opened up in front of them.

The door thudded to a stop and the echo faded into the derelict. No-one said or did anything for several seconds as they listened, straining their ears for any kind of noise. There was nothing - just the familiar dirt and filth.

Tracker went first, taking his time to study the patterns in the dirt on the floor. Toze expected he might find tracks that would make what had followed them more physical and less like a ghost. But the tracks were the same tangled mess that they had been the day before with no signs that anything else had been there.

"Looks like we got ourselves chased by a phantom," said Tracker, straightening himself up and rubbing the dirt from his gloves. He voiced the thoughts that the officer had not dared to.

Following the trail left by the salvage crew would not be difficult. The drive cores had been bulky and had taken them several trips. Leaving the relative safety of the *Magellan* would be the difficult part. Even though there had been nothing to show anything had stalked them to the airlock, it still felt real on tortured minds.

*   *   *   *   *

The trail had taken a direct route from the airlock to the second level of the atrium. Here they had found it the previous day, and their footsteps still showed clearly in the dirt. Now it was uncharted territory branching out into a part of the Starliner that was unfamiliar.

From the marks along the floor it was obvious the crew of the *Magellan* had passed several times. The equipment had been heavy; that was quite clear from the damage to the ancient carpeting. It had pulled apart with frayed seems and had been kicked aside leaving unusually clean black underlay underneath. Even this too in places had ripped and torn leaving balls of foam scattered across the floor.

A number of times Tracker stopped to look over sets of boot prints that led away from the corridor into other sections of the Starliner. It was becoming apparent that the salvage crew had explored this area thoroughly before they had taken the drive cores from their own ship and brought them here. It was as if they had been looking for something, though it was not clear what that something might have been. On several occasions doors had been forced open into cabins along the corridor, revealing the ancient splendour of what had once been a flagship of interplanetary cruising.

At the side of the first corridor they found a door left ajar with the tattered remains of its lock smashed strewn across the floor in pieces, and they had ventured in to take a look. The cabin's lights were not on, but their own lights picked out the shell of a four poster bed whose base had long since deteriorated and sagged away so that now it was nothing more than a shell. Along the walls fine ornate panelling in mahogany was hung with the threadbare remains of tapestries and oil paintings that had fallen from their frames and curled, cracked and broken, on the dirty floor.

At one end another doorway led into an annex where they found a palatial sized bathroom, its cream tiles decayed to a jaundiced shade of yellow. Alongside lay a dressing room with floor to ceiling wardrobes pulled open wide. On the floor were bundles of clothes that had recently been pulled out. They were reasonably free of the dirt and muck that seemed to have settled on everything else.

Tracker nudged the pile with a foot and noted the sparkling of jewelled sequins and gold threads.

"That's some fine threads in there."

Toze looked around the room. "There's something not right here. I can feel it nagging at my mind."

"What's not right is that some-one was in here recently and they left in a hurry."

"How can you tell?"

He stooped down and pointed to the tracks on the floor. "See here. Three tracks come in not including ours. You can see them at the doorway through. They messed around in here after paying the bathroom no more than a glance." He paused a moment, rubbing his hand gently across some of the débris on the floor. It seemed unusually sticky and came away as a black mess on his glove. "Then," he finished slowly gingerly lifting his mask to sniff the goo on his fingers, "Two of them left in a hurry."

"So where's the third?" asked Toze as he gingerly moved the clothes that remained in the wardrobes apart with the barrel of his gun.

"That's what I'd like to know. Each of them wore distinctive patterns on the soles of their boots. Three in and two out – one never left unless they carried him, and I don't see evidence of that." He stood up slowly and looked the room over nervously, "Just like Exbo."

"Let's just get out of here."

Tracker turned and made to leave. On the way he reached up and flicked the light switches set into the panelling on the wall. There had been no expectation for them to work. It had been more habit than anything that he had flicked them at all.

The lights came on with a muted glow seeming to gain brightness then lose it a little as if an electric circuit somewhere was struggling with being asked to cope with use after so long a period of inactivity. Toze had his back to the bathroom when they came on, but Tracker was looking that way as the lights glowed bright for a moment. He inhaled sharply in surprise; in the bathroom he saw in the mirror the figure of the tall woman again stood impassively seeming to be watching him. She did not react to the light at all.

The thoughts raced in his mind. Had she been in there watching them all this time? The lights flickered and died within a heartbeat, and darkness descended again taking with it any night vision that they had had.

"Hey Tracker, what's up?"

He ignored the voice and fumbled with his shoulder light moving it around to point into the bathroom illuminating the yellowed ceramic tiles. Frantically he played the light back and forth exposing every possible hiding place, but the woman was no longer there.

"You look like you've seen a ghost," said Toze.

Tracker looked around, shocking the officer with the sweat that trickled from his face.

"I saw a woman, standing in the bathroom in the brief moment that the lights were working."

Toze looked past him and played his light across the bathroom too. "There's nothing there now. Are you sure it wasn't just a trick of the light?"

Tracker shrugged. As the seconds ticked by he began to wonder whether he had really seen something. "I've seen her before. She was in the gym when we were there, right before Exbo got wasted."

Toze hesitated. "You didn't mention this?"

He shrugged. "I thought I must have been mistaken then. I forgot about it after we had to go and try and get to Exbo." He knelt down on the floor and let his light scan over the dust and dirt that covered the tiled floor of the bathroom.

"No tracks," said Toze slowly, "So either she wasn't there, or you saw a..." The words faded out.

Tracker looked around, his face creased into a smile under his mask. "A ghost?" He stood up again and gave the room one last glance over. "Perhaps this ship is getting to us all. Considering all we've seen and heard, maybe we're going to see spooks all over the place that aren't really there."

They turned and left the suite of rooms, heading back to the corridor.

*   *   *   *   *

Repairs on the *Magellan* were a slow affair. Dezza found that most of the circuits were missing key modules that had simply been disconnected and taken away. Some of the main drive control circuits he found were burnt out. It puzzled him how the crew could have come to be in this situation until he realised that some of the circuits showed a pattern of damage that was consistent with power spiking. With a cold knot of fear twisting in his gut, he remembered the same fault on the Tug that had only been prevented from getting so bad by Tubs' quick thinking.

He checked through what he could find of the logs on the ship's computers, looking for the telemetry that might give him some clues. It was difficult to decipher an unfamiliar system, but eventually he found the computer files that he was looking for. With an icy realisation he found himself looking at a mass of figures on the screen that showed him that the *Magellan*'s main drive core had simply been switched off and removed. It was not a power spike as had happened to the Tug, but simply the actions of the salvage crew.

As for the reason they might have stripped what they could from the *Magellan*, he could only guess. It suggested to him though that they might have been trying to repair something aboard the

Cerberus. Could it have even been the Starliner's own drive and propulsion system? He could not know for sure.

Popping service panel after service panel, he found that they seemed to have grabbed modules at random from the most accessible areas first without concern for rendering systems inoperative. They must have been in one hell of a hurry, he thought to himself. It would have been for him only a method of last resort to cripple his own ship. But that was exactly what they had done.

Some of the modules were standard components, and he found that by removing some that remained from one system and plugging them into the vacant ports on another there was a chance he might find enough workable parts to re-energise some of the more minor systems. It occurred to him that he could perhaps re-initiate the communications console. With a leaping heart he realised that it might give him the means to get the *Magellan* to once again send her distress signal out into the vacuum of space back towards the far off pinprick in the starscape that was Sol and the Earth.

The circuits were simple and only a few modules were missing. He found these in some of the control consoles on the command deck. He had no qualms about pulling them from there; the *Magellan* was unlikely for now to be moving again. The exercise gave him a renewed hope and he found the time flashing by in an instant as he worked hard at repairing connections that had been pulled apart in a rush by the ship's former crew.

Making the last connection he flicked the power switches with baited breath and was rewarded by banks of tiny lights flashing from red, to yellow then sticking on to green. The communications worked! Tentatively he pulled up the headset and placed it over his ears.

He felt his heart fall. The set was dead. Desperately he adjusted the controls listening for any crackle of static even that might tell him that something was working. There was nothing, so he rested the headset back on the desk and crawled back underneath into the maze of wiring to test connections with a scanner looking for the one that was stopping it all.

It came as a shock when he heard the voice. It was faint and tinny seeming far away. He nearly banged his head in surprise before he wriggled back out from the mess of cables. At first he thought there was some-one else aboard. It sounded like a television left on in another room. But he knew there was no-one else here.

He kicked himself for not realising sooner when it clicked that it was the sound of talking coming from the headset. Picking it up he pressed it to an ear and listened.

The shock of recognition of the voice ran through him like a hot knife. It was Zoë with a voice that he would never forget, even though it sounded slightly hoarser and more weathered by life than he had remembered.

He tried to talk back, but the voice kept going in monologue and he realised with disappointment that this was no more than a recording. Somewhere under the console the circuits must have become crossed; this was some kind of personal log.

He settled down on the floor with the headset on and listened to the voice. It made him feel slightly odd; a mixture of relief to hear her and despair that even this was not proof that she was all right. She seemed to be detailing something about the Starliner, and he realised that she was talking about events that had happened to her crew when they had arrived to salvage the ship. With renewed interest he concentrated on her words.

*   *   *   *   *

The *Magellan* had docked without incident, and Zoë had found the Starliner just as it had been left by her crew before, all those years ago. No-one else had found the ship in its time away in the Rösenbridge, and the salvage crew had discovered only the boot prints of the three members of the Tug crew, still fresh as if they had been left only the day before.

The salvage crew had been more interested in profit. Like so many over the years, they viewed Zoë's story of what had happened aboard the *Cerberus* as a tall tale and nothing more. To them the Starliner was a floating paradise of profit.

They had wanted to start breaking into the passenger cabins immediately, looking for booty that they could carry away with ease. This was a high-class ship, they had argued, and being abandoned in a hurry meant the state rooms would still be loaded with the finery of a life cruising pre wars out amongst the stars. They might not have known a lot about this particular vessel, but they knew their history of a time when decadence and wealth with its trappings had been the hallmarks of the cruising generation that could afford it.

Zoë had persuaded them to check the lower levels first. She had argued that if the *Cerberus* had dropped on its own into the Rösenbridge once, then there was no certainty that its drive system was stable and would not accomplish the same feat again without notice. Reluctantly they had agreed, and she and two others had set off through the vessel into the atrium and down the grand staircase following the trail of boot prints whilst the rest of the crew waited impatiently aboard the *Magellan*.

She had not liked the experience. From the moment she and her crew had set eyes on the Starliner, she had felt the bristling feeling that told her she should turn and run. It was a marked change from the enthusiasm she had had the first time she had set eyes upon this derelict, and the irony was not lost on her. How she wished she had never convinced Tubs and Dezza to go along with her lust for the big prize.

Her crew now had rushed before her with a disregard for any of the warnings she had given them. She had hurried to keep up with an ever-growing feeling that she was losing control over them.

At the base of the staircase she found herself hesitating, knowing that in the lift would be Tubs' body. The salvage crew had not been afflicted by such qualms; they had never known the man. She had turned, and waited expecting the crew to call her over at some point and she wanted to prepare herself for the shock. Curiously the call had not been to identify a body, but to question why there was no body at all.

It had shocked her to be told, and when she had walked to the open lift she had found to her amazement that whilst the two ancient skeletons had remained, of Tubs there was no trace.

Whatever had happened to his body she did not know. Where it had lain there was a mark in the dirt, but no trace of it now.

Her mind had raced. Had he really been dead when they left him? At once the seeds of doubt were sown, and she began to question her recollection of the events. Could he have still been alive and had come round after she and Dezza had left, and found himself left to wander aimlessly the derelict?

But the two salvos had pointed out that there were no other tracks. They could account for those they knew who had left; only two sets of tracks left the lift to climb the grand staircase back to the airlock levels.

It was a mystery to her. How could a dead man rise up and just evaporate leaving absolutely no trace? One of the salvos had asked her whether her memory could be mistaken and that maybe this was the wrong location. She had snapped at him that she would never forget that day, but deep down she began to find herself questioning what might have really happened after so many years of being fiercely certain.

The lift controls had worked, just as they had when she had been here last. The two salvos piled into the car and she found herself obliged to follow even though she did not really want to. The ride downwards had been conducted without a word from Zoë. The salvos had talked; laughing and joking about what they would each do with their share of the salvage. She had found the talk so familiar to the talk she had had all those years ago before stepping aboard the derelict for the first time. How tables turn, and how much she felt disgusted at how she had been as she saw the same attitude in these two men. Had only the money really motivated her?

At the final deck as the lift car slid to a halt and the lights flickered for a moment. She warned the men about the unsafe deck, but they were already ready. With their lights switched on, they had stepped out into the darkened and shredded corridor and in a flood of emotion Zoë found all those memories again flooding back to her. She saw the hole that Dezza had fallen through. The deck plating still hung at a dizzying angle drunkenly into the void underneath. It seemed to her like it had been only yesterday.

The salvos had led the way gingerly following the single set of boot prints that showed where Dezza had come back from the machinery spaces. They already knew from what she had told them and from the reports of the tribunal that he had come straight from where the main reactors were. Step where he had stepped and follow where he had been and there was little chance of putting a foot wrong and disappearing through the deck.

From here, it was new for Zoë. This had been only where Dezza had gone. She remembered with a shudder that she had gone after Tubs, and found only his body. She shut her eyes and tried to erase the image from her mind, but the thoughts still haunted her. At least this was new territory now that she had never walked in. Maybe she could kid herself that this was a different derelict in space.

They had found the staircase and taken it down to the engineering spaces, ignoring the signs that announced that only the Starliner's crewmembers were allowed any further. Notices for a passenger compliment that had long since disappeared – it seemed somewhat surreal to read signs so normal in the midst of a sea of destruction that was picked out in the beams of their lights.

The lights were on in the engineering spaces and that was stranger still. It seemed wrong to be in a ship that would have been more at home as a museum and for decks to be almost as if the crew had left out of another door moments before they had arrived.

They had seen the toroidal structures just as Dezza had described at the tribunal. Everything was just as he had said they would be. They had found systems returned to standby and the reactor back to minimal power again. The Starliner appeared to have dropped from the Rösenbridge simply because of a failure in an ancient component that could no longer take the punishment of use.

The salvos had looked the old equipment over with knowing and experienced eyes and nearly whooped with joy. Maybe they could get the Starliner running under its own power and pilot it back to civilisation? Zoë had tried to warn them, but blinded by their own greed they had usurped her authority and pushed her aside. There was nothing she could do except watch from the sidelines as they made plans to reactivate the derelict vessel. There was nothing that she could say that they would listen to.

The main computer system, strangely docile compared to the reports given in the tribunal, had yielded finally a full deck plan. Armed with this the *Magellan*'s crew had taken the decision to remove their own drive core and ship it down to the engineering spaces through the service shafts and use it to bring life back to the Starliner. No-one else would side with her.

Furious at their stupidity, there had been nothing they could do but leave them to their foolery. How she despaired at seeing men consumed by their lust for wealth to the point that they became blind to the truth. Deep down she knew that there was more to this Starliner than just aged and decrepit circuits. Above all the thought nagged at her of where was Tubs' body?

The salvos poured scorn and said she had to be mistaken, but she knew she was not. They lampooned her and jested until she felt her cheeks flush with pent up rage. How cruel grown men could be!

She had left them alone and moved off to the solitude of the Starliner's corridors. Even as she walked the last of the stairs to the base of the atrium and away into the dark and dusty corridors, she could hear the echoes of laughter of fools stripping their own ship bare in a foolhardy plan.

*　　　　*　　　　*　　　　*　　　　*

The service shafts stretched through the centre of the Starliner in a pit of darkness that went far beyond the feeble glare of their torches as Tracker and Toze moved through the corridors. Some of the shafts contained lifts, though their controls remained stubbornly dead. Another shaft contained nothing but pipes and cable trunks whilst a final one housed only a utilitarian switchback staircase that thrummed eerily under their booted footsteps. They had been forced to take the laborious route after the lift cars had all failed to respond. Judging by the tracks in the dirt, they had worked recently for the salvage crew. Maybe another weary circuit had failed after years of disuse? Again, there was nothing that would give them more than the vaguest of clues.

The descent was a sapping affair. The Starliner possessed many decks, and without the use of any lift it was a long way down needing to check every floor for signs that the salvage crew may have got off there. But there were no signs, and they kept on climbing down the seemingly endless switchback.

It was easy to sink into a monotony of the task. Twenty steps that echoed loudly in the shaft, then spin around a landing to take twenty more steps in the other direction before looking back in the beam of light for footprints that were never there. Then it was time to repeat it all over again. They had long since lost count of the floors by the time the beams from their lights picked out the fresh trail on the landing.

Tracker called a halt simply by raising a hand in the air, and the echo of their footsteps died away to be replaced by the sucking blanket of silence. He knelt by the edge of the tracks, just as he always did, but Toze did not need any special skills to see that these were the tracks of a single lone person and not the massive jumble they had been expecting.

"Just one. In a hurry," whispered Tracker. He followed them away along the service corridor that stretched from the landing with the beam from his light.

Tracker played his light on the trail too. "Never came back either."

"Could be one of the tracks we saw when we first came aboard?"

"Could be. That might help to explain why everyone who got here before us seemed eager to never retrace their steps."

The prints were smudged and darted left and right. Whoever had been here had been running without much care for where they went as long as they went somewhere quickly.

"Follow the tracks or keep going down and see where the salvage crew took the cores?" asked Toze.

Tracker sucked his teeth for a moment as he thought. "We need the cores more than we need one lost salvo," he replied, "I say we get down into engineering. Leave this one for later."

So they turned and kept going down the stairs, the sound of their footsteps once more echoing eerily about them. But neither could shake off the thoughts about the tracks. The file had said the salvage crew was five men and one women. So far they could only account for one, and that remained a mystery all in itself.

It had only been a few more floors to the bottom. At the final turn they realised that this had to be the level as there was nowhere else to go. Beneath their feet the metal grill of the walkway gave way to solid metal plating covered in the tired remains of rubber matting and slicked in years of filth.

Their lights picked out the continuation of the trail. A lift door hung open at the base of the shaft, and it was clear that it had been used several times; the floor inside was cleared of dirt and the control panel had been wiped clean. Apart from that, the power was dead when Tracker probed the panel with his scanner.

The trail led along a service corridor. Here they were well beyond any area that passengers were meant to go, and wooden panelling had long since given way to utilitarian conduits and pipework strung along the walls on brackets for ease of maintenance. All were hung with the same drooping mass of blackened filth that they had witnessed hanging from air vents on the upper decks. As before it revealed nothing of its origin to the scanner when they took the time to check it.

At a closed hatchway they saw the pale glow of lights on the control panel and found that it opened with a hiss of hydraulics at the touch of the buttons. On the other side they hesitated, feeling the change in the air. It felt hotter and humid here, though a probe with the scanner showed nothing poisonous.

*   *   *   *   *

At a second hatchway they found the controls still operative, letting them move through with more confidence.

Then the trail stopped. Playing the lights left and right they saw that the dirt in this compartment was gone replaced by the same clean floors and walls that they had seen in the gym area.

"What do you make of it?" asked Toze hesitantly.

"I'd say we just found another area that the cleaning robots are still doing their rounds."

"No lights though."

Wherever their lights were not pointing this compartment was completely dark.

Tracker shrugged. "I guess the cleaning robots just aren't bothered about seeing or not, they just get on with the job."

The compartment contained a number of consoles with screens and assortments of gauges. All looked dead at first glance until at a closer look they realised that there were some lights still on dimly on the consoles.

"Still got power," said Toze.

Tracker tried the controls at one of the consoles. He had not really expected much to happen, but it seemed he had done something to wake the computer system back up off standby. As the screen glowed into life and rows of controls blinked and gauges flickered they both instinctively took a step backwards.

"What did you do?" hissed Toze.

"I don't know."

They watched as the screens began to flash on one by one around the room banishing the darkness with the strange ethereal light as reams of text scrolled across them.

Tracker moved back closer to the nearest one, as it flashed up logos for a long gone shipping line.

"Operating system coming online," he said, "Looks like it might be navigation."

He looked over the consoles and suddenly it seemed to make more sense to him. "Yeah, I'd say we're in the control centre for the navigation system. That means we must be close to main engineering and wherever the salvage crew took those cores."

"Warning messages," said Toze as red lights began to flash across screens.

Tracker leant in close. For a moment they both scrutinised the glowing display, trying to decipher its archaic design. Some of the displays seemed to show a sweeping sensor scan around the Starliner.

"Long range scan," said Toze at last. He cast his fingers across controls, and a projector unit hummed into life.

The pair shrank back.

"What did you do?" asked Tracker.

"Activated the main display."

The air began to shimmer above the console as images began to coalesce in the airspace. Gradually shapes took form, and they were left squinting at a series of dots and spiralling lines that showed intercept vectors and trajectories of various objects picked out in the glowing ball of ozone-laden air.

Toze wrinkled his nose despite the screening of his mask. "They can't have been overly health conscious. Think of the free radicals."

Tracker pointed a finger into the haze, and the image crackled and distorted angrily as the computer tried to compensate for this new obstacle. "Forget the gas hazards – looks like there's a bigger crimp on your health coming this way."

Toze squinted, as he tried to read the lines just above Tracker's finger and ignore the crackles of static that leapt along the gloved finger. "Meteor swarm?" he said at last.

"Yeah. Looks like it from what I can tell."

"Is it going to intercept? Can the Starliner's navigation fields still deflect them?"

Tracker removed his finger, and the projection shimmered back into its correct shape. He typed quickly at the controls, and the images changed. "Questions, questions. Are there any answers?" he muttered.

The projection sped up and they watched the swarm encroach the dot in the centre. Finally they sat back and thought in silence. Both had realised the same thing.

"No wonder we've got a console here flashing like Guy Fawkes Night and New Year rolled into one big shit sandwich," said the officer blankly breaking the silence. He read off the numbers from the display. Whichever way they looked at it, it was not good. They had a few days at most before the swarm would hit. Whether the Starliner could shrug off a hit or not, it would be safer to be away from the sector by the time it came. They needed to find the core.

Something caught their attention and in a split second they turned. Afterwards Toze would claim that he thought he saw a ghostly figure, but even in his own mind he was not completely certain. Too much had already happened aboard the *Cerberus* that had set him on edge.

His gun spat a burst of bullets and spent cartridges flew into the air and clattered all over the floor. A shower of sparks exploded from fused electrical equipment illuminating the control room in a blinding flash.

"Hey! Hey!" called out Tracker until the gunfire stuttered and stopped.

Over the drifting haze of cordite smoke they peered together at the disintegrated mound of metal and electronics. Tracker took a step forward and nudged it with his foot.

"Easy now Rambo! Looks like you managed to waste yourself a service robot on the cleaning rounds."

He paused a moment looking over the smouldering machine remains and then to the doorway behind through which it had entered creeping up on them with barely a sound. Then he slid the gun back over his shoulder.

"I guess the maid service won't be running any more."

He ignored the machine remains and checked the doorway through which it had come. There was a corridor outside painted a dull shade of battleship grey which was clean though a little faded looking. Without any trace of footprints he could only guess at which way the salvage crew might have gone.

Tracker was unfazed. Taking his time to analyse the paint on the floor and walls he ran his fingers over what looked like to Toze to be insignificant scuffs and scrapes. Finally satisfied, the tracker looked first one way down the corridor, then back the other before turning to the officer.

"I'd say they went that way."

"You're certain?"

"As certain as I'll ever be." He pointed to the scuffs in the paint. "Something heavy made those marks recently. It wasn't the maid service either."

Toze did not need to wait; he trusted Tracker implicitly. Taking a final glance at the wreckage of the robot they edged down the corridor to where an open hatchway led through into the darkness of the next compartment.

*   *   *   *   *

Zoë had wandered the decks of the Starliner, consumed at first by the anger. But the anger faded, as it always did, and before long all that was left was the growing realisation that she might be lost. Every corridor looked the same, and with a feeling of unease she had realised that she had come a long way. No longer could she hear the sounds of the salvage crew making their noise. Actually, when she put her mind to it, she realised that she had not been hearing them for some time.

It felt cold now as if the atmosphere were chilling down like a clear winter's night as the sun slips below the horizon. Her breath curled into the air in an opaque vapour cloud and she realised she was shivering.

Stopping for a moment, she turned and looked at the trail of her footsteps leading back in the beam from her helmet light until they faded beyond where it could penetrate. Turning around she saw the virgin carpet that covered the corridor ahead, undisturbed for decades. How strange to be the first person to come here after so long. It was a secret world left and forgotten by its occupants. In her mind though she tried to shut out the stories she had heard about why the Cerberus was here.

The tribunal had rekindled the myths that had sailed around the bars and the way stations faster than a Chinese whisper and gaining an extra twist every time. By the time the stories had come back and been told to her it was hard to pull what little truth might be left in them from the cumulated tall story telling.

Where had all the people actually gone? She remembered the two skeletons in the lift; that had been the only evidence they had ever seen. But with an icy shiver gripping her spine, she wondered what had happened to Tubs' body.

Suddenly she realised that it was not as quiet as she had assumed down here. There was an echo, faint but getting louder, that came to her along the deserted deck. How long it had been there she did not know; it had built up from nothing. Listening intently, she thought it sounded like the screech of metal on metal, like the sound of machinery neglected to the point it is ready to seize and fail. The noise grew louder until she felt the deck beneath her feet begin to shudder and vibrate and little clouds of dust began to flutter from where they had been dislodged.

Her forehead wrinkled into a frown. What were the salvage boys doing? She took a step back in the direction she had come, meaning to return and find out but she got no further. The air began to move around her, slowly at first, bringing with it a coating of fine dust caught in the movement. Then it grew faster until she feared there might be something heading at high speed towards her pushing a vortex of trapped air ahead of itself.

She side-stepped into the recess of a locked door and pressed herself against the stained wood as the tide of dust grew and grew. The noise too had changed and had become an eerie moaning sound like wind moving in a gale through a ruined building. As it grew louder so the floor and even the walls beside her began to reverberate to the vibration. The dust rolled by like a fog, threatening to choke her. In the last minute she remembered her helmet visor and fumbled to drop it into place and latch it shut.

With the visor shut she could inhale sweet clean air from the suit's recirculation system, no longer tainted with the musty smell of the Starliner. The beam of her light made the passing dust glow in front of her like a wall of fog. Then, as fast as it had begun the vibration ceased and the dust slowed and began to settle back onto the floor.

She fumbled for her scanner and realised that her hands and body were shaking with the fear. Had it been a decompression of the Starliner's hull? She checked the readouts, but they showed the atmosphere still present and pressurised to the level it had been before. She wondered what else could have caused the air in the derelict to circulate so quickly under a forced pressure. What the hell had her crew been doing?

Tucking the scanner back into her belt, she pulled herself from the recess and looked up and down the corridor. She saw the dim flashing of a far off light stabbing through the darkness and immediately drew back in genuine fear. Fumbling for the controls for her suit she switched off her own light and huddled, listening to the rasping of her own breathing as the stabbing light moved closer and closer.

*   *   *   *   *

The banging on the airlock filled Dezza with a knot of fear as it echoed through the tiny *Magellan*. Almost as soon as it started, it stopped: three sharp raps, then silence. He looked around, frightened even to breathe. Fumbling with a hand on the console he paused Zoë's log playback. With this off there was no noise, save for the faint rustle of the air circulation system.

He wondered if he had imagined it. Sliding from the chair he made his way back through the *Magellan* until he was stood amongst the hung up suits by the inner airlock door. He did not know exactly what he expected to find here. There was not anything to see but the matt black steel of the door. He rested his hands against it, feeling for any vibration, but there was none. The metal felt icy cold to his touch, chilled by the air behind it in the *Cerberus*. He placed an ear to it, listening hard. He could hear the rumble of the *Magellan*'s air plant, but aside from that there was nothing. He wanted to know what was outside, but remembering Spanners he hesitated without turning on the video link. Instead he fumbled with the audio link.

"Toze? Tracker? Is that you?"

He waited for a reply, counting the seconds by. Through the audio he could hear nothing except the hiss of static. He wondered whether it was working or if it was another circuit compromised by missing circuit boards. But when he tapped his fingers experimentally on the airlock door, he heard the reverberation coming back at him over the hiss.

The seconds ticked by turning to minutes before he lost all track of time, listening hard. There were no more noises, and he began to wonder if he had imagined it all. Looking at the panel for the video link, he tried to suppress the urge to flick it on and take a look. But as each second ticked by and nothing happened he began to wonder why he was so scared at all.

Finally he swore quietly to himself, and flicked the feed live.

In a wave of anticlimax he saw the shape of the airlock flicker onto the screen and beyond it the corridor of the Starliner. Both were empty.

The buzz of a radio communicator on the command deck made him jump. What now, he wondered? Flicking off the video link he moved back through the living area and onto the command deck. The log was playing when he got there filling the deck with the muted soft tones of Zoë's words through the tinny speakers in the headset. He froze as a wave of cold sweat rolled over him. Had he not specifically turned that off when he had gone through to the airlock? Yes, he remembered specifically clicking the switch. It had made a satisfying clunk under his fingers. He searched the panel and found the switch and pressed it. Immediately Zoë's voice was gone again. How had that got back on? The circuit could have a bad connection on the controls, he surmised. But the explanation did not fully convince him.

He slid himself back into the chair and checked the radio panel. Confused, he noted that it showed no channel open and no incoming transmissions. So what had made the buzzing noise? Deep down he was unsure he really had heard those bangs, and the log left on or the sound of the buzzer could easily have been a hallucination brought on by fatigue and exacerbated by fear.

Switching off the frequency he sat back in the chair, listening. There was nothing but the background rattle of the air circulation. He wondered whether he should go down and check over the machinery deck of the *Magellan* again. He had gone over every circuit he could find up here and maybe there were circuits down there that he could look at. But the thought of that body sealed in the empty chamber filled him with a little bit of dread. There was something about the idea of working so close to it that he did not relish at all.

He thought he saw something move back in the living section through the connecting corridor. It was not much other than a sensation of something moving in the edge of his peripheral vision. When he turned and looked there was nothing there.

Easing himself out of the chair he found himself fumbling for the gun but his fingers found nothing, and looking over the consoles he realised the gun was not there and he could not remember exactly where he had put it down.

He called out through the corridor. It seemed to him after he spoke to be slightly silly to call to a person he knew could not be there. The airlock was sealed and there had been no-one else aboard.

Except the body in the chamber below. He froze as a memory triggered. What had Zoë said about Tubs' body? He had not seen it for himself, but he had felt the hairs go up on the back of his neck as he had heard her voice recount the fact that Tubs was gone. It did not matter that the salvos had made her doubt; he knew on that fateful day they had left the man's body in the lift. In his mind the memory was still as fresh now as it had ever been. There were some things you never forgot.

No answer came, but that did nothing to calm his nerves. He stepped cautiously into the connecting tunnel past the empty escape pod bay and around the open hatch into the machine spaces below. Like a young child with a fear of an open closet door, he suddenly felt very uncomfortable with that hatch open. Fumbling over its catch he slid it shut and flicked closed the locking bolt. He felt a little better now, not having to step over that space. It did not pray on his mind so much as he walked through into the next compartment.

The area was just as it had been when he had left it before. The sleeping pods were empty with blankets in dishevelled heaps, and the remains of discarded food from the hurried meal that morning remained on the surface. Dezza felt foolish; getting all worked up over nothing. He forced himself to relax. He was just on edge, he told himself.

He turned to leave, to go back onto the command deck, when something caught his eye. On the utility surfaces behind the discarded food there was a small, black rectangular object. He felt questions whirl in his mind; he did not remember that there before. He edged around the room and gingerly picked it up. At first he thought it might be something the others had left behind. Tracker's belt had seemed at times to contain everything that anyone could ever expect to need. But on closer inspection the object was not his. It had a symbol on the back that showed it belonged with the *Magellan*. Turning it over he saw that it was some kind of personal log.

It made him think hard. Why had he not seen this before? He racked his memory, scrutinising the mental image of the sleeping quarters. He was certain there had been nothing there. A thought occurred to him and he placed the device back where he had found it before nervously ducked through into the final passage to the airlock area. Was there some-one else in here hiding after all?

He felt his heart begin to race as he stepped into the airlock anteroom. The airlock was still sealed. On the wall the same row of suits hung that had been there when they had entered. They looked almost human in shape, though they hung limp and still and lifeless. Gingerly he poked at the closest one. The rubbery material yielded under the touch until he felt the hard smoothness of the bulkhead behind. It was empty. He tried the next one and that proved empty too. He worked his way around until the final suit faced him. He prodded at it even more gingerly this time, half expecting to feel the warmth of a person through its material. But like the others it yielded and deformed flat until his hand felt the bulkhead behind. None of the suits hid anything, and there was nowhere else to hide.

A sound from the sleeping quarters made his ears prick up. Again, it sounded like voices on a radio channel, tinny and with all bass stripped away. He thought he must be imagining it, but stubbornly when he listened hard, the sound remained. He could feel the sweat on his back slicking his clothes against the skin as he tiptoed back through the passage.

It was just as he had left it, except for the sound of the faraway voice. He saw it was coming from the device he had found and replaced only moments before. Confused, he picked it up to see that it was switched on and was playing back an entry. He knew it had not been switched on when he had looked at it last. Had he accidentally activated the device when putting it back? Curious, he listened to the man's voice that played from the machine. The recording was not very long, and seemed to loop at a point as if the device had corrupted its memory file. But the words spoken were enough that before it had finished the second loop he had already donned his breathing mask and had activated the airlock back into the Starliner ready to head back into the ship.

*   *   *   *   *

The reason for the Starliner's reappearance from the Rösenbridge could never have been clearer. Two of the toroidal structures were dark and inactive, just as the report at the tribunal had said. The third however had suffered partial failure, and scorching covered nearly a third of its outer casing. At some point, an increase in power had caused the ageing device to overload. Instead of tripping out completely and plunging the Starliner into total darkness and inactivity, it had instead defaulted back to standby. In this way it might still remain for years, providing enough power for lighting and the air recirculation system, but never enough for the main drive to initiate the Rösenbridge again.

But some-one had recently thought otherwise for the fate of the vast ship. Each of the inactive toroidal cores had opened access panels and inside showed where vital components from the *Magellan* had been used to repair and replace failed circuits that had long since been dormant.

It took Tracker and Toze only a few minutes to trace the pattern of work and deduce what plans the salvage crew had had for the Starliner.

"Those gutsy sons of bitches," cussed Tracker in respect, "They really were going to try and bring this baby home under her own power."

A bundle of cables stretched from the improvised repairs to the engineering consoles. They hung loose, pulled apart at a connection. Toze nudged it with his foot.

"What do you make of this?" he asked.

Tracker took a closer look. Frayed ends around the connection caught his eye along with deep gouge marks in the insulation around the bundle.

"Looks to me like some-one changed their mind right after they plugged all this in."

"Yeah, maybe," said Tracker slowly, "Except I bet you have to be awfully desperate to pull out a plug with an axe."

"You reckon these marks were made by that axe?"

Tracker nodded at the main consoles. "Same way some-one once tried to shut this lot down with an axe too."

"It says something like that in Dezza's report."

All across the consoles were deep gouge marks. The axe had been used to smash at anything and everything. It was not systematic, but instead seemed to be a desperate fleeing attempt at vandalism. Most of the marks were very old and the bare exposed metal had faded and had gained a layer of oxide from years in a slightly humid environment. But other marks looked fresh and there was barely a dulling of the metal edge. Some-one had made a second attempt to finish what the *Cerberus*' long gone crew had started.

Tracker found what seemed to be the main computer terminal, and moved a small piece of the ripped up fascia that lay across the screen. A cursor blinked at the top left; the system was still running. He tapped at a few keys on the dusty keyboard, and the letters appeared up on the screen.

"I think we got a command line prompt here. Know any computer basic?"

Toze looked to the screen. "None at all. Can you make it do something?"

"I can make it play Space Invaders."

"Something helpful, I meant."

Tracker laughed as he typed. "Just kidding with you. I'll see if I can bring up the root directory and see what where it can go from there."

He typed quickly, trying to dredge commands learnt and forgotten in a childhood long ago when, for a while, computers had been a passing vogue for him. The computer system he faced now had been considered old even before he was born. Even the keys felt odd and archaic under his fingertips as they clunked noisily. He tried a few of the commands he could remember, but they did nothing except turn up error messages. At last an obscure command dredged from the depths of his memory sent text scrolling up the screen.

"All right!" he exclaimed. He read the data. It seemed as though the system had partially crashed though something was still running. Something was running, but not the core operating system. It was not crashed out, but instead had failed to activate properly.

Typing some more he found more commands that worked until finally, bathed in the glow of the screen with his nose barely inches from it, he found what his computer skills had told him he was looking for. Could it really be this simple?

"Here goes nothing." His fingers glanced across the keys and the screen went black.

"What happened?" asked Toze.

"I don't know. It should be running." He swiped at the keys but it did nothing. Perhaps the sabotage with the axe had damaged too much after all. He turned from the console in disgust. Whatever the salvage crew had done, it seemed to have rendered the *Cerberus*' systems beyond his skills.

Toze looked over the silent machinery and sized up the parts that the salvage crew had jury rigged into the toroidal reactors. It did not matter any more about the Starliner. Without their dropship there would always be only one way back out. They had ventured back into the derelict looking for the *Magellan*'s removed equipment and had found it. They began to assess the pieces.

It was possible, they decided, to retrieve the parts for the *Magellan*'s secondary core and stand a chance of getting it working again. It would not give them the power to enter the Rösenbridge, but it would allow them to keep alive and leave the *Cerberus*.

Starting on their task they used tools found discarded to start to dismantle the parts they needed and stack them carefully ready to be carried back up all those stairs. That was a task they did not relish, but they put the thought of it from their minds for now.

A vibration rocked the floor and both men looked up from their task wide-eyed and afraid. Neither said a thing. Looking around slowly, there was no change in the engineering spaces. Consoles still blinked intermittently and the three toroidal structures remained grey and silent.

170

"What do you think that was?" whispered Toze slowly.

"I don't know, but I think we need to hurry."

Taking the tools again, they moved to continue their work with increased pace, filled with the unease of the memory of that noise.

*   *   *   *   *

When the light had come, Zoë moved back into the shelter of the recess, pressing her body into the gap as far as it would go. Yet, this still felt like not enough. The light picked out the edge of the frame and she held her breath. In her mind the fear grew greater and in that moment she found the feeling of calm washing over her as she felt so close to the end. What was there left she could do? So she stepped out into the corridor ready to face whatever was coming, and stood defiantly in the sea of settling dust.

She gasped and fumbled for her helmet light, switching it on again. In its beam it picked out a moving shape - the dirt-streaked suit of one of the salvage crew hurrying towards her. All their suits had a coloured band on the helmets to tell them apart, though this one was so filthy it was impossible to tell. She flicked on the short-range communications and spoke despite the trembling of fear in her voice.

"Who are you?"

The figure faltered a moment; they had not been expecting to meet anyone here. For a moment she thought they might turn and run, but they paused only a moment before she saw their hand steal towards their own suit controls and she heard the pop of static as he spoke.

"Shit! Zoë!" The voice panted breathlessly in a mixture of fear and relief.

She recognised them as one of the crew. Red they called him, because of his hair. She had never seen hair so red before and had called him that on the first day he had come aboard and the name had stuck.

He struggled to her and stood before her quivering as he struggled to get his breath back.

He told her what he knew, that something had attacked them. They had been shipping the core parts into the engineering spaces when it had come. Whatever it was it had come out of the electronics until it had surrounded them all. When she pressed the matter, he could tell her no more other than the same garbled story over and over again. Perhaps he was not so certain of what had happened; she could sense the confusion in his voice.

He had turned and run, so he seemed to be saying, whilst the others had stood fixed to the spot. As he had escaped into the darkness he had heard their screams behind them and the clatter of equipment dropped in fright to the floor. And there was a noise, he said, like flesh being squeezed and bones crunching. He had not looked behind but carried on running; even when the decks and bulkheads around him had begun to shake and the dust cloud had rolled past him. Eventually he had seen a figure step out in front of him, before her voice had spluttered in his ears from the radio channel.

*　　　*　　　*　　　*　　　*

The voice on the log had seemed so clear to him. It was a warning from the grave now; the salvo that had made that hurried recording was long gone, lost somewhere in the Starliner. His fate would probably always remain a mystery, though Dezza could not help but wonder whether the body in the core chamber might belong to the man?

The Starliner was infected. The thing that had been there dormant when he had been there with Tubs and Zoë had been roused. Whatever it was, it would not rest until it had destroyed those who came aboard the derelict.

He tried the radio link, but it did nothing but crackle and hiss and he cursed. Damn this structure! Unless he was close to the others, there was no means of communication.

He thought he heard a noise echoing in the darkened atrium and he wished he had thought to look for the gun before coming. It was too late to go back now; he had to get to the others fast. He took the stairs two at a time as his light picked out the trail that was easy enough to follow.

The noise came again, this time louder and drawn up at the end into a cross between a wail and a shriek. There was no mistaking it; he could not blame it any more on his imagination. Below him he had only one more flight of the grand staircase before he could see the trail branching off around the balcony level.

A shadow flickered against the backdrop of the starscape beyond the domed roof and he looked up desperately, too late to see anything. More shadows moved in his peripheral vision, hugging close to the top level of the atrium. But every time he turned to look there seemed to be nothing there.

Glancing nervously around himself, he took the last of the stairs slowly trying to make as little noise as he could whilst all the time listening hard for any alien noise. But there were none. He could not, however, shake the feeling that all the time he was being watched. He dared not call out, even though the screaming voice in the back of his mind begged him to. At the bottom of the stairs he judged the distance to the open corridor, took one last look around the atrium for safety, and ran.

The distance narrowed and he felt closer and closer to the relative safety. All the time the mental fear of the open space behind him filled his mind with dread. It was almost as if he could imagine unseen creatures swooping after him ready to pounce.

The distance narrowed to ten, to five, to one metre. Then he lunged and was in the corridor. Sliding himself sideways into the recess of a doorway, he turned to face the atrium, panting and out of breath. But where his paranoia had expected to see evil shadowy creatures, there was nothing but empty space.

For a while he watched as his chest heaved and he caught his breath. There was an expectation that something would happen. But nothing did. Eventually he had to concede that nothing was going to come; at any rate, what did he expect to do if it did? He had no weapon and nothing else he could use as a weapon, and weapons had not helped Exbo.

He glanced down the corridor. There was nothing there either. Summoning up the courage he began to follow the corridor leaving the atrium behind. Once or twice he thought he heard a distant noise echoing from there, but he could never be certain despite stopping several times and listening.

He found the service staircase and quickly saw which way they must have gone. The tracks made by the salvage crew ended at the lift, but Tracker and Toze's footsteps took to the parallel stairs. Dezza considered pressing the call button to try and ride the lift down, but remembering the incident earlier, he decided there had to be a reason why the others had taken the safer stairs. He did not trust the ancient equipment aboard the Starliner.

The stairs thrummed under his feet, but the tracks were easy enough to follow. He felt exposed in the stairwell and could not help but glance up through the metal grills of the walkways above at every switchback. Once or twice he thought he heard the sound of the steps vibrating under footfall somewhere above him. But every time he stopped to listen, the sounds seem to fade in time to the echo of his own until he was stood in silence save for the rasping of his own breathing. It was probably just the reverberation of his own footsteps, he kept telling himself, but the explanation did little to appease the paranoia he felt.

He descended the last few levels at a hurry. It was more than his mind could cope with to be in that stairwell with all those empty landings above him separated only by a mesh. Yet again he felt the feelings of being watched that made his back shiver and the hairs stand on end. But no matter how many times he flashed his light upwards through the metal, all he ever saw was the inert underside of the grills receding beyond the limit that the light could penetrate.

At the bottom he hurried into the corridor checking only to see which way the trail went before following it along to where they disappeared through a hatch. The hatch was shut, though the panel alongside glowed, showing that it still had power. It had to still work, he thought, or else the others could not have passed through. Jabbing at the buttons he expected it to slide open smoothly, but instead it juddered a few inches before wheezing to a halt. He pressed the pad a second time, impatient for it to open. He did not feel comfortable to be exposed in this corridor with nothing but open space and darkness that his light could not fully penetrate behind him. He still felt that unseen eyes were watching him from beyond the arc of his light.

174

The hydraulics wheezed again, but the door did not budge. He peered through the gap and shone the light through. He caught a glimpse of a room with consoles whose panels held a Christmas tree of lights. But before he could take it all in the door suddenly lurched and slammed shut violently like the jaws of a hungry predator. He reeled back in surprise; he had not been expecting that. His heart thumped loudly in his ears as he tried the panel again. Nothing happened except the lights flickering a moment as if something was shorting in the controls.

He muttered an expletive and looked for an access panel, but there were none. Hitting the controls in frustration with a clenched fist, he was rewarded with the lights flickering once then dying altogether. No matter what he did the panel remained dead. He must have shorted out the controls. But there was no access panel on this side of the hatch, so there was no way he could gain access to the circuits.

Looking around he realised that there was no way to proceed other than to retrace his steps. He had to find another way to get around into the compartments beyond the hatch. With a sinking feeling he realised that he was isolated and lost somewhere in the depth of the derelict without knowing any way to go.

He toyed with heading back to the stairwell and climbing up one level. If the engineering spaces were laid out like any other ship, there should be a duplicate of this corridor and a way through above. Then all he would have to do would be to find a corresponding way down into the adjacent compartment. He was not sure that there would be one though, and there was a very real risk of getting even more lost. At the same time he knew that the failure of the door mechanism might now trap the others on the other side with no way to return. He cursed the ageing equipment on the ship. Why did it have to fail now?

A high pitched sound made his ears prick up, and for a moment he hesitated as he thought it could be the power to the door. But realisation dawned that it was not coming from the hatch or the panel next to it, but instead seemed to be humming in the air from beyond where his light would penetrate. He took a few steps forward as the sound seemed to gain in intensity. He could see the edges of the way through from the stairwell now, and he wondered whether it might be coming from there.

It felt now as if all the air around him was buzzing. When he stopped to listen hard he realised that there was a strange feeling in the air, as if it was becoming charged with static.

He cast his light up and across the sides and ceiling of the corridor. The light picked out pipework and cable ducts. A thought occurred to him and he gingerly put his ear close to one of the ducts. He pulled away in surprise when he realised that the buzzing was louder from there. His mind raced as he tried to think. What was in those ducts? He figured that they would contain electrical systems for the Starliner. Fumbling with his belt he took out the scanner and gingerly pressed the probes to the metal casing of the ducts. He expected they could be charged, but the scanner showed nothing. He found an access cover and popped it open.

The buzzing grew even louder now, and was definitely coming from the cabling inside. He knew that something was passing through it even without the scanner; he could feel the warmth radiating off, and smelt the acrid smell of the dirt that had coated the cable bundles beginning to heat up. He wondered if the fused circuits in the door could have triggered this, but that was unlikely. Whatever had caused this had to lie in the now inaccessible compartment beyond the hatch.

He considered the stairwell, but his light picked out a large opening further back along the corridor. It was a massive rectangular doorway which ordinarily would be sealed by a hatch, but this was rolled back leaving the opening through which once upon a time the Starliner's crew might have moved big equipment on trolleys between the service lifts and the area beyond.

He faltered at its edge, taking the time to play his light over the room beyond and to listen. The buzzing seemed to be fading now, and he could hear nothing from this new area. Again the light was not powerful enough to pick out more than a tiny sphere, but it was enough to tell him that this was a cargo hold.

There was a cool breeze coming from within the hold, and he could sense that it was a big space. His feet scrunched on dirt

176

underfoot, and he heard the sound seem eerie and loud in the vast open area. He could feel it opening to either side and above him. It sent a shiver down his spine; he did not like the feeling. Without light the place had an air of foreboding, and he turned and headed in a hurry back to the stairwell instead. The buzzing had faded now, though he could hear the metal of the ducts ticking slightly as the heat began to dissipate.

The staircase seemed colder and unfriendly now. Stood at the bottom and looking up through the grills he could see nothing but the dull grey of the tarnished metal. He knew there could not be anyone there, but the bristling sixth sense of being watched still continually washed over him as he began to climb.

He did not like the noise his feet made as the walkway vibrated. It seemed too loud in the confined space, and made it impossible to hear any other noises as anything other than confused background that never seemed to stay when he stopped moving to listen. Maybe they were just a product of his overworked imagination, but he kept thinking he could hear *something*.

At the level above he stopped to look over the heavy hatchway door. There were no footsteps at its base; no-one had been through here in a very long time and the dirt and dust had settled almost to the depth of the rim. He regarded it with a sinking feeling, remembering the failed hatchway in the deck below that had thwarted his progress. But the panel at the side when he looked was still glowing strongly. Perhaps it was on a different circuit?

He tapped the panel. Nothing happened. He tapped it again, a little stronger this time. An angry beep echoed from the panel, though the door did not slide back. On a tiny screen above the panel a code flashed up in tiny green letters. He read the words: 'access denied'. What was that about, he wondered?

There no markings on the door that he could see, and nothing to suggest that the area beyond might be any different. He tried following the landing to the end to see if there might be another way though. All he found was the shut doors leading into the cargo lift shaft, and a large rectangular hatch opposite it that would have given access to large objects coming from the lift.

There were no access panels he could see alongside it, and he surmised that it had to open from the other side.

Returning to the small door he tried the panel once more and heard with disappointment the same beep and read the same error code. Deciding to try the next level, he climbed the switchback of the stairs only to find that the hatch there returned the same error message and refused to budge. One by one he checked the levels, until he came to the level where marks on the floor showed where one of the salvage crew had taken to his heels. The hatch was shut here also, but the footsteps clearly had gone through, meaning the hatch must have been open. Checking them over in arc of the light, Dezza was confused. He was sure that this hatch had not been shut when he had climbed down this way. What was more, he could see the boot marks of Toze and Tracker where they had gone through then come back - so it had to have been open for them. Try as he might though, he could not get the hatch to yield and open.

It seemed that every level he climbed up to was exactly the same. Hatch after hatch returned the same error code until he was forced to return down the stairwell to the bottom corridor.

He planned to go back through into the corridor and to have another look at the hatch. Maybe there was a way to dismantle the panel and see whether the power rail could be jumped, bypassing the security. He surmised that the security on the Starliner should not be too hard to get passed.

He was caught unexpectedly by the sight of a hatchway sealed shut. For a moment he thought that he had misjudged the levels, but when passing his light over the stairs he realised he was on the bottom level. Looking further he saw that the marks in the dirt did pass through where the hatch was shut. He could even see his own distinct boot marks half under the rim of the door.

He thought at first that perhaps it had been triggered by power fluctuations, but pressing the panel just resulted in the same error code. This confused him. Why would the door have latched shut like this? He remembered the hatch he had seen several floors above and realised that something must have shut and locked them all within the last few minutes. Was it something that the others had accidentally triggered?

Unscrewing the panel cover revealed only a mass of wiring and some chunky archaic circuit boards. He tried probing with his scanner, looking for a power line he could use to try and jump the lock, but when he pressed the device against the wiring he saw a wisp of white smoke coming out from behind the circuit boards. Pulling back, he saw the wiring flare for a moment spewing out acrid smoke. Then the flames died back leaving only a scorch mark and crumbling remains inside the panel.

A cursory check showed him that the lock was useless and the controls were now fused. Looking over the door he saw that it would be far too heavy for one man to ever hope of moving aside so he did not even bother trying. With no other options he could only turn and face the stairs again and make the long climb back up towards the corridor to the atrium.

*   *   *   *   *

Neither man knew what had activated it. One minute they were alone, and the next minute the air on the gantry seemed to shiver in a haze. It was Toze who had pressed the buttons, not expecting anything like this to happen. The console had been damaged, but the marks across its front seemed superficial. He had not expected much, but instead a pattern of lights had flashed up, then this.

Tracker pulled the officer into the shadows of a hatchway. Toze opened his mouth to say something, but Tracker planted a hand there to shut it. Gesturing for him to remain quiet, he let his hand slip away.

The shimmering air seemed to take on a form and expand. Ozone crackled around its edges as a bank of screens burst into life on the console behind. Slowly the distortion became a tall cylinder of colour before beginning to form into a humanoid shape.

Watching it take form, Toze realised it was some kind of hologram. He must have activated the projection unit. Finally the humanoid shape became a figure which became the outline of a tall, thin woman wearing a uniform that looked many decades out of style.

He did not know what it was that happened next exactly. Tracker had seemed adamant that staying still in the shadows was the best option and had gestured so. Just creep away and leave an ancient computer programme to go through a loop, just like the cleaning robots had elsewhere in the ship. Something must have been on the floor amongst the dirt. As he stepped to follow Tracker through the shadows it made a loud crunch, and he jumped with surprise.

"Identify," came the soft and slightly digitised voice of a woman with a hint of an accent he did not recognise.

He felt the alarm as the hologram's head darted round and the eyes seemed to bore into the shadows.

"Identify," the voice repeated. This time he saw the hologram's mouth move.

The voice froze him to the spot. He felt compelled to answer. "Just passing through," he said. It was all he could think of.

Behind him Tracker moved uneasily.

The woman glanced briefly over the consoles beside her, then moved in slightly unreal stiffness towards them.

"You do not appear on any crew or passenger manifests," she said before tilting her head at a slight angle, expecting an explanation from the pair.

It seemed strange to Toze to be face to face with what his mind was unsure about whether it could be real. "Who are you?" he said.

Her head tilted the other way. For a moment he thought he saw a flicker in her eyes, but it could only have been a glitch in the projection. It seemed remarkably odd to him that when he looked closely at the woman he could see ever so faintly through her. Yet those eyes seemed so piercing he almost took a step backwards to retreat from their gaze.

"I am the onboard Host," she said, "My purpose is to provide information to passengers or crew as required. My system logs show that I have been reactivated now after an enforced shutdown."

Tracker took a hesitant step forward. Toze noted that his face showed an unease and concern.

"When?" he asked.

The woman's head tilted again. It seemed to Toze to be the computer's attempt at animating the hologram when considering questions so that it did not stand there like a statue. Maybe its designers had thought that passengers would find some sense of movement easier to interact with. It struck Toze that they had not particularly managed. Little wonder that no ship he had heard of used such holograms now.

"I do not understand your question," the woman said after a moment's pause.

"When were you shutdown?"

The eyes seemed to flicker, but the head did not tilt this time. "Ship's chronometers indicate a time period of ninety-five years, four months, twelve days, fourteen hours and thirty-two minutes."

Tracker looked to Toze with pleading eyes. "I need to speak to you, Sir, in the next compartment." He turned to the hologram and added, "You might want to go and look for the passengers and see if you can help them."

The hologram's head tilted and her facial expression looked perplexed, though she said nothing.

Toze followed Tracker through the hatch into the next compartment and watched as the man marched up and down the small anteroom to make sure that they were alone. When he seemed satisfied they were, he marched back to the hatchway and glanced through at the hologram. The figure was still stood where they had left her.

"Creeped out?" asked Toze quietly.

"Not sure."

"Why? We just activated the ship's hologram system. That's all it was. You heard her say so much herself."

"That's not what bothers me."

They watched the hologram closely, looking for signs of a reaction. It seemed that the computer processing the image had decided for now just to leave the figure standing in the centre of the floor. She was not still like a statue, but seemed to sway a little like a real person might.

"I know this ship is enough to make anyone jumpy, but it's just a hologram. Maybe some things just are what they are."

Tracker turned to him, the look of concern etched back on his face. "She said she had been offline for over ninety years until we switched her back on. But that's a lie. I've seen her before."

"Are you telling me that some bird you saw in a bar on Titan has decided to come all this way just to jilt you?" scoffed Toze.

He seemed hurt a little by the comment. "No. She was in the gym, and again I saw her in the atrium. She says she was offline, but I don't believe her."

"She says we switched her on, and that does tally with the consoles."

Tracker was adamant. "I think that system has already been on. How else could I have seen her before twice?"

Toze looked back to the figure. She was still stood where they had left her. "Are you sure it was her."

"I never forget a face." He shivered. "I never like the feeling of being watched, and there have been too many times that I got that feeling it was going on."

Toze considered this. He believed that Tracker would never forget a face. The guy was too good to make mistakes, or so it had always seemed. "Then what does that mean?" he said at last.

"I don't think things are quite what they seem."

"You think the hologram is lying?"

"I think something is up, even if I don't know what."

Toze nodded. "Then we leave that thing a wide berth."

"It could be dangerous. If it's lying then there has to be a reason." He looked at the dulled grey walls around them and the damaged consoles. "This place is not good. If we could I'd order in a strike team and just blow this hulk out of the stars."

"We don't have that luxury. We need that drive core back on the *Magellan* just to stand a chance of staying alive if we want to get off the Starliner."

They left the figure of the woman and made their way back through the other corridor. Toze suggested finding a way back around to pull the plug on the consoles and to shut the ghostly figure down. But Tracker stopped him. Their time was best spent elsewhere, he argued, and the hologram could just be left where it stood waiting for the return of a crew that would never come.

                    *   *   *   *   *

If a hologram could think about what it saw, the hologram might have wondered why the two men chose to hide from it. But holograms do not think, and neither do the computers they are connected to for the runtime they need to exist. Nonetheless, the figure of the woman stood and waited with the patience of a machine.

Time meant little to a computer. It could wait for a millennium with the same patience that it could wait for a mere millisecond. Only the chronometer ever told it how long had passed, and in truth the figure was not significant to a machine mind in any way other than the way in which it had been programmed.

So the figure stood by the console, animated by the computer in a programme devised by developers over a century before to make it more 'user friendly'. Like most computer developers, they merely wrote into programmes as many problems as they wrote out.

A flicker ran across the woman's facial expression. One moment it was blank and expectant and the next it seemed to possess an altogether different aura. If either man had been there to see it, they would have seen a change from inanimate machine mind to something else. But no-one was there to watch as the figure shivered a little then stopped still, no longer controlled by the ancient programme of user friendliness. Tracker and Toze had already gone.

For a moment the figure regarded the hatchway through which they had left, as if considering whether they might return. Turning slowly they looked over the console next to them, over the smashed fascia panels and damaged controls until their gaze – if indeed a hologram could gaze – rested on the screen and terminal that Toze had activated.

The screen still glowed, but at the bottom of the screen a cursor blinked and several lines of text hung in the green glow of the projection. They read: 'programme not found. Unable to complete initialisation - programme aborted'.

This did not bother the figure of the woman. It seemed as though she smiled, and the eyes flickered once more as the image dissolved away into the air.

*   *   *   *   *

Even before Red had finished telling his hurried and panicked tale, Zoë knew they had to get off the Starliner. Faced with a frantic Dezza all those years before, she had been sceptical, she remembered. Now it did not need much evidence to make her believe what had been so hard then.

The pair ran, snaking their way though corridors that lay thick with virgin dirt and decay. In some places it was like wading through sand, though this was fluffy and left black streaks wherever it touched. It stirred up an acrid smell and much dust, and more than once they had to lower their visors to avoid choking in the clouds of filth. But their suits were already low on oxygen, and each time the audible warning buzzed in their ears warning them that the re-circulators were almost expired and could not be guaranteed on to work for much longer if pushed. All they could do was struggle on, breathing from the suit's systems sparingly only when faced with no other option.

Small sections of the corridors had lights on. It was strange to them to suddenly find themselves running in light, but the areas were few and far between and usually they stumbled along by their helmet lights alone. Occasionally they stopped to regain their breath. Most times the break would be cut short as they heard the noises again coming from afar and felt the deck vibrate underneath them. Once more they would head wearily into the darkness trying to find their way back to the *Magellan*. Slowly they were putting distance between themselves and what had attacked the others as the noises became more muted and far away.

The pace gradually slowed, as fatigue moved over them and the noises all but disappeared behind them. But the urge to keep moving was never far away and they would always begin moving again as fast as they dared.

It was easy to get lost in the corridors of the Starliner. They had been laid out like a maze, and no two decks appeared to be exactly the same. When the corridors ended, they took to the lifts. When the lifts did not work, they took to the stairs. They passed massive rooms once brightly lit and ornate with decorations, but which were now no more than broken down shells. They went through a shopping mall where the windows of the boutiques were dulled brown and opaque and obscured much of the contents save for a few tattered remains of clothes and degraded remnants where food once might have been.

Connecting corridors here were vast affairs flanked by promenades that had splendid views out over the stars through massive Perspex screens. Once painted white and decked with teak, these areas seem to have been made to imitate the ocean going liners of centuries before. Now they were mottled with tarnish and even the Perspex took on a blackened tint where mould and algae had briefly flourished before fading away as the atmosphere in the Starliner had changed. White paint peeled and without power to the wide promenades they felt the penetrating cold leaching through from the vacuum beyond the clear screens.

They caught a view through the arching roof of the *Magellan* still attached to the airlocks with her navigation lights flashing as if nothing had ever happened. It renewed their hope; the vessel did not seem far away. All they had to do was to follow the promenade along and find a way to climb up just a few decks. But the Starliner was not about to let their return to their ship be that simple. The promenade ended at a wall flecked with peeling paint and a mock life buoy with the faded lettering *Cerberus* in gold copperplate letters that had dulled almost to black. The only way to go was back into the derelict's interior with a last glance and a falling heart at the view of the *Magellan* that was so near, yet so far.

They tried to keep their bearings, but the corridors here seemed to twist back and forth until it was hard to remember which way they had intended to go. They looked for any signs of deck plans that might show them the way, but infuriatingly there were none. Light beckoned to them from beyond the end of a filthy corridor, and they slowed their pace to ease out of the darkness and into the light.

Blinking in the unexpected brightness, they found they were in what had once been the largest room they had ever seen. Chandeliers still glowed, retaining some of their magnificence despite the tarnish and dirt. A bar ran the length of the bottom floor that they were on, whilst above towered tiers of balconies whose empty levels overlooked them with empty menace that filled them with unease.

The bottles rattled as a vibration ran through the deck again, reminding them that they must hurry on. It came again, louder still as they turned in the dark corridor outside. They could hear something coming, preceded by the same moaning whine that they had heard before. The dust around them began to smooth out and settle like a liquid and the floor beneath almost seemed to sing to the reverberation that was building in pitch.

Red fumbled with his belt and withdrew the gun he carried there. The fear that had made him run before had been replaced with a mix of anger and grim determination. As the wall of dust came, he fired the weapon blindly into the mist. It was all Zoë could do to scold the man to keep moving as his face contorted to screams of fury and the gun kept spitting bullets.

Still the dust rolled on. The gun was nearly drowned out by the screams that came with the wall of dust. They came to a mound of detritus that seemed to block the corridor, and with a feeling of despair she thought they might have reached a dead end. But when she tilted her light upwards, the faltering beam picked out in the haze a tiny crawl way through at the top.

Red gave her a leg up before following too. The air screamed past them in the tiny crawl space carrying with it dust so strong now that both had to close their visors and hope that their perilously low supplies of oxygen would not fail on them just yet.

The tunnel in the débris felt like it was going to narrow and end, leaving them trapped inside at the mercy of whatever was in the corridor behind them. But it did not. Instead it opened out into another corridor, and they jumped down thankful to be out of the worst of the dust and able to open their visors and conserve the remaining seconds of oxygen that their suits might be able to provide.

Whatever had followed them seemed to be unable to get through. Dust fluttered through the tunnel in the piled junk, but nothing came after it. Not wishing to remain here, they turned and ran aiming to put as much distance between them and it as they could.

*   *   *   *   *

At the opening into the atrium Dezza stopped and listened. Pressing his body back against the wall, he looked out over the vast open space and tried to visualise what might lie hidden in the shadows that shrouded the lower balconies. The starscape above still provided illumination of sorts, though it was feebler than moonlight would have been on Earth. He longed to use his helmet light, though the fear that this might attract whatever had lain here in wait for him before gnawed at his mind and prevented him from doing so.

There were no sounds, except for the rasp of his breathing. For a while longer he stood, just looking, and weighing up what he wanted to do. He could see the grand staircase, and knew he must head up that to get back to the *Magellan*. But he could not shake off the feeling that he was being watched by something unseen, scrutinised by an entity that was content to watch and wait for now.

The moments slid past, and he began to doubt his own feelings. Nothing had happened and there were no sounds no matter how hard he listened. This was foolish! He cursed himself, and not for the first time wished he could have had that gun. Still, there was no point in dwelling on what could not be.

Judging the distance in his mind, he reckoned it would be maybe thirty seconds to trot around this balcony to reach the grand staircase. Then maybe a further ten seconds for each pair of switchbacks on the wide stairs to get to each level. Finally, away where he could not see from here, there was the run to the corridor then a further flight of stairs to reach the airlock level. He reckoned that it would all take six minutes, maybe seven at most.

Taking a moment to summon up courage, he took a glance to the corridor behind him then lunged out into the atrium. Following the tracks, it seemed to take an age to work around to where the grand staircase opened out. Finally he reached it and began to take its steps two at a time.

He made it up that flight, then onto the next. Pausing on a balcony, he took a moment to catch his breath and look out over the atrium. He was a good deal higher up now, and from this vantage point it was possible to see almost all of the open space. He saw the husks of what might once have been vegetation in large raised areas, and in his mind's eye these began to form into sinister figures of things lurking in the dark. But the atrium was still and quiet, and the strange forms were just figments of his mind.

He cursed himself for letting his mind wander in such a way, and took to the stairs again. He took another flight before he became aware that there was a new noise that had not been there before. With a pang of fear, he recognised it - the same moaning wail they had heard in the laundry room when they had made their escape through the chute. Whatever that thing had been, it had found him.

It spurred new speed to his motion, and he rounded the final switchback on the stairs. Just one flight remained then a dash to the corridor. Perhaps he could lose this thing in the stairwell that lay beyond? He pushed aching limbs on, never daring to look behind. But the noise increased as if echoing from the corridors below that led into the atrium.

Finally he dared to look at the top of the last flight. Looking back over the atrium, he saw the dust beginning to roll from the balcony where he had been minutes before contemplating this dash to relative safety. Had it been following him? He knew he had felt the feeling of being watched, but he had tried to put it down to the fears induced by the derelict. Now he began to think that maybe there had been something in the shadows, regarding him through alien eyes.

The dust was growing stronger all the time, rolling across the atrium and beginning to make the floor disappear under its dirty haze. In the dim light afforded by the stars, it looked as if the floor was beginning to seethe like an agitated sea. He turned and ran and did not look back again. He saw the lights that still glowed in the final corridor, and without hesitation ran for their inviting glow.

As he reached the door for the stairwell he felt the air in the corridor beginning to move. He felt the floor move as a vibration rumbled briefly through the structure, and his back bristled with the sixth sense that something had entered the space behind him, as the walls around him grew darker as the light from the wall brackets dimmed and flickered.

He saw the door and dived for it. It's handle seemed stiff and his hands weak as he wrestled to get it to yield. All the time he felt the air moving, growing clammy and cold. The handle seemed to have seized, dropping only a small way before something caught in the mechanism.

The air around him grew thicker and bristled with static charge. It gave off an incredible feeling of foreboding. He realised that the dust that was blowing past him seemed to be glowing, and tiny patterns of blue static discharge flickered in the dark.

Putting his shoulder to the door he pushed his weight against it. The door was old and was not meant for much more than decoration, and he felt it bow under his weight. He tried again, pushing with all the strength he had. This time he was rewarded with the sound of aged wood splintering. The handle flicked and with a crash the door gave way taking him with it as the frame cracked and peeled away at the lock.

Picking himself up he pushed the door back shut on the corridor, shutting out the worst of the dust and wind, though he could still hear it rushing past. On the landing he saw a ceramic pot filled with dirt and a skeletal stick that might have been a decorative bush a long time ago. Pulling it with both hands he managed to drag it across the landing and wedge it under the door. It was not much, but it would be enough to stop the door from blowing open.

Taking to the stairs he heard the door begin to creak. Something was testing it from outside, and his heart leapt. He heard the handle drop, and the sliding of ceramic on dirt. He reached the door at the top of the stairs and piled through into the airlock corridor. Unseen in the stairwell below, hidden by the

189

bulk of the stairs, he heard the sound of splintering wood and the crash of exploding ceramic. The noise only made him run faster.

He saw Neptune flash by in the weaving light of his torch; there was no time to stop and look. He saw the myriad of tracks left in the floor, from the salvage crew, his crew before, and the marooned crew of the dropship that he was part of now. He saw the airlock open and waiting as behind him he heard the mounting wail of rushing air within the stairwell that made the door at the top begin to knock and flap.

Skidding into the airlock bay his heart leapt as he saw the power was still on. It had been a fear that he would return to find it dead again. He hammered on the panel and the airlock door began to slide shut; it seemed so painfully slow. Outside he saw the rising dust fluttering along the corridor and behind it the heavy clouds that rolled like fog.

He gasped, as the clouds seemed to gain in speed before coalescing together and down. Before his eyes the dust seemed to be separating out and becoming something else. He saw the dirt dropping to the floor to leave behind a mass that seemed to be glowing a white that seemed unnatural alongside the mess and filth.

For a split second he thought he saw a figure coming out of the white, and he reeled in shock. It was only a moment he had to view it before the metal of the airlock thumped home. The lights on the panel changed from red to yellow, and the moaning wail from the corridor disappeared to no more than a background hum.

He remembered the image; it was one that felt like it had been burnt onto the back of his eyes and into his mind. Yet, it seemed impossible to believe that he had seen a ghostly figure that seemed to have at one moment been Tubs, and at the next Zoë. In his mind it was not possible that either could be there, and yet his eyes were telling him that they had been.

The airlock cycled and stopped, and the panel lights flickered to green before the inner door slid open. He contemplated going back, then cursed himself for such a stupid suggestion. Whatever that had been out there, it had chased him and the others throughout the *Cerberus*.

Dust fell from him as he took a step into the interior of the *Magellan*. He had not realised quite how much filth had been stirred up until now. It left a dirty trail across the floor and on everything he brushed against or touched. He could still smell it: the stench of death. He remembered that smell with a shiver that ran through him. He remembered the first time he and Zoë had watched the Starliner evaporate into the Rösenbridge and they had been left with nothing but the stink of dirt and tarnish.

There were spare overalls in lockers in the living quarters, and he thankfully found a pair that were the right size, and stripped off his dirty clothes to change. Not wanting the stench to linger, he stuffed the old clothes into the garbage disposal unit, though he stopped short at activating the compacting mechanism; without a core, battery power had to be saved. It felt good to be rid of the smell though.

A buzzing echoed briefly from the command deck and he tensed. Listening, he heard it again, and ventured slowly through the connecting corridor. At the opening he paused, listening to the steady on-off pattern of the buzzer. It sounded like the communications desk. When he peered around the rim he saw one light flashing from the console. Looking around, the command deck was still empty, just as he had left it. He felt a little relieved; after all he had been through he had half expected there to be some-one there, waiting to taunt him.

He sat at the console and picked up the headset and slipped it on. The panel showed that a frequency was open and a call was coming through. For a moment he wondered if it might be another ship, but deep down he knew the Starliner was adrift far off the beaten shipping lanes, and rescue without a distress call would be very unlikely.

Adjusting the controls he reeled in surprise at the sound of the familiar voice.

"Toze? Where the hell are you?" he demanded.

He could sense the relief washing over Toze as he whooped in joy at the other end of the line.

"I got through! Goddamn it! I got through all right!"

*　　　*　　　*　　　*　　　*

The hatchway had refused to yield, either to probing of the electronic lock, or to brute force. Designed to seal compartments from the vacuum of space in the event of a hull breach, they realised that there was no way they would be able to smash through. It had been open when they came through; their tracks proved that. Whatever had happened since had happened without any warnings in the control room.

Retracing their steps, they found route after route blocked by yet more sealed hatchways. Every one returned the same error code when they tried to activate the panel. Occasionally they passed through hatches that were still open, though always they would come to a dead end and be forced to retrace their steps.

Then they retraced their steps to find a hatchway they had come through moments before had closed soundlessly in their absence. There were their tracks, clear as day in the dust on the floor, but the way through had been sealed.

It had felt like they were being herded. A pattern of hatches both open and closed that forced them to take a certain route. Gradually it dawned on them that they were being prevented from finding a way back to the *Magellan* as well as back to the room where the drive cores were.

At an open hatch, Tracker gestured for the officer to pause. Scouting around he found a length of pipework along the walls whose brackets had rusted in the passage of time. Rust patterns down the wall showed where water had once leaked out, but the water was long gone and the pipe proved easy to remove a length.

The hatch had a lip that allowed its workings to seal and make the fitting airtight. Checking the gauge of the pipe with the groove in the lip, Tracker looked up and smiled behind the mask. It would be a perfect fit. With Toze's help he fed the pipe into the groove and wedged it at either end so that it could not pop out if the door shut, only be forced in tighter.

If the Starliner was playing tricks with them, then they would play it at its own game. Finally satisfied that the pipe was in place, Tracker levered several more lengths off the corroded brackets to carry with them for wedging the next hatch. Stepping over their work, they carried on through the maze of compartments.

Sure enough, they came to a closed hatchway, and were forced to retrace their steps. Deliberately they followed them all the way back to the hatchway they had wedged.

Rounding the corner, Tracker turned to the officer and signalled with a jubilant hand signal. The hatch was halfway down, but the pipe had done the trick and the door had jammed with more than enough room for them to clamber back through. At the next hatch they took the precaution of laying another piece of pipe into the groove of the rim, and then another and another. Some hatches were still shut, forcing them to double back, but now they found that the hatches they had wedged remained open; there had been no attempts to close them.

In places they came across their own tracks criss-crossing in the corridors, and it became apparent that some of the doors that had been shut before were now open again.

Stopping in the shadows of a compartment whose lights were out and whose control consoles glowed dimly, they huddled in a corner and each raised the same thing that the other had been thinking. They were being herded around the engineering decks by a pattern of closed and open hatches. When they had thwarted the pattern with jamming the hatches, so the pattern had changed. Whatever was trying to lead them had altered its methods with bluff and double bluff. But if it had not been for the tracks left behind in the dirt on the floor then in all likelihood they would not have noticed.

If they were to keep going, where would the maze lead? They could not open hatches that were already closed and they had exhausted the supply of pipes to jam more.

Searching the compartment they found themselves in, they found little that would be of use to block more hatches. Just a few old chairs so broken down with age that they would be unable to support a person sitting on them and certainly not the mass of a hydraulic hatch.

For a while they sat, unsure of what to do, until Tracker seemed to become alert, and gestured for Toze to stay quiet and in the shadows.

At first Toze was unsure what had caught the tracker's attention. But he said nothing and pressed himself into the shadows as the man had indicated for him to with a hand signal. He watched as Tracker edged to the hatchway out of the compartment. It was not a hydraulic door, and would have to be closed manually; there was no risk of it unexpectedly sealing.

Slipping his gun to one side out of his way, his left hand stole to his belt and fumbled in a pouch. He brought something out; Toze squinted to see – it was hard in the dark to see anything. It looked like a slender metal rod that widened out into a lollipop shaped piece at the end that seemed to catch the light from the corridor.

He realised it was a mirror, not unlike those that Dentists used. He watched as Tracker eased the mirror to the edge of the hatch and let the glass slip beyond the edge and angled himself so he could see down the corridor. For a moment he paused, scrutinising the tiny reflection, then he rotated it so he could see down to the other end of the corridor.

Then the man froze, stiller than a statue. For a moment Toze thought he might be about to fall asleep, but then he realised the expression on his face was changing. From the usual calm, he saw surprise and then fear wash over it and the eyes opened wider and wider until the whites seemed to dominate his face.

He dropped the mirror with a suddenness that startled the officer. Even before the mirror had hit the floor, Tracker had leapt up and had grasped hold of the hatch. Toze scrambled up as he managed to unhook the catch and swing the door around. He found himself washed along in Tracker's panic, helping him to flick each of the deadlocks until the hatch was secured.

He slid back against the metal of the hatch, breathing heavily.

"What the hell was that all about?" Toze demanded.

Tracker did not answer at first. Instead he rushed across the compartment looking for other ways in. In an anteroom he found another hatchway like the last, and sealed it shut. Then he rushed across to a short passageway and disappeared into it at a run, forcing Toze to follow.

The bounded down the passage with Tracker skidding briefly into each of the small rooms off it, but each seemed to be nothing but a small store or office room, and he carried on with barely a grunt of acknowledgement.

Toze shouted after him, but he did not stop until he reached the end where another hatch lay ajar, partially blocking the way. He threw his weight into the door, forcing it against hinges that seemed to be rusted solid. Heaving hard, the sinews on his neck and arms bulged as he put a superhuman effort to the door.

Toze found himself rushing to help. There was something about Tracker's urgency; what had he seen in that corridor?

Only when he was satisfied that there was no way in from where they had been did he settle and slump to the deck, his chest heaving.

"What did you see?" repeated Toze.

"I saw..." he faltered, "I saw the creature. It seemed to change from physical to just, well, pure energy. One minute it was there, the next minute the figure folded in on itself and looked like it was, well, pouring parts of itself into the electrical system."

"You're saying it can move through the power?"

Tracker looked up. "You think that's how it got onto the dropship maybe?"

Toze shrugged. "Maybe. But what are we going to do?"

"Something. I don't know what yet."

Toze tried the radio, but static and distortion buzzed loudly. "There's going to be no help from Dezza," he conceded.

Tracker looked over the corridor they were in. The small rooms had no other way out through them and contained electrical equipment. He eyed them all with suspicious eyes. "It can get into the power; it could be anywhere, including here!"

Grabbing an access panel he wrenched it from the side of equipment and began pulling wiring out in tussled loops.

"Get in here and help me," he called out, "We need to kill the power. Short it out. If that creature is trying to find a way through the power, we can try and kill it, or at least buy ourselves a way out."

They pulled off any access cover they could find. Soon there were coils of wire laid out across the floor. Taking a cutting tool from his belt, Tracker began sawing into the bundles. In a moment he had cut through the armoured shielding of the bundle and exposed the shiny metal of the core. Repeating the task, he worked until several different cables were treated the same. Careful not to let any ends touch, he checked them with the probes on his scanner.

"They're all live at different voltages. Good," he said, "Shield your eyes; this is going to make hell of a bright spark."

He hesitated a moment, then rammed the exposed ends against each other. There was a flash and a bang and the air filled with the stench of vaporised metal. Lights flickered on, then died. From beyond the corridor and rooms, as if emanating from within the structure of the Starliner, they heard a tortured high-pitched whine that hurt their ears. Then it was gone, and there was nothing but the lingering stink of burning and clouds of fog-like smoke from the still smouldering cable ducts.

Toze flicked the radio switch again idly in the gloom. To his surprise instead of buzzing and static, there was nothing but clean silence of the carrier signal. They looked at each other.

"Interference has gone," said Tracker slowly.

Gingerly Toze tried the send button. It took another couple of goes, but he was eventually rewarded with the sound of Dezza's voice.

*   *   *   *   *

The radio was clear now, and they could stay in contact with Dezza. They did not know whether they had killed it, but the clear radio signal suggested that at the very least, it could not be close by.

Further along the corridors the lights were still glowing. The current surge they had caused had not spread through much of the ship, and it was apparent that circuit breakers would have protected most of the Starliner's frail systems. Hatches still remained locked down though, and no amount of probing at the dead panels would make them yield. It was probably a safety device that the hydraulic clamps locked shut in case of power failure. At any rate, they were forced in a new direction to find a way through to access stairwells and make the long climb back up countless decks before they found the tracks to the atrium and retraced their steps.

They barely said a word, but at the opening to the atrium both found themselves hesitating.

"Do you really think it's gone?" asked Toze at last.

Tracker looked out over the gloomy bulk of the open space, lit by the dim light of far away stars. It seemed empty now, but no less menacing. "I'd like to think so, but I doubt it. If it had been that easy to kill it, this hulk wouldn't be floating out here as a derelict."

He flicked on the radio. The carrier signal was still there, and he knew that if he wanted he could send the call and Dezza's voice would come right back to him. But there were the beginnings of interference forming.

"I can hear it licking its wounds," he said. As if in answer the radio's signal hissed a moment with a staccato of noise that waxed and waned annoyingly. "Listen to that," he continued darkly, "It's there all right, just waiting for its moment."

"What about the meteorite swarm?" asked Toze.

Tracker paused. It had been on the back of his mind, but he had not really thought about it properly until now. "We need to find a way of getting that core. If we can't get through those hatches again, then we have to find another way."

The radio buzzed with a burst of static. From somewhere far away in the Starliner, a vibration rumbled through the structure. The two men looked around as a few stray patterns of dust were dislodged and fluttered before the reverberation died away.

"You hear that?" said Tracker. "It's going to be back if we don't move fast."

Toze shivered. "Let's get back to the *Magellan*." He looked over the foreboding bulk of the atrium. "This place gives me the creeps."

*   *   *   *   *

Dezza had not wanted to go down into the engineering spaces because of the body in the chamber. Toze had hesitated, but Tracker had chuckled and stood up to go.

"When you've been on as many hot missions as I have," he rumbled, "You don't get scared by dead meat any more."

If it was the man's attempt at humour, it fell on deaf ears. They waited as he popped the hatch that Dezza had sealed out of fear, and opened the way into the spaces below. Dezza held back from the edge, remembering the feelings he had felt before, but Tracker was not easily riled. Swinging his body onto the ladder, he had slid down in one movement and disappeared without a moment's hesitation into the unseen portion of the crawl space.

The news from the gauges was not good. They had expected at least five days of battery power left, but the gauges had shown only three, and that was on the proviso of if they conserved power.

Tracker hung on the ladder, head and shoulders through the hatch as he relayed the news. It seemed that in the panic, systems had been left running that were not needed, impacting on the consumption.

Dezza felt the pang of guilt knot in his stomach; it had been his foolish fears that had left them down on reserve power.

"If we're going to act, now is the time to do something," Tracker said without showing any hint of annoyance. Now was not the time for any pointing of fingers of blame.

"We need a core running," said Toze blankly.

"Isn't there another way?" asked Dezza.

Toze shook his head. "With the swarm approaching, we have to get clear."

"We don't need a core to do that," offered Dezza, "The ion drive will give us enough propulsion to get out of the path."

"No good," said Tracker, "Three days and we're out of air."

"What about the quo-fields? We could ride it out in stasis."

"Still takes power, and that's something we don't have at the moment whichever way you look at it. We'd drop out of the stasis booths just in time to see the power die and the air system go offline."

"So we're dead either way unless we get back inside the *Cerberus* and drag one of those cores back and get it up and running in under two days before the swarm hits?" said Toze.

It began to dawn on them that without a core it did not matter what they did, they would be out of options whatever else they did.

Tracker nodded calmly. "Pretty much, yeah."

Dezza thought for a moment. "All we need is the secondary core. It would provide enough power for the life support systems and guidance. We wouldn't have the option of the Rösenbridge, but then with the ion drive we would not have to."

"It shouldn't be too hard to shift the secondary core; we already disconnected it. We'll double check our chamber, but I don't think any of the other critical components are gone," said Toze thoughtfully.

"Just have to get past whatever is stalking us in there," said Tracker.

*   *   *   *   *

Toze had wanted to use the explosive charges that the salvage crew had stored in lockers. The shaped charges were for removing damaged plating but they would be equally at home at slicing the plate of the Starliner's hull. They could charge the suits with enough air that they did not need to put themselves at the mercy of the Starliner's atmosphere. But Dezza had warned against it. One explosion in the wrong place risked starting a chain reaction that could make the Starliner's hull fail catastrophically over a wide area. At worst they could find themselves blasted off into space, at best they could render the Starliner impossible to enter again as safety systems activated to prevent compartments from just peeling themselves inside out into the resultant vacuum. So instead they opted for simultaneous entry at two different points. Dezza would go after the core, whilst Tracker would play the game of chicken with an entity they did not fully understand.

After so long of being used to the synthetic gravity of space stations and space ships, it filled Dezza with a mixture of dread and excitement to know he was going on his first space walk in more than five years. It had been something he had loved doing, but to his surprise he realised that in those passing years he had never thought about doing it or missing it.

Now he stood alongside Tracker in the *Magellan*'s tiny external airlock, waiting for the controls to flash as ready. They wore the suits they had found in the salvage ship, left behind by its former crew. They were just like the ones Dezza remembered from the Tug. It seemed odd to be looking to Tracker now encased in the skin hugging white material and hidden by the oversize helmet. They had supplemented the basic suit with small thrust packs for moving outside in zero gee and utility belts for the tools they might need.

He could hear only the sound of his breathing now; it sounded sharp and raspy in the echo of the suit. Somehow the noise seemed to fill him with reassurance and an inner calm. It was just like old times.

Static buzzed in his ears bringing him from his moment of memories.

"Okay," buzzed Toze's voice from the safety of the *Magellan*'s command deck, "I have green lights for go. Everything good in there?"

Tracker signalled back on the channel he was ready, and Dezza did the same. They heard Toze signal he was going to activate the airlock, and a moment later the panel flashed up its amber warning lights and he felt the tug on the suit as the air began to be pumped out.

At first the noise of the pumps was loud, but as the vacuum increased so it became muted until he could hear it only through the vibration of the deck beneath his feet.

Finally the panel clicked over to green, and he saw the external door pop a little, and a flutter of dust edged around the rim. Tracker grasped the handle and pulled it across. Swinging himself around he pulled himself to the edge of the rim, then felt for a grab rail outside and pulled himself out.

Dezza went to follow and realised he was floating up off the floor. No more synthetic gravity until they re-entered the Starliner.

It was an odd sensation, and he was not sure that he was ready for it. It would take a while to get his space legs back.

Outside the airlock he found Tracker floating just off the hull plating. He had tethered himself to the *Magellan* by a hook on his suit and he indicated Dezza to do the same, for now.

"Check your thrust pack, and use it wisely," Tracker's voice came calmly across the radio into his helmet, "There isn't enough to be wasting any if you want to get yourself back here."

Did nothing unsettle this man, Dezza wondered? Faced with the void of space and a starscape that gave a stomach churning illusion of falling in all directions at all times, he seemed as at home as he had been perched nonchalantly in a chair in the sleeping quarters.

Toze's voice buzzed in their ears again as he told them he would keep on the radio for as long as possible. If they were lucky, they might stay in contact all through, but it was likely the connection would drop at some point as the signal was screened out by the structure of the Starliner, just as it had been before.

Tracker set off first. Unclipping his tether, he said nothing and just calmly activated the thrust controls for the backpack. White gas jetted out, silent in the vacuum, and he began to accelerate away alongside the bulk of the 'liner towards the set of pressure doors they had picked out from the comfort of the *Magellan*'s command deck.

It seemed so different now, thought Dezza, to be faced with the reality. He felt the doubts creeping of whether they would be able to open the doors from the outside at all.

As he watched, the graceful motion of the white suited figure came to an end in a silent burst of jetting gas. He had made it with pinpoint accuracy. He watched the figure remove tools from his belt and do something with the pressure door.

For a moment nothing seemed to happen, and Dezza wondered if his fears had been borne true and that Tracker might at any moment jet back, defeated by the door. But he saw a jet of silver dust flutter into the vacuum and a second later the radio crackled with his calm voice.

"I'm in. The door mechanisms are stiff, but they release manually. Give me a minute to get clear." Without waiting for a reply, the white figure levered the door open a fraction, then disappeared inside. Finally the door revolved back into the frame, and it was like Tracker had never been there at all.

"Okay, you know what to do," came Toze's voice, "I'll be here for you on the radio if you need me."

"Okay," was all he could say.

Unhitching the tether he felt the sudden rush of fear to know that he was floating in space. But he pushed those fears down and pushed his mind back to the days when he had done this for a living; it seemed so long ago now. Almost in another lifetime.

His fingers remembered though, and they jabbed at the controls without hesitation. He felt the jolt as the jets fired, and the noise vibrating through the suit. It was a weird sound; he had not been able to hear the jets on Tracker's suit. He remembered just in time to shut the jets off. There was no prize for arriving too fast and bouncing off the Starliner's hull. At any rate, he needed the precious propulsion gas to get him back again.

The journey across was exhilarating as he felt like he was free falling. He concentrated on the dark bulk of the Starliner moving past, to distract himself from what felt like a drop into infinity alongside, above and beneath him. It was easy for a man to go crazy faced with such distances.

Reaching forward with his gloved hands he braced himself and caught the plating to slow himself down. Under the fingers of his gloves he saw the dust that had collected over the decades on the Starliner's hull puff into clouds like it was suspended in water. He had not had as good an aim as Tracker, but he was close enough that a tiny application from the jets brought him to where he wanted to be.

He saw the panel and quickly opened it with a flick of his fingers. To his surprise he found it was difficult to grasp anything properly. The cold of the vacuum was leaching the heat from his body despite the best efforts of the suit, and he realised that he would need to get inside the Starliner as quickly as possible.

Inside the panel was just a handle that fitted almost flush to the recess. It felt like ice to his touch as he pushed his fingers through the handle and pulled. For a few seconds nothing happened despite his best efforts, and not for the first time he felt the feeling of failure wash over him. But finally the handle gave a fraction, and he felt the mechanism start to yield after years of neglect.

Suddenly it gave completely and thumped to the open position and the door let go a crack revealing the darkened interior of the Starliner to him.

He saw something move inside, and he reeled in surprise. It was something mottled and old and, somehow human in shape. It caught Dezza by surprise and he nearly lost his grip. In a panic he flailed but managed to catch back hold of the handle.

"What's up?" demanded Toze's voice in his ears. He must have been watching closely on the *Magellan*'s external video monitors.

"There's something in here," he heard his voice falter. Then he caught another view, and a shiver ran through his body before he breathed a sigh. "It's okay. Must be one of the original crew."

"You stay cool down there. It's easy to lose your head."

"I know."

He levered the door open a little more. It was difficult to do when he had to wedge one hand onto the popped out handle to stop himself from floating away into space. But he managed it, and made a gap wide enough to slip through.

It surprised him just how much darker it was inside. Of course outside there had been a glow from the stars that his eyes had grown accustomed to, but here there was no light source at all. He felt something brushing against his boots, but tried not to think about it. His outstretched hand found the inner door and the panel alongside it. Fumbling for his helmet light, he turned it on to reveal the tiny little space in which he was now in.

The remains on the floor were the first thing he was drawn to. The body had been here a long time, and it had not so much decomposed as been freeze-dried by the cold and the vacuum. It looked so mummified that it was impossible to know gender or age. It had looked in that moment that the door rolled back that the body had been waving its arm, but it had merely been the effect of the zero gravity. The clothes were old and it was definitely not one of the missing salvage crew. In a locker that sat ajar he saw an old archaic pressure suit. The airlock had been intended as an emergency escape hatch, but for whatever reason the crewmember had never got as far as donning the suit and stepping out into the stars.

He tried to ignore it and looked over the controls inside the tiny airlock. Closing the outer door was easy, and he felt the mechanism slide home much more easily from this side. Stepping over the body he turned his attention to the inner door.

There was a panel here and he slid it open easily. Without exposure to space the lever inside slid effortlessly, and he heard the brief deafening hiss as the air rushed in to equalise and the strange feeling of gravity returning as his feet pressed into the deck.

The door opened into a darkened space deep within the machine rooms of the Starliner. Leaving the inner airlock door ajar, he cast the helmet light first over the floor; there were no tracks here. Good – that meant this are was undisturbed by the salvage crew and might pass unnoticed for now from the thing.

The sound of his breathing and the noises of the air recirculation in his suit reminded him that he did not have time to waste. There would be only so long that Tracker could provide a distraction for.

Reaching for his wrist controls he tried the radio. To his relief after a brief pause, Toze's voice came back to him.

"I got you. Where are you?"

"Engineering levels, right at the bottom."

"Okay, as far as I can tell from the computer construction, you need to head up a level, and towards the centre of the ship. What does your scanner show about air content."

Dezza flicked the scanner from his belt and took a sample. There was a delay whilst it processed the results, then he read the numbers off the screen to Toze.

The air was slightly humid, with a mix of chemicals that seemed to be consistent with having leaked from the coolant of the Starliner's fusion reactor cores.

"Coolant mix," he said into the radio confidently, "Looks like we're in the right compartment after all."

"We got lucky," warned Toze's voice, "But let's make that luck stick."

It had not taken Tracker long to open the inner door and venture into the Starliner. He found himself in a service corridor that stretched beyond the distance his helmet light could penetrate in each direction. It was interspersed by other corridors heading off at right angles, and he checked the first couple cautiously.

In one he found a set of lifts, and pressed the call button. Almost immediately the doors juddered open, giving him a start and sending him slipping back into the shadows.

But the car was empty, and after checking the corridor up and down, he stepped in and pressed the button for the upper decks. As the doors shuddered shut and he felt the car begin to rise, he hoped that activating electrical systems around the ship might draw the entity away from the engineering spaces.

He did not wait for the car to reach its floor; he had other plans. There was a hatch in the centre of the ceiling of the car, and he hoisted himself up and popped it open. The shaft above was illuminated dimly with lights that showed him there would be maintenance catwalks that he could use.

Pulling himself through onto the roof of the car, he paused a moment to judge the distances between the passing structural beams. He could see the catwalks at regular levels silhouetted in the lights and connected by bare steel ladders. The lift was moving fast, and he would have to judge the moment to jump just right if he did not want to get caught between the lift car and the structure of lattice girders. He counted the gaps, then took a breath and jumped.

He landed heavily, but nothing was broken. He watched the car climb on higher without him, and heard the sound of its runners fade into the tall shaft above. If the entity was interested in following the pattern of use of the ship's systems to track him, then let that confuse it.

Picking himself up, he swung himself onto the ladder and climbed deftly until he reached a catwalk level that intersected with the access doors into the lift shaft from the floors. Normally they would only open when a car was alongside, but he found a release lever and popped this one open and jumped through onto the corridor beyond.

The lights were on here, which he found disorientating. Looking to the dirt in the floor though he could see he was the first person in decades to have been in this area. There were ripples in the muck that looked like sand on a beach might when the tide had gone out, but these were more likely caused by patterns on the breeze from the air circulation.

The sound of the lift car many floors above faded to nothing, and he heard the pause then the clunk as its doors rolled open high above him. He did not know what he was to expect, but there was nothing. The minutes ticked on by, then he heard the doors thud shut again, though the lift car remained where it was.

So that had not brought the thing out of hiding. Had it anticipated this, and instead gone after Dezza? He had not heard anything, and the deck was still without any hint of vibration.

He decided the best way to go would be to head on upwards and work his way though the Starliner. Anything to get him far away from Dezza and lead the thing on. He went to push the call button for the lift, then stopped. Suddenly he felt uncertain about using it again. He had used it once and sent it onwards as a bluff. That bluff would be undone to use it now.

So his fingers wavered and never pushed the button. Instead he walked through the dirt to the stairwell that opened out alongside the lifts. The lights were on here too, and he could see the stairs heading both up and down interspersed with large balconies on three sides at each level. It was not on the scale of the grand staircase of the atrium, but it came close. The lights let him see up all the way to a glass covered domed roof that provided another spectacular view out on the starscape.

But how was he to attract the attention of the thing? He searched up and down the corridor, looking for controls he could activate. There was the lift, and the electronic door locks on the passenger cabin doors. But the lift he felt reluctant to use again, and all the door circuits were dead and latched tightly into the locked position. He toyed with using his tools to try and search the circuit panels for a power line he could try and short out, but then his eye fell upon the fire alarm panel on the wall. Would they still work after all these years?

He wiped the dirt that had gathered on the glass, and rubbed the tarnish that had prised away some of the red paint leaving a mottled brown colour underneath. Inside the glass he saw the release button, clean and protected just as the day it was new.

'Break to activate' said the legend on the glass that was just about still readable. Well, nothing to lose, he figured. With a last glance up and down the corridor he took from his belt a small pair of pliers and after a moment's hesitation, jammed the head into the centre of the glass.

It splintered, but did not break. He felt his heart beating as if he was back at school setting of the fire alarms to disrupt classes as part of some freshman prank. Another swing brought the fragments outwards and the button in the middle popped out with a satisfying click.

Almost at once he heard the klaxons wail. Not all were working, and some of those that did sounded pitiful and muted as if their inner workings had all but decayed over the years. But it was enough to know that somewhere on the Starliner a control panel must be lighting up like the town Christmas lights at switch on.

He ran for the stairs and jumped them two at a time climbing to the next deck. Here the klaxons were wailing too, and a soft feminine voice seemed to be soothing pre-recorded advice for passengers who no longer existed to assemble at predetermined lifepods that he knew had long since been launched.

He ran on up the stairs, suddenly mindful about what if the alarms had been set off all over the ship? But by the third balcony, the klaxons were off and he found a series of firedoors half closed that had jammed in their runners, twisted and destroyed by years of decay. He squeezed under, glad that there was no real fire to worry about.

He could still hear the warnings echoing up from the decks below, seeming somehow less urgent now. But what now? He paused a moment, unsure of what to do and where to go. He looked around this new deck. It must be above the passenger decks now as the space opened out in a large shopping mall that stretched on in a mock Elizabethan street. How strange to see half-timber buildings on either side of a fake cobbled street with a canopy overhead through which the stars would always shine, with no two nights' star constellations ever the same. There were no lights on along the mall, and he had to switch on his helmet light to see beyond where the lights from the stairwell illuminated.

The upper floors of the buildings were fake, with windows painted on for effect. The lower floors were shops that advertised on their hoardings the names of chains that he had never heard of in fonts that looked beyond even being dated. The whole place was a time-warped homage to the tacky consumerism of a bygone and almost forgotten age.

He looked for a deck plan. Perhaps there would be one here? It took a bit of looking around the balcony that surrounded the stairwell, but he found it. As he rubbed the tarnish off though, he felt a shiver run down his spine; the alarms from the lower decks had cut off. What did that mean? He found himself concentrating, to listen hard until he could feel the blood hissing through the capillaries in his ears.

He thought he felt a vibration beneath his feet. It was not strong and felt maybe as if it was far away. He was not even certain he had felt it, but he decided at that moment it was time to move on.

The deck plan showed where he was. He had come almost to the top of the Starliner where malls and recreational facilities were shown stretching the length of the ship. It also showed the command deck; there was a viewing platform where it appeared passengers on the Starliner had been encouraged to come and watch the command crew piloting this behemoth through the stars. The thought occurred to him that maybe from there he could do a lot more to attract the thing away from the engineering spaces.

His radio crackled giving him a start.

"Hey Tracker," hissed Toze's voice through the static, "If you can hear me, what the hell did you just pull?"

He breathed a sigh of relief. "Shit. Don't scare me like that."

"All the panels on the *Magellan* lit up with warnings that the fire alarms were going off in the *Cerberus*."

"Must have picked up some kind of signal from the fire system," replied Tracker with a smile, "I thought it was a good way to attract that thing's attention."

So the fire system must have triggered more than just a few control panels hidden away in some forgotten engine room compartment for the *Magellan* to be able to intersect a signal.

"There's something else," came Toze's voice, somehow a little fainter as the static rose.

Tracker was forced to fiddle with the radio controls, trying to get a cleaner signal, but it seemed to be degrading fast. "Oh?"

"I'm picking up something going on about fourteen decks below you. The sensors on here picked up something, but I can't identify what. It seems to be heading upwards."

He felt the sweat on his back. "How fast is it moving?" he asked.

"That's the weird thing," came the muffled reply, "It jumps around. First it's here, then it's there. Difficult to tell, but I've also got you showing at the limit of the sensors. It's coming right your way whatever it is."

He grimaced as the transmission buzzed and disappeared into an angry noise of electronic hiss. "Damn!" he exclaimed, but no amount of adjustment on the suit's radio controls seemed able to bring Toze's voice back.

He felt the deck shudder. That time it was definitely real. Whatever was causing that vibration was getting nearer. The deck plan showed the way to the command deck viewing platform, and an inner feeling of calm told him that was where he needed to be.

Memorising what he could of the plan, he turned on his heels and ran.

*   *   *   *   *

Dezza found the main engine room almost by chance. He had been following the ducts towards where he guessed the centre of the ship was when he saw a tiny object in its own impact crater in the dust. It looked new and shiny, and he recognised it as being like the tools that Tracker carried in his belt.

Dezza looked up and down the duct. It was low and lined with cabling and the floor was a few inches deep in grey dust that was flat and undisturbed. He frowned, trying to work out where the tool had come from. Reaching out, he gently plucked it from the dirt and held it in the beam of light. It was certainly fresh and had not been here long. Aside from what it had picked up from the ground, one side was clean.

His helmet light picked out no side tunnels, but above a short shaft rose an opening that his helmet light could just about pick out. The tool must have fallen from there, and that meant that the others – or at least the salvage crew – had already been there. He wagered that meant there was a trail he could follow up there.

Climbing fast, he cursed the suit's backpack for forcing him to hold his body at an awkward angle. But the shaft was short, and he found himself at an opening set alongside a mesh catwalk. There were no lights here, but he could see on the opposite side of the catwalk a large void in which his helmet light could only just pick out the edges of colossal machinery criss-crossed by other catwalks.

It seemed familiar to him, though he was stumped for a moment as to why. Looking down at his feet, he could make out the disturbed dust that showed people had been along here before. It was hard to distinguish how many people might have gone this way; the mesh showed only that the dust had been disturbed.

The beam from his helmet light picked out a bulkhead that seemed to run the full width and height of this compartment where the catwalk ended at a hatch whose access panel still glowed active at the side.

With an icy cold feeling that made every part of his body go numb, he realised he had been here before. Looking up, the light picked out the puckered metal of the deck above, ruptured by the firefight that had raged in the distant past. This was where he had fallen through into the engineering spaces on that fateful day with Tubs and Zoë.

The hatch opened smoothly, just as it had done all those years ago. He felt the temperature change through the material of his suit as he stepped through, just as he had done the first time he had been here. Looking round, he felt like he was looking into the

210

most lucid of dreams. It was just as he remembered it when he had naïvely assumed he could power back up this behemoth to get her back to the shipping lanes.

How little he had known then and how much he wished he could go back and change it all. But it was too late now.

He saw the cores and the jury rigged equipment that the salvage crew had worked to install, blinded by their own greed. He asked himself repeatedly: what could they have been thinking? It was unlikely anyone would ever find out now.

There were too many components that would need refitting to bother with the main core; the *Magellan* would never enter the Rösenbridge herself without a refit at a shipyard. The secondary core would need only a minimal amount of work to be able to bring it back online. It would provide enough power that they could survive once the ion drive had taken them clear.

Looking the device over he saw that the salvage crew had been more concerned with getting the main core working. The secondary core had been left to one side, as if only a backup to their plans. How foolish, he thought, to have stripped it out. He did not dare touch any of the looms of cables that connected the larger device in case it attracted unwelcome attention.

The core was not heavy, though he touched it gingerly. In the wrong hands these devices had the power of a hydrogen bomb, and it made him feel uncomfortable to know that he was going to have to drag the device all the way back to the airlock. It occurred to him too, that exposure to a vacuum might not be helpful to the core's integrity. He remembered long ago on a salvage mission where the Tug crew had gone in to salvage a Bulker that had suffered decompression. They had entered the drive section to find the ship's core bleeding plasma through a crack that had begun to lengthen even as they had watched it. They never knew whether it had been damaged by the exposure to the vacuum or something else, but they had all found themselves exposed to dangerous levels of radiation.

He thought about taking the core up through the decks to the atrium. He could carry it; it was not so heavy as to be unmanageable. But he remembered the thing that had been there in wait for him before. The thing knew where the *Magellan* was docked, and had on a number of times been there in wait. He did not relish the idea of braving that open space weighed down by something so delicate and vital as the core.

What other options were there? Then he thought of the ancient suit that had been hanging in the locker in the airlock. Would it be big enough to protect the core in, he wondered? Possibly it would. If it worked, it would protect it from the worst of the vacuum. Then all he would need to worry about was getting back to the *Magellan*'s airlock.

He checked the tools he had brought with him. It would be a quick enough job to free the core. Then it was just a matter of carrying the cumbersome object back through the machine spaces to the airlock. He was not sure he would remember the way, though he knew all he had to do was to follow his own boot prints. As long as the core would fit easily down the crawl spaces, he thought. It was a risk that he would have to take, and hope it did not get stuck.

*   *   *   *   *

Tracker was running through a part of the ship he did not recognise. They had not been this far forward in all the time they had been roaming. Judging by the dirt underfoot, nobody else had been up here either. It made it feel even lonelier as he ran breathlessly.

"Anything on the scopes?" he hissed into his radio.

Toze's voice buzzed back through the static, distorted but just about decipherable. "Hard to pinpoint. Some patterns of energy. It's weird: first I'm getting something with mass, then nothing but energy fluctuations that move like lightning, then it's back to mass again."

"You must be getting interference on the readings."

"No interference. I already checked."

He heard a rumble echo through the Starliner, like a scream and forlorn wail combined. It sent a shiver through his spine; the thing was gaining again. How did it know where he was?

He came to an area where the corridor opened out into a long wide area. A bar ran down one side, and windows opened out on the starscape along the other. In between were a scattering of tables, upset and overturned long ago and now shrouded in the same blanket of filth and decay that the rest of the ship was. In its day, this place might have looked spectacular as passengers sat and sipped their drinks and looked out over the heavens. Now it felt cold and lonely.

He began to move through the room. Looking for a way out on the other side when he noticed a pattern in the dust near his feet. The more he looked at it, the more it seemed to move. The dust seemed to be flowing, like a liquid. Confused, he looked around the room, and realised there were similar patterns elsewhere. The dust really was moving.

"Hey Toze," he barked into the radio, "Give me a reading on my present location. There's some weird shit going on here."

Static hissed. He thought he could hear a voice, far away and indistinct through the noise, but it was impossible to make out. He tried again, still with no success. Switching the channel off with disgust he realised that the distortion was too much and he was out of contact with the *Magellan*.

He wafted his hand through the closest area of moving dust and the stream began to move as if directed by his hand. It wavered, then fell to form a ridge in a perfectly straight line. It looked too geometrical to be a natural phenomenon, and he realised that the floor about him was beginning to crawl with dust.

He felt afraid; this was not right. What was going on? Suddenly the whole room felt even more unfriendly about him, as dust slid from overturned tables and trickled across the top of the long abandoned bar.

"What the hell," he murmured under his breath.

Then as fast as it had started, it stopped, and the dust settled silently down across the floor in a perfectly flat blanket. Turning around he saw that the entire floor was now a flat unblemished sea of grey. Even his boot prints had been erased. It was like he had never been here, except he was here stood in the middle of a long abandoned room.

His breathing notched up a rate, and he felt his heart thumping. Something was wrong; he could sense a kind of apprehension in the air, as if something was about to happen. For the first time he realised all was deathly silent; the vibrations through the ship and the wailing moan had gone. He was alone here in a silent world.

He tried the radio again, but got nothing except static. He cursed the device. Why could it not work right when he needed it? He wanted to ask Toze where the thing was. But there was no contact left. His entire body prickled in a bristling sixth sense. For a moment he felt alone, and then the feeling returned. It was the feeling of being watched, being observed. He did not like this at all.

Tracker looked back the way he had come. There was nothing there but a dark corridor. Even his helmet light failed to penetrate more than a few metres before the arc faded to grey and black. Looking the other way, there were two other corridors, equally as foreboding and a staircase whose walls were panelled with mosaics whose patterns were almost lost beneath the tarnish.

He took a step towards the staircase, and froze. The air seemed to be boiling with a charge, but everywhere he looked he saw nothing there. Still the feeling persisted, getting stronger all the time. For a moment he got the feeling that he was being watched, and toyed with.

Then the charged feeling of the air went away, and he turned and saw the woman watching him from the staircase. One moment she had not been there, the next she was; he could not recall there being an in between.

"What do you want?" he whispered hesitantly.

She tilted her head in that same way that she had in the machinery spaces. He could see partially through her; there was a body but beyond, ever so faintly, he could still see the patterns of the mosaic. She took a step towards him; her feet left no mark in the dust. He could almost believe she was nothing more than a hologram, even though everything in his mind told him to turn and run. But he did not; he stayed rooted to the spot.

The same look flickered in her eyes that he had seen in the machinery spaces, and he shivered. He did not like that look; there was something beyond it that stared back with a sense of almost evil. Then it passed, and he was looking at the same vacant expression of nothing more than a computer generated hologram.

"You're not real," he said at last.

"Oh?" she said, "I am the ship's hologram." Though that look flickered in her eyes as she spoke the words, and it did not seem as if she was being sincere.

"Bullshit."

She smiled. "Then you tell me what you think I am?"

Her sudden directness shocked Tracker a little. He had not been expecting her to fully understand him, but it seemed as though she did.

He plucked up the courage to voice those thoughts that had lurked in his mind and which he feared. "You were active before we found the consoles in the machinery spaces. You lied to us when we spoke to you there. You said we had activated you, but I saw you elsewhere before."

She nodded and smiled. There no longer seemed to be any hint of those computer-generated mannerisms anymore as if pretence was not necessary. "Very good."

A part of him wanted to turn and run. She was dangerous, but he could not work out how.

"I'm going to go now," he said slowly, starting to edge back towards the corridor behind him without taking his eyes off her.

The look flickered again on her face. This time it stayed, and he saw the expression change to that of calculating calm. For a moment the room flashed again with the feeling of enormous static charge, and he winced as if a current had been run through his body. Flecks of light speckled in his vision and he sank to his knees, drained. Then the feeling went, and he was left panting and weak.

"Where are you going to go?" she said, "I know your every fear. That which you fear the most is the creature that has been chasing you throughout the ship. You cannot visualise it and that is what makes it so powerful a fear. It is the monster from the closet in your childhood: you never saw it, but your imagination always filled in the details. You think you can keep me from the machinery spaces and finding Dezza, but are you really prepared for facing me at all?"

He said nothing, dragging himself upright. What had she done? Could she really read his mind? He tried to edge back towards the corridor again, wanting to run but afraid to turn his back on her.

"What would you do," she said sweetly, "If I told you that the monster from which you had been running, was standing in the corridor right behind you? Could you really turn and face it?"

That was when he felt it, the sixth sense of something behind him. He felt the icy cold breath on his back and could almost sense the noises of something in the shadows.

Suddenly it was as if he was aged six all over again, and this was the closet in his bedroom.

*   *   *   *   *

In the panic and the rolling dust, Zoë had become separated from Red. She had called out to him, and checked every frequency that she knew on the radio, but there was nothing. Once again she heard the echoes of the creature vibrating through the ship, and the realisation came that maybe Red had been the prey it had stalked.

There was no time left to contemplate it. She knew that if she remained long on the Starliner, it would find her too. She could not afford to stay still. More than once she heard those echoes again as she wandered the empty corridors and rooms. Sometimes the noises were close, and she would feel the fear rising within her. At other times they were muted into the distance and she felt she had bought herself some time.

Time became meaningless to her in the quest to survive. She did not know how long had passed by the time she managed to find her way back to the atrium and on upwards to the airlock level. The *Magellan* was still there, silent where it had been left. She saw the airlock left open, and felt the shiver of uncertainty of what she might find inside. Summoning courage, she knew she had to get inside and seal herself from the Starliner. That might buy her a little more time. So she stepped forward and into the light of the open airlock and activated the controls to run the cycle and enter the *Magellan*.

*   *   *   *   *

Dezza got the drive core as far as the crawl spaces before it stuck. There was a bend in the pipework, and it had forced him to try and place the core on the ground and push it past. There was very little clearance, and he remembered he had struggled here to get through with the backpack of his suit. It did not matter which way he tried to tilt the core, it seemed to catch on something and wedge in the narrow space. Finally he despaired and called up Toze on the radio. He felt the relief wash over him as the officer's voice came back hissing over the fuzz of static.

"I can't get the thing through. I'm going to need to take a different way through. Can you guide me at all?"

Toze hesitated. For a moment Dezza was frightened that the connection had faded into interference, but finally the voice came back. It was weak, but he could still make him out.

"Okay, I have your position just about. As far as I can tell if you can go back to the last junction, there's a way into the service corridor there. I can guide you around."

"Any sign of the thing?" Dezza asked, not liking the idea that he would have to step out again into unknown areas of the Starliner.

"Not sure. There's energy levels peaking all over the ship, and I can't get a good fix on Tracker."

Suddenly Dezza felt alone and exposed in the forgotten passageways and crawl spaces of the *Cerberus*.

*　　　*　　　*　　　*　　　*

As soon as Zoë entered the inside of the *Magellan*, she knew something was wrong. There were boot marks on the deck – fresh. With a cold realisation she knew that they were Red's. He had got back here before her, but a bristling sixth sense told her this was not right.

She took a look through the connecting corridor that ran from the airlock anteroom into the living quarters. The trail went through, onwards towards the command deck.

"Red?" she called out pensively. There was no answer. She stopped and listened, but there were no sounds of life.

"Red?" she repeated again, this time a little louder and more urgent.

The interior of the *Magellan* remained strangely quiet, with just the gentle hum of the air conditioning units. After the gloom of the Starliner, the bright and somewhat harsh lights of the tugship seemed strange and unreal.

She edged into the living space and looked around. It was just as it had been when she had left it, even down to the discarded meal one of the salvage crew had put to one side when called out into the Starliner by the greed of his colleagues.

There was no-one here. Moving through towards the command deck, she stopped at the open hatchway in the floor. Here the fresh boot trail of dust ended. Peering through she saw more dust on the floor of the spaces below.

"Hey Red! Why are you hiding?" she called out. Her voice echoed hollow from the machinery spaces, but she heard little more than the hum of auxiliary equipment.

She considered that maybe the tracks were not Red's. Maybe one of the other crew had come back for something they had forgotten before heading back out into the Starliner. But the trail only went one way; unless he had taken his boots off to return, he had to be down there.

Plucking up the courage, she stepped onto the ladder and gingerly climbed the rungs into the crawl spaces beneath the *Magellan*.

*   *   *   *   *

Tracker had never moved so fast in his life. He remembered those fears as a child. They had been at the time completely irrational, and his Father had told him so on many occasions. But that did not stop him from harbouring the fear of the closet. Maybe all children had that? He did not know; it was something from his life he had never talked about. Yet the hologram just *knew*.

He dared not go back, in case the woman told the truth. In one leap he had cleared the tables and chairs and had passed the figure and was on to the mosaic-lined stairs. There was no turning back. He heard the sound of movement, and the shrill-pitched banshee moan he had heard so many times before. Only now it was right behind him.

At the top of the stairs there was a balcony that opened out onto a covered promenade. This really was the very top of the Starliner, laid out just like the ocean going liners on Earth from many centuries before. Everything was perfect, even down to the pseudo liner deck fittings, lifeboats on davits and teak decking underfoot. Looking above at the rolling starscape it might even have been possible to imagine that here was a ship at sea at night.

But the stars were wrong, and the creature was gaining. He swung under a lifeboat and skidded sideways under faded white railings. There was another, lower deck and he dropped down onto it. Pressing back against the wall behind him he fumbled in his tool belt for the things he knew he was going to need. Above he heard the sound of something prowling, looking for where he had slipped. It would only be a matter of seconds before the creature would find him.

*　　　*　　　*　　　*　　　*

Even before the voice finished echoing in his headset, Toze sat bolt upright. It took a few seconds for it to sink in; had he really heard that? It was just one voice for no more than a couple of seconds, nothing more. He had been watching the long-range scopes, watching the trail of the meteorite swarm getting closer and closer. On the displays it seemed to move at a crawl that felt as if it would not take much to outrun it. But it was an illusion brought on by the scale.

He played those words over in his head: "I can see your mind."

It filled him with a gnawing sense of foreboding. It was not the voice of Dezza or Tracker, but that of a woman. He could almost convince himself that it could be the voice of the *Cerberus'* hologram, but he was not sure. Had it even come from the headset? He tore it off and rubbed his face with a sweaty palm before glancing back from the command deck through to the living quarters and beyond. Suddenly the little tugship seemed like a lonely and frightening place that he was no longer comfortable being in.

He checked the adjacent console: the airlock still showed sealed tight. There was no way anything could have got in through that; they had been careful. His ears strained for a sound that did not fit with the routine mechanical noises of the life support, but there was nothing.

A voice echoed tinny from the console and he jumped. It came again, more urgent, but he recognised it as Dezza and he grabbed the set and jammed it to an ear.

"Toze, are you there!"

"I'm here," he replied, faltering over the words. He still remembered the words spoken by that female voice, and they sent a shiver through his body.

"I'm at the junction," came Dezza's voice, "But I've found a trail; one of the salvos must have got this far. There's something odd. You have to warn Tracker, and then keep all the audio channels locked down and offline."

Toze leant close to the microphone, the woman's voice forgotten, for now. There was something in the urgency and fear that carried on Dezza's voice that made him listen. "What's up with the audio feeds? All I'm getting is static most of the time anyway."

"You don't understand. The trail just ends. One set of boot prints in and nothing goes back out. There's something else. There's some personal kit, just like when Exbo went missing. There's a recording device that was running when it got him." He paused, seeming to choose his next words carefully. "It can move through the power lines and anything else it chooses."

Toze did not understand. "What the hell are you saying?" he demanded.

"The thing. It goes from physical matter to energy and back. E equals M C squared. The thing can convert itself to pure energy and back. It's moving through the electrical systems and manifesting as something physical only when it wants to. That's how it's moving so quickly."

Toze realised the significance. He remembered the voice. "Shit, so it can come through the audio?"

"I think so. I'm going offline. I'll call in only if I have to."

The line clicked dead before Toze could answer. He flicked shut the relays on the console and threw the headset to one side as if suddenly it had become a deadly wild animal. It skidded on the floor and bounced to a standstill, sitting defiantly in the harsh glare of the command deck lights.

He reached for his gun and made to move to search the ship, the voice still ringing in his ears. What if the creature really had seen his mind? What if the creature was already here aboard the *Magellan*?

*   *   *   *   *

He dared not use his light and had to fumble along the wall behind him. His fingers brushed against a light fitting, dead now, but which would have once illuminated upwards over the planking of the lifeboat hanging over the lower level. He found himself praying silently to a God that he did not believe in as he fumbled to remove the cover from the fitting.

Straining his eyes in the gloom he pulled out the wires and found the circuitry beyond. Pulling enough of the wiring through he used a cutting tool from his belt to pare back the insulation. The wires showed shiny underneath. He shut his eyes, and hoped, and jammed the bundle into the exposed steel of the fitting.

He felt the heat as the power arced across from the line and despite having his eyes closed, he saw the flash that must have lit up the promenade deck like a Roman candle. He heard the tortured scream and the vibration of the deck. It was so violent that he lost his balance and stumbled headfirst. In the darkness, blinded by the flash, he felt something hit him hard and he slipped away into unconsciousness.

*   *   *   *   *

It had hurt mentally to cut off communication, but Dezza knew he had to do it. The sounds he had heard from the portable recording device had been enough to convince him. He could not bring himself to play them again, and tossed the device to the ground where it bounced into the dirt.

The salvo had not even heard it coming; there had been no warning. The creature had attacked him from his own radio as he had paused a moment to try and raise the others.

There were a few other scattered belongings on the floor. A torn scrap of suit material, frayed around the edge and an empty holster for a gun. Of the man, there was nothing; he had vanished into thin air, just as Exbo had. With a shudder Dezza realised that if he had stayed with the private and not walked off in disgust, he too might have shared the same fate. It was not a thought he liked to think about, and tried to shut it from his mind.

The instructions that Toze had given him before had made the route to drag the core through seem quick and easy. But faced with the maze of service ways, it was anything but. Without Toze to guide him he found himself cursing his luck and hoping that he was remembering the instructions correctly. He did not dare now to use the radio to call in for help. Silently he cursed himself for not realising sooner. The crew of the *Cerberus* had known, and he had read their logs from the computer screen by the main reactor cores all those years ago without realising the significance. Shut down the systems, and the entity would die, they had said. They had nearly succeeded too. Whatever it was, it needed the power to survive.

The floor began to vibrate, and he felt a sense of urgency; the creature was looking for him. Hoisting the core delicately in his arms, he kept moving. He had to find that airlock, though as the vibration began to increase, he felt that any escape hatch would provide a welcome sight.

He could hear the sound of moving air. It moaned like he had heard before in the atrium and elsewhere in the derelict. It was a sound that he had learnt to be afraid of. He moved faster, despite the cumbersome weight of the core. More than once he wished he could dump it, to be free of its bulk to let him run faster. But he knew that they were dangerous thoughts; without it, they would all be cursed to float with the *Cerberus* as the meteorite swarm hit. Even if the Starliner survived intact, there would be no future without power for their own life support systems, and the derelict promised to offer them little better.

*   *   *   *   *

There was no explanation of why he had done it. Hell, Zoë did not even know how Red could have made it back to the ship before she had. Whatever the reason, she found the body hunched in a foetal position locked in the otherwise empty drive core chamber.

She placed her hands on the Perspex inspection glass and her breath fogged the surface up. Why had he done it? Had he really believed there to be no hope? She did not understand why a man would give up so easily. He had probably died of asphyxiation, a nasty way to go.

Zoë did not know what made her skin prickle, but it was as if the temperature in the crawl space had dropped. There was no sound, but she sensed there was something behind her. For a few seconds she waited, not knowing what to do. Then she realised she was holding her breath, and let the breath out.

She turned, pushing herself to overcome the fear she felt. For a moment, all she saw was a shimmering haze, but then it coalesced and suddenly where there had been no physical object there now stood Tubs. Or at least, Tubs as she had remembered him five years ago. Even down to the suit he had been wearing, though the helmet had gone.

She felt confused. "Tubs?" she faltered, "Is that really you?"

Something flickered in those eyes, and for that split second she felt as if she was looking into the soul of something that was neither Tubs nor human. It filled her with dread.

The figure said nothing, and she found herself fumbling for anything she could use as a weapon. She felt something hard under her fingers and wielded it around. It was only a pry bar, left behind by the others, but it was enough.

"You aren't Tubs!" she screamed, and the bar swung around with all of her force behind it.

It should have hit the figure, and in her mind she never worked out the moment he was there before he was not. At any rate the bar clunked heavily into the plating behind, bouncing from her grasp, and the figure of Tubs was gone.

She looked around the spaces, not knowing what to make of it. For a moment she thought she saw a haze in the air, then there was nothing. From the deck above she heard the sound of movement, edging towards the open hatch.

*　　　*　　　*　　　*　　　*

For a while, Tracker could not remember where he was. He saw lights spinning, and wondered what they could be. Then he moved his head and felt the wave of pain wash over him and the flashing lights flitting around his vision increased. There was a smell burning in his nostrils, but at first he could not place it. Then he realised that the stink was ozone.

He struggled to cast his mind back; thinking was an effort over the pain. But gradually he pieced together where he had been. There had been the creature, and the woman who he realised now was probably an extension of the creature. Whatever had been the ship's hologram was long gone when the thing had oozed its way through the Starliner's computer systems.

He tried to move and found down his left side that every muscle felt weak and ached from the exertion. He opened his eyes, and immediately was forced to shut them; the lights were bright here, wherever here was. He remembered the promenade deck and the flash of light when he had shorted out the power.

The memories came back, and he felt the icy feeling as he wondered whether he had managed to kill the creature. In the engineering spaces it had retreated. What had happened here? Had it gone too?

He tried to open his eyes again. The light hurt, but slowly he was able to open them a little and try and force shapes to come into focus. He tried to move again. There was something pressing into his back, and the angle he was lying at was uncomfortable. It felt like there was a great weight on his legs. No matter how he tried, he could not move them.

Looking around his eyes grew stronger and more used to the light, and he began to realise that this was not the promenade deck. He saw consoles and screens, some on and some blank and defunct. It looked like the bridge of a starship, but somehow old and obsolete.

It had to be the command deck of the Starliner. The icy feeling came again as he realised he had no knowledge of getting here. Looking around he saw he was lying between a set of holo projectors. One was silent, but the other was glowing and a shimmering sea of stars and green vector lines hung in the air. He caught another whiff of the ozone smell; it was coming from the charged air.

How had he got here? He looked to his legs. His right one seemed okay, and with some effort he could start to move it. But the left leg was twisted and hurt at the slightest movement. He was not sure that it was broken, but it sure as hell was badly twisted if it wasn't.

Beyond his legs he saw the grey of the deck, shrouded in a blanket of dirt and filth. The filth was undisturbed. It did not look like any of the salvage crew had made it this far. Looking to his left and right he saw there were no marks on the floor there either. Turning around he realised that however he had got here he had not left a trail doing it. The fear gripped him and he felt with a hand to where his belt should have been; it was gone.

This was not where he had been and he could see no way that he had got here. Remembering the radio he tried to call in, but the static buzzed and hissed and he realised he was completely cut off.

In the engineering spaces the radio had become clear when they had used the power spike against the creature. With a sinking feeling he knew that that meant the same trick had not worked twice. The creature had been ready for him.

*   *   *   *   *

The face on the figure that smiled back at him was a face he remembered all too well. It filled him with dread, even before he noticed that the shape of the body was wrong.

"Hello Toze," said Spanners' head.

The body underneath writhed and changed with nauseating speed, as if the creature it belonged to could not decide exactly what it wanted to be. There was a woman's body, then a man's. Then it dissolved into a creature that was alien and strange and that Toze did not even recognise the origin of before finally settling on the figure of a man's in khaki military issue slacks and shirt.

"You're dead. I saw you die," Toze heard himself saying; it was all he could find to say.

Spanners' head smiled, and the body seemed to morph a little in a way that made it seem as if it was made of clay before it settled on the physical form that Toze finally recognised as Spanners'.

"Seeing is believing."

Toze tried to dart past Spanners' form, but an arm moved with such speed that it was hard to tell whether it actually did move, or was just not there one moment and there the next. It grabbed hold of him and threw him back with such force that he travelled the length of the connecting corridor from the command deck and slammed into the central console in the sleeping quarters.

He lay there, stunned a moment, but recovered quickly as the form of Spanners seemed to melt into something else and move in a blur. In the blink of an eye the blurry mass was gone, and once again Spanners was stood there in front of him.

An arm reached out and grabbed him. Or at least, Toze realised there was a hand gripping him by the shoulder. It felt almost real, but his brain insisted it could not be there. With seemingly effortless ease it lifted him until his feet were barely touching the floor.

"What do you want?" spluttered Toze. He struggled against the grip, but the grasp was like iron and would not yield.

"You know; stuff," Spanners said in a vague voice.

He threw Toze again and the officer bounced off a wall with a groan and slid to the floor. Spanners' grin twisted and there was a laugh, but it was not Spanners' laugh. It sounded like the banshee shriek they had heard on the Starliner mixed with the whoop of a Hyena.

Toze dived for the way back through to the command deck. He made as if to charge the figure, then last minute feigned a duck to the left and rolled underneath Spanners. He felt the creature move, and saw as he passed the shape ooze from the figure he had recognised through an assortment of other shapes in a sickening fluid-like speed. He felt something graze across a shoulder with a sting. He reached the corridor and tried to scramble through, but he felt something grasp his foot tightly and begin to pull. Rolling over he saw the creature had transformed again. He saw the face of Spanners, but the expression was something else. He saw the flash behind the eyes and could not meet their stare. Around his leg a tentacle tightened its grip.

He flailed around for something to take hold of and managed to wedge his arm around pipe fittings.

"There's no escaping," taunted the creature in Spanners' voice.

From the corner of an eye Toze saw the edge of the airlock The panel was close to his head, and he realised the safety release was within his grasp. As the creature pulled, he freed one hand, held as tight as he could with the other and tried to grasp for the lever.

The creature seemed to sense what he was trying and jerked hard as his fingers brushed tantalisingly close to the lever. Then his grip failed and he slid too far away.

"The woman salvager already tried that," said Spanners' head, "But we did not let her win."

With a lunge the creature changed shape again and became a haze of energy. Lightning crackled across the deck, and fingers of blue tinged forks seemed to reach out all over his body racking Toze with an agonising pain.

The centre of the haze swirled and coalesced and a voice came once more over the crackle of power and the stink of burning and ionised particles. It was no longer Spanners' voice, but instead barked like a dog and was edged with harsh bass that hurt Toze's ears and reverberated through his body.

It sounded like an alien language; he could not decipher a single syllable. Then he felt the pain lance through his body and a wall of static seemed to envelope his head and he felt his thoughts being ripped from his mind out into the swirling maelstrom of the creature.

*   *   *   *   *

She had known what she had to do. All the power had to be switched off. She pulled open the console and pulled out the breakers. The lights flickered once, then died. The sounds from the deck above immediately stopped. All she could hear were the sounds of her own tortured breathing and the thump of her heartbeat.

She fumbled for her light and was rewarded with a wavering glow as her fingers found the right controls. A part of her had expected that the beam might show the creature, stood looming over her ready to pounce. But it didn't. Instead she saw the empty crawl spaces and the consoles now devoid of any electrical life.

She climbed the ladder slowly. Near the top she stopped, waiting and listening. There were no sounds. Even the air recycling had shut down, and she really could truly hear nothing but silence. Seconds turned to minutes that passed with agonising slowness. Still nothing happened. Finally she said the silent prayer in her head, and popped her head above the rim.

Her torch beam stabbed back and forth across the deck, picking out the edges of the bulkheads. She turned it upwards, but there was nothing unexpected. She could see the command deck one way, with the faint glow of starlight coming through the screens. Beyond the living quarters, her beam faltered over ghostly forms in the anteroom to the airlock, but they were just spare suits hanging there lifeless.

Had the creature gone? She pulled herself up off the ladder. At any moment she expected something to leap forward and attack her, but despite the tension she felt, the minutes dragged by and nothing happened.

On the command deck all the consoles were dead. Without cores or connection to the battery banks, the *Magellan* was truly dead. It had been the inspiration of what the *Cerberus*' crew had tried so long ago to do and fail that had made her do it. Without

228

power, the creature would die, they had said. And they had almost managed it. Had she killed the creature by denying its source of power? The more she explored, the more she wondered.

The anteroom was empty, and the airlock controls were dead too and sealed. There really would be no way back off the *Magellan* now. She wandered back through the living quarters, and then the beam of her torch began to falter. Its batteries were running low and where the beam had once been a powerful arc of brilliant whiteness, now it glowed a feeble orange getting weaker all the time. She cursed it and shook the battery packs, but the light glowed only slightly for a few moments before continuing to fade.

That was when she saw the control panel glowing ever so faintly. It had been easy to miss when the beam from the torch had overwhelmed it. She hurried over to the connecting corridor from the living quarters to the command deck, where the external airlock and the escape pod bay were. The airlock was dead, just like everything else, but of course the escape pod had its own power, and the systems were ready.

She cursed herself for not having thought of it. Of course when the power failed the computer in the pod was designed to activate an emergency beacon and be online. With a sinking feeling, she knew the call back to the inner system had already been made and there was nothing she could do except enter the pod and try and disable it. Only then would the *Magellan* be truly dead and she could guarantee the end to the creature.

That was the theory, anyway.

She tapped at the controls and the hatch slid open. Ducking through she clambered into the main body of the pod, trying to remember where the main circuit controls were. The pod was a small thing, designed to take two people, maybe three at a pinch. It was woefully too small for the normal crew of the *Magellan*, but the safety rules for certification of a space vessel were notoriously vague, and the company had got away with having the very bare minimum. Besides, salvagers would boast that only those who made mistakes needed escape pods. She shuddered at what her crew had been thinking when they had been blinded by greed and striped out the *Magellan*'s cores.

There was a control console at the front of the tiny craft. A small screen looked out at the outer airlock in the *Magellan*'s hull and a tiny viewing hatch gave a small snapshot to the stars beyond. On the inside of the Perspex the dimmed light of the console reflected in hues of green and yellow.

Zoë slipped herself into the seat and typed quickly at the controls. It had been a long time since she had had to go through the sequences of the codes. Most of the time the crew used the pod if they wanted a quiet hour alone for privacy. Some of the salvos, she knew, kept their secret stashes of alcohol in here. At least then it never had to be found on inspections.

Reams of text scrolled on the screen as she typed, then suddenly the screen began to blink. A shiver ran down her spine; this was not meant to happen. Her brow furrowed and she tried typing again. This time the screen blipped to black. The computer refused to let her shut it down.

Only too late she realised the significance, and felt the presence behind her. She saw the reflection on the Perspex, indistinct, but moving slowly.

"You're here," she said softly, sliding her fingers off the panel.

The reflection folded in on itself. By the time she had turned to face the airlock, all that was there was the patient figure of Tubs, sitting like he had been watching her all the time. But it still wasn't Tubs, she told herself. There was the look in the eyes that he had never had. Tubs was gone; this was nothing more than a sick facsimile.

The creature was entirely within the pod. In a moment she realised that there would be no turning back. The beacon the pod had activated would be picked up, and others would eventually come. The creature would do to them what it had done to her crew. She saw the look in those eyes again and realised that no matter what the facsimile said, the words it spoke were no more than its approximation of what it thought a human would say. It was an alien pulling the strings; there would never be any reasoning with it.

She flicked a series of buttons on the pod's control panel behind her, and the airlock slid shut and sealed. The creature's eyes darted back and forth and in a gut wrenching morph the face of Tubs seemed to fold into itself, then back. She reeled at the sight, but refused to let it stop her. Typing again she gave the console her full attention. Outside of the Perspex the outer airlock opened onto the starscape.

The creature howled, but with all electronics on the *Magellan* dead and severed, it must have realised for the first time that it was trapped.

As the pod rocketed away into the stars it folded into a haze of energy, and the tentacles of energy lashed at her mind. She arched in pain as lights danced across her vision. The feeling was intense. Words were spoken, but not out loud. Somehow the creature had access into the void of her mind.

"We will survive. We are many and one. You cannot purge us all; others will come and we will have them too."

In that moment, she realised that the *Cerberus* was infested. As the pain became more intense, she knew only too late that it was the *Cerberus* she should have shut down when she had the chance. Only then might the creature be slain. Then blackness overcame her, and there was no more.

Nearly eighteen hours later the pod's electrical systems overloaded, and its own emergency beacon spluttered to a halt and the transmission was finally silenced.

*   *   *   *   *

The vibrations had subsided, but he knew the creature still prowled for him. From the safety of covered cable runs he had heard the movements, but it had never found him. But the core was cumbersome, and he found himself making slow progress.

The creature knew he was here. Checking the digital display on the suit's readout he felt the pressure and he knew that time was short.

*   *   *   *   *

He heard footsteps, and for a moment he thought that Dezza or Toze had come looking for him. He banged his fist in anger on the floor; how could they jeopardise their safety like this?

"What the hell are you thinking?" he called out, dragging himself up against the side of the projector.

His hand sliced effortlessly through the projected image, and renditions of meteorites and vector lines wobbled angrily about his fingers.

"Hello Tracker."

The voice filled him with surprise, and he froze. He recognised the voice, but it was neither Toze nor Dezza.

"Exbo?" he said with some uncertainty.

The footsteps scrunched closer. He sensed the person getting closer. "I thought you were dead?"

A shadow cast across the console, and Exbo rounded into view. "Close enough."

For a moment he could have believed, but in the eyes he saw the same expression that he had seen in the ship's hologram. It was not Exbo, just as she was no longer the real ship's hologram. It was nothing more than the creature. He found himself slipping back to the floor.

"What did you do to him?" demanded Tracker.

The creature did not seem to understand. It cocked Exbo's head, and with a shudder Tracker recognised the mannerisms that the holographic woman had had.

Exbo's body shrugged. "Don't you believe it's me?"

"Not really."

A smile spread across the face. "Is it too hard to believe?"

"Yes," he replied blankly, never taking his eyes off the figure.

Exbo smiled. It was the same smile that Exbo had had when he was planning something. The man had never been the brightest tool in the box, and had been only one step up from moving his mouth when he was thinking. Tracker realised that to see it again made him almost want to belief that Exbo could be alive. But he knew it could not be. Even the real Exbo would not stand there and leer. Besides, the figure in front of him was still holding his gun, and they had found that discarded in the bar.

Tracker smiled. "You got the details almost right, but not quite."

The creature looked to the gun, and laughed. "I know you think I'm cannon fodder."

"Exbo didn't know."

"Are you so sure?"

"Yes."

For a moment Tracker thought the creature was going to continue bluffing, but it seemed that despite having been able to manifest itself as those it had assimilated, it could not fully grasp the nuances of what it was to truly be human.

"Spanners did though," it said.

The figure seemed to loose stability, and began folding in on itself. There was a flash of light, and Tracker blinked. Then there was nothing. He was left glancing up and down the command deck, looking for where the creature might have gone.

Footsteps scrunched behind him and he turned.

Stood behind him was the woman, wearing the tennis outfit he had found in the locker in the gym. He realised that the creature had assimilated over time many forms. Perhaps every form it took was a casualty of its past.

"What are you really?" he asked blankly.

The woman tilted her head in the manner that he had found so disconcerting. This was the archaic programming of the hologram now.

"Please repeat command," she said without emotion, "Invalid prompt."

"I know you aren't the ship's computer either," he said.

She tilted her head the other way, but said nothing.

He waited and she took a step towards him. He reached out suddenly, trying to grab at her leg, but in an instant it dissolved away, and the figure was gone, and he seemed alone on the command deck once more.

He pulled himself upright again and tested his leg, wincing as the pain shot through it. It did not seem broken, but was injured. He might be able to hobble slowly if he tried. He pulled himself to the console to look out of the viewing screen. He saw the front of the Starliner stretching out to its scarred prow, and beyond that the vacuum of space stretching out like an endless black sea flecked with a wall of pinpricks of light. Somewhere out there was the meteorite swarm getting closer. Even as he watched he saw intermittent tiny green streaks zip past as the dust that would precede the swarm folded around in the ship's navigation field. How long could it keep doing that? There would not be long before bigger chunks would follow. The prow of the Starliner already showed the grazing damage of a close call that had come decades before. The field could not stop everything.

The lights on the command deck flickered and died leaving it bathed only in the glow from the projector. He sensed the air move behind him, and saw the reflection in the screen. For a moment he could almost believe that the air had become humid, as if fuelled by the breath of – something. He felt the childhood fears rising again, and this time there was nothing he could do to stop it.

"You ain't so clever now," said Exbo's voice from alongside him.

He turned his head a little, not daring to look behind him. He saw the figure of Exbo stood, almost gloating. It was if the creature was getting off from taunting him, and playing his fears out at him. Did the creature really know what it was doing? Was this how it fed: on emotions?

He heard the grunt from the thing behind him and sensed the pulsating movement of a mass far greater than he could have imagined could fit on the command deck. It was like the whole world behind him was taken up with his childhood fears.

*   *   *   *   *

He felt the pain as the creature lashed out again, trying to punish him for going for the airlock. In that instant he realised that the creature knew the danger it was in if he succeeded. It had an instinct for survival, even if it did not fully realise the manifestations that it was putting itself into.

He saw it change shape again, seeming to scroll its form through any number of figures. He saw humanoids dressed in archaic clothes. Some in fancy gowns and suits, and others in stylised uniforms. Then he saw alien forms that seemed to scroll and change. He felt the whiplash of static charge again, and for a moment the creature was in his mind. He felt it probing, looking

234

for his fears. It took no more than a moment, but in that moment Toze had a brief insight directly to the creature's mind.

He saw a history spanning back millennia over galaxies and star systems many millions of light years away. He saw the creatures it had taken, and the paths it had led. It was only a brief look before the creature pulled away from the link, but he saw enough to realise that the creature was many and one at the same time. Killing this one small part would not kill the entity.

He felt the fear rising, and the despair setting in. There was no hope. He felt the creature leaching its way through his mind, searching his memories and personality and assimilating them. Before him the creature's form appeared to writhe and change with nauseating speed, and in the creature's image he saw himself forming. Within moments he was looking back at a mirror reflection of himself.

Then the pain stopped, and Toze fell forward, feeling the weakness in his body brought on by the savagery of the attack. In his nostrils the harsh tang of ozone lingered in the stale atmosphere. He gasped at the air, finding it hard to draw breath.

The image of himself seemed to be eyeing him through alien eyes. Why had it stopped? It had not shown the others such mercy.

The creature seemed to sense Toze's confusion, though it seemed to struggle to form the words and meaning. It was as if the creature had not finished assimilating him. Again the thoughts drifted in his mind: why had it stopped?

Then he heard the sound of the airlock hissing open, and he knew why.

Caught between morphing forms and with thoughts it barely understood cluttering its mind that it had stolen from him the creature was defenceless. But it would be likely not to be for long.

From the airlock Dezza stepped deftly. He seemed to have a purpose and already knew what he was going to do. The visor flicked open only a moment, and relief washed over Toze as he saw the determined look of the wily salvager.

"Grab onto something and don't let go," he commanded quickly, "Scrunch shut your eyes, take a breath and just hope this works."

Then the visor snapped shut and there was no time for a reply.

The creature began to whine. It was the same banshee-like sound that they had heard many times before within the Starliner; it was getting ready to attack again. Looking around, Toze saw the shape morphing again, and his own features began to dissolve away and be replaced by an assortment of other forms that the creature had taken in the past.

Dezza reached the airlock control panel and wrenched it open. The creature seemed to pour itself after him, flowing around the central console in the sleeping quarters as if the console was merely a rock subsumed in a turbulent river. Flashes of static laced out in the air as the creature morphed again, turning from matter to energy. Toze flinched; knowing that the lash of pain would begin again, and the creature would do to both of them what it had done to the others before.

But the moment of pain never came. Dezza seemed to move as if in a blur, never shying from his task. The panel swung down and the salvager's gloved hand wrenched at the lever beyond.

In a moment, with a flurry of anger, the creature seemed to falter. The airlock doors popped a fraction, and in a moment the moan of air rushing between the crack became a deafening roar.

The creature seemed to be confused. The static discharge increased, but without focus. As the door slid further still and both men braced themselves, and the atmosphere of the *Magellan* began to scream past.

Toze scrunched his eyes shut as tightly as he could. He could feel the tug of the vacuum, trying to pull him away from where he had braced against the panelling. Objects whipped past him catching him a glancing blow, but he dared not look. His skin grew cold and he felt the enormous pressure mounting on his lungs as he fought the urge to try and gulp down more air; there would be none to gulp. His head began to tingle and he felt as if he was spinning around.

The creature screamed again from somewhere close by. He almost felt it touch him as it streaked on by, and then the scream was lost to the moan of air, and was gone.

Toze felt unconsciousness reaching out to him. Fighting hard, he tried to stave it off, but there would only be seconds before unconsciousness would win.

*   *   *   *   *

Dezza stepped from the airlock with a sense of purpose; he knew what he had to do. He had seen the flashes of electrical discharge reflected through the screens of the *Magellan*'s command deck and had known then that something was wrong.

As the airlock had cycled, he had found himself peering through the tiny observation window, seeing the attack that the creature had set upon the officer. He had known he had to act quickly before Toze's fate became the same as that which had happened to Exbo.

The airlock door had hissed open and the creature had seemed to falter as if caught unawares. Half way through a morphing into Toze's form, it stood blank-faced watching Dezza as if trying to reorganise thoughts that were still new to it.

By the time the airlock opened onto space with the safeties disabled, the creature had recomposed itself. He felt his heart rate notch as the creature seemed to flow at speed towards him, but as the air began to evacuate, the creature rolled back on itself, uncertain yet angry.

The vacuum pulled hard at the suit, and he felt himself sliding towards the airlock door. There was a safety clip on the suit, and he clipped it to the console, hoping that the structure would be enough to take the strain. Things whipped up and whirled around him, dashing through the vortex. As for the creature, it seemed to be searching out a hiding place to avoid being sucked out. It tried the consoles, looking for a way in to the circuits just as it had moved freely through the Starliner. But the pull of the air was too strong, and before the creature could change from mass to energy, it whipped in a serpent-like mass and hissed away through the airlock emitting a screech that faded then was masked by the roar of the air.

For a few seconds longer the air rushed, then he felt the flow subside, and no longer were his feet sliding on the plating.

Hurriedly he reached inside the open panel and forced the lever back up. The airlock door slid shut again, finally sealing the ship from space.

From the corner of the visor he saw Toze's limp body slumped against the edge of the sleeping area, arms locked around the pipework. He was unconscious, and Dezza knew that he had only seconds to re-pressurise the ship before he would die of asphyxiation.

Unclipping his safety line he pulled himself through to the command deck and checked along the consoles until he found the one he needed. They had never needed to check before whether the *Magellan* had any spare air left in her tanks. With the recirculation system working, there had never been a need to check. But now it was imperative, and he desperately checked the computer's readout until he found the systems that he wanted. A recirculation system was useless without any air to move around.

He felt the relief wash over him as he found what he was looking for. The readout showed that there was enough spare capacity. Tapping at the controls he sent the command for the computer to dump the tanks into the atmosphere, and was rewarded by the feeling of positive pressure start to build up against the suit. He had done it.

Popping the visor, he rushed back to check on Toze. Even before he reached the sleeping quarters, he saw the man begin to stir, and smiled. There was no keeping military men down.

"What happened?" gasped the officer, disorientated. "Did we get the bastard?"

Dezza smiled. "I smoked them back out into space."

"You know, you're all right by me, Dezza."

"I'm glad to hear that, but if you can still move okay, we've got a core to fix. I stashed it in the tool locker in the airlock and sealed it before I came through."

"You never cease to amaze me."

*   *   *   *   *

238

He felt every bone in his body protest as the creature slammed him hard across the command deck. It was Exbo's form, but the effortless way in which he could just reach out and toss Tracker across the room like he was nothing more than a rag doll was not Exbo.

Before he could stand up, the creature had morphed from mass to energy and back to mass again, flowing across the consoles like a flash flood waiting to strike. At its head, the grinning face of Exbo never changed; it was like the creature knew that to see a fallen comrade would unnerve its prisoner.

"He screamed like a baby when he died," taunted Exbo's face.

Tracker sensed the creature was trying its hardest to drive fear into him, to provoke a reaction, and refused to rise to the bait. It had killed others with barely a blink, but it seemed to be faltering, and he wondered if it might be desperately trying to provoke emotions, to feed off them.

"You should have heard his bones crack."

"Exbo was a prick," said Tracker calmly, never taking his eye off those of the creature, "He deserved to die."

This seemed to confuse the creature. The eyes flickered, just as he had seen them flicker time and time before. The creature was stopping to think, having received an answer that it did not expect.

In the moment of hesitation, Tracker forced his aching body to roll. As the creature moved into life and darted after him he feigned left and moved behind the consoles. He heard the creature following, but he did not look back. There was a tight gap behind the projectors, and he wriggled through it. He heard the creature try to follow, but its physical form was too big to fit. There was a sound like creaking leather, and he sensed it was changing from physical to energy to follow.

The blow that hit him caught him completely unawares. He had assumed he had made some distance on the creature, but it had moved in the blink of an eye to catch him and had tossed him over the consoles as if he weighed nothing at all. He heard the snarling banshee wail as he landed heavily on the consoles, and saw the reflections of blue static as the creature prepared to lance after him.

He felt a control panel underneath him, its keys yielding to his weight as he rolled. He caught sight briefly of a screen glowing green with reams of text before he thudded to the hard floor. As the first of the lancing blows of energy streaked across the command deck greedily probing the gaps between the consoles to search him out, the creature's shrieking seemed to turn to a squeal. He clenched his eyes tight, waiting for the lance of pain from the creature, but it never came.

The squeal turned to a revolting wet squelching noise, and he dared to open an eye to see what was happening. There was a green-tinged glow across the command deck, but he saw it was not coming from the creature. Instead it flowed through the screens from something outside the Starliner. He looked for the creature, and saw it only a brief moment as it writhed at the entrance to the command deck before folding into several parts and seemed to pour itself in pieces into a companionway and electrical terminals. There was a moment when one small piece remained, churning between different forms then it emitted a loud shriek and he saw the image of the woman appear again, contorted as if in pain. The image flickered, and something seemed to flow away from the woman as a white vaporous ooze before the figure was left upright, flickering but no longer contorted. Then the sounds of the creature were no more.

"What the hell?" muttered Tracker under his breath.

The figure of the woman flickered and the head moved in the manner he had seen before. But this time the eyes did not flicker too; they were just ordinary renditions of plain human eyes.

"Unknown order, repeat?" said the woman in a voice that seemed familiar yet not as he had heard it before.

He eased his aching body upright, and took a step towards the woman. "Perhaps you could tell me," he said slowly, "What the hell just happened?"

The woman's head tilted. "Boot time thirty seven seconds. Insufficient data."

He remembered the console he had landed on and took a look. Sure enough on the screen the reams of data showed programmes that had been reactivated. The ship's hologram was one of them.

He remembered the way the creature had seemed to be ripped apart, and that the figure of the woman had separated out just as it had left. What if the ship's hologram was now real, and had somehow been parted from the entity?

The green haze from beyond the bridge screens increased in intensity, and he was forced to shield his eyes and look away before he could read any further on the screen. He saw the woman look towards the bridge screens, apparently immune to the glare. Her image flickered with lines of static as if there was interference from something. He saw too that the hologramatic projector too was beginning to falter.

"Radiation levels above safe levels," she said in her faraway voice, as if anticipating his question.

The green haze faded, and he risked a look out of the bridge screen. His heart jumped as he saw the entire Starliner's navigation field glowing, as particles streaked through it.

"What is that?" he asked.

"Cosmic débris," replied the hologram, "First wave of a meteorite swarm. Collision risk imminent. Advise evasive action."

He remembered the navigation readouts he and Toze had witnessed in the engineering spaces. It had been only a matter of time before the swarm would reach the Starliner. This must be the dust that preceded it; they had not thought of that possibility and the particles must have been so small as to not show on the Starliner's aged scopes.

"It's being deflected by the navigation fields," he said slowly, "But how much longer will that last?"

The woman and the projector flickered in unison, and he realised that the radiation generated as the dust grazed the fields at high speeds must be well up. That must have affected the creature and sent it scurrying from the command deck seeking shelter, for now.

It was strange though that he felt very little except for a tingling on his skin, and he was not sure whether that was real or imagined because his mind thought subconsciously that there should be a feeling from the danger.

"Dust field will end in approximately four minutes," said the woman after a moment's contemplation as the computer processed the calculations. The projector image folded in on itself and changed to depict the approaching swarm. Vectors and numbers appeared as the computer projected the course and speed. "The *Cerberus* will graze outer edge of swarm in twelve minutes with risk of collision at sixty-two point eight percent."

Tracker leant close to the shimmering projector image until his face glowed in hues of blue and yellow from the reflected image. It was clear that the Starliner would pass unharmed through the dust cloud, albeit irradiated by the interaction of the particles in the navigation field. After that there was a risk of being hit by a real meteorite, though he pondered the computer's percentages.

If the creature survived the swarm, then he knew that others would come to the *Cerberus* in time. He realised that he had to do something to stop the creature for good.

Looking back out through the bridge screen he noticed that the green haze of particles grazing the field was already less; there would not be much time before the creature returned to try and finish him. Glancing along the consoles he looked for ways in which he could ensure the Starliner would be destroyed, taking with it the creature.

"What systems still work?" he demanded, glancing over a sea of controls.

"Air recirculation on-line, auxiliary power down to forty-seven percent efficiency," the woman began.

He shook his head and cut her off; time was too short. "No. What propulsion do we have?"

The woman tilted her head as the computer did the checks. At last she replied in the same faraway voice that he was growing quickly to hate. "Rösenbridge unserviceable and offline with unknown fault. Docking thrusters offline and unserviceable with unknown fault."

He listened as she continued through system after system, each one as unserviceable as the next. With a sinking heart he began to wonder whether there was any way he could alter the *Cerberus'* course.

"Manoeuvring thrusters gas packs depleted and inoperable. Ion drive offline and presumed functional," finished the woman, and tilted her head as if waiting expectantly for any answer.

Tracker found himself latching onto her final words in his mind. "Ion drive?"

"No diagnostics available," she replied stubbornly.

He shook his head. "Oh no. You don't just brush it aside like that. Tell me how to get it working, bitch."

She ignored his insult and tone of voice and moved to a set of consoles by the bridge wing, then turned to face him. "Computer control offline. Unable to initiate or check." She indicated with a hand to the adjacent console. "These are the manual controls."

The wailing banshee shriek of the creature echoed up the companionway from somewhere several decks below, and with a stab of fear he realised that it would not be long before the creature would return and would almost certainly try to stop him. Outside the screens the green glow was still fading fast. Soon it would be gone, and there would be nothing to hold the creature at bay.

He looked over the console's controls and blew a layer of dirt from them that had accumulated over the decades. For a few seconds he tried to read down the controls, but he was constantly aware of the image of the woman hovering at his side. It bothered him that she was there - not because she seemed to be looking at him blankly, but because of what the creature had done whilst manifesting in her form.

"Can you not be there?" he asked without looking up. He felt the perspiration brought on by anxiety beading on his forehead.

"Unknown order. Repeat?" she said innocently.

He tried not to get angry. "I'd just rather you not stood alongside me. You give me the creeps."

The woman tilted her head in that infuriating manner that the computer had been programmed. It was as if she did not understand. Perhaps she didn't, he thought. He sighed and returned his attention to the console, trying to ignore her.

Some of the controls were dead. Others seemed to have become victim to the decay, and switches pushed through the rotten fascia under his touch. But some still worked, and the control screen soon glowed as systems began booting after decades of disuse. Tracker crossed his fingers, and hoped.

"Fuel cells at eighteen percent," chirped up the woman, much to Tracker's surprise. "Drive three inoperable. Drive one manifold chamber failure imminent."

"You told me that you didn't know whether the ion drive would work or not," said Tracker slowly, testing his words and watching the woman's translucent face for any signs of emotion that might betray the returning presence of the creature.

But the woman looked back blankly. "System now booted; information available."

He grunted, not really that convinced at her explanation though right now he had little choice.

The main ion engine firing controls flicked uselessly under his fingers. Testing the panel, it felt loose, and he found he could pull it out of the main console and turn it upside sown. There was a loom of wires, but he could see crusty white patterns of oxidation on the terminals and the insulation was cracked and dusty.

"Damn," he muttered under his breath. It would take hours to trace the wires and find the faults; time he did not have.

"Can you control the firing sequence?" he asked the hologram.

Her head tilted. "Indeed."

"Then stop stalling, HAL, and get those engines online."

*   *   *   *   *

The core had not taken long to reinsert to the chamber and connect. When the salvage crew had removed it, they had at least left everything else around it intact.

They had both been too engrossed in their work to feel the first shudders running through the *Magellan*. They had been only faint, and in the bustle of work were easy to miss. But they slowly grew.

Toze signalled Dezza to silence.

"What is it?" hissed Dezza, but Toze waved him quiet.

"Listen."

They listened. There was no mistaking the noise. A study thunder deep in bass rumbled through the plating.

"The entity?" Toze hazarded.

244

Dezza shook his head. "No. Feels more like a drive unit firing." He scanned across the adjacent consoles, but the *Magellan*'s systems still showed as being offline save for the life support systems.

"It isn't us," he said at last.

"You think it could be the *Cerberus*?" asked Toze.

Dezza thought for a moment. "Nothing else it can be."

They scrambled out of the engineering spaces up the ladder to the command deck above. Here too the consoles showed blank. Outside of the screens a faint green glow seemed to envelop both the craft and the bulk of the Starliner beyond.

"What is that?" exclaimed Toze; his face illuminated a ghostly green in the wavering glow.

Dezza checked readouts from gauges. "Dust zapping through the *Cerberus*' navigation fields I guess."

"Are we safe?"

"For now. Just worry if the particles get any bigger."

Toze did not reply. They jumped as Dezza's suit radio crackled into life.

"Anybody there?" crackled a familiar voice beyond the static. It was Tracker.

"Hey, where are you?" replied Dezza hastily.

"No time for stories," interrupted Tracker's voice. The static was getting stronger now and it was getting harder to make him out, "I'm taking the Starliner into the swarm."

Both realised the consequences. The Starliner would be pounded into dust for sure. Anyone left aboard would suffer the same fate.

"Are we crazy!" barked Toze.

"Not crazy. If the *Cerberus* survives, some-one will come poking their nose in where it isn't wanted. Unless this hulk is pulverised there will always be a risk. I can't the opportunity go; I need to destroy the creature. I've got the ion drive working and I'm changing the *Cerberus*' course directly into the swarm. You've got to detach now and get away from here."

"What about you?"

"Don't waste your time with me. There's no way back through the Starliner without running into that thing, and it's going to be gunning for me."

"But…"

"No buts. Haul your arses out of here right now."

"Hey!" scolded Toze, "I'm supposed to be in charge making the decisions around here."

"Sorry Sir. Sometimes there's just something a man's got to get on with."

The line clicked dead before either could answer. Dezza tried the channel a couple more times, but it seemed that Tracker had simply turned his unit off.

"What now?" asked Dezza.

Toze peered through the bridge screens at the slender length of the Starliner. It was easy to see its full bulk now, bathed in green from the radiation in the navigation field. Far away at the stern end he could make out the faint orange glow of the ion particle stream from the engines of the Starliner.

"That crazy son of a bitch managed to get her engines going," he muttered in partial admiration of the tenacity of the man.

Something streaked through the navigation field, adding a painful red glow to the green haze and they both winced at the closeness of it.

"That one was close. It's going to hot up around here even more," said Toze, "All right. We had better juice up that core and hope with fingers crossed that it works. Whether we like it or not, we are out of here."

They slipped into the seats on the command deck and began running through the initialisation sequences for the core. Now would be the test of whether it would still work after all it had been through.

"Manifold pressures good," said Dezza, reading off the gauges.

"Looks like we got lucky for once."

"Save the celebrations. There's still a long way to go."

As the core switched live, the Christmas tree of diagnostic lights on the panel flickered from red to amber to green one by one with agonising slowness. Finally the last light turned, and remained green.

Almost disappointingly, there was nothing other than the lights on a panel to tell them it was all working. Perhaps it would have been better if there had been some audible sign.

"That's it?" said Toze at last.

Dezza nodded. "You were expecting something better? A fanfare perhaps?"

"No, maybe not. Let's hope it holds."

The ion drive was a different matter. As soon as the relays were opened they felt the steady rumble of the drive winding up. Compared to the gentler vibration that had fed through from the Cerberus' drive firing, this was far more aggressive.

"Locking clamps won't let go," said Toze.

Dezza felt the sinking feeling he had felt all those years ago. The Starliner was not going to let them go so easily. It was just as it had been before. He notched up the ion drive, and through the bridge screen he saw the green haze become drowned by the yellow glow of the Magellan's exhaust.

*   *   *   *   *

As the haze of the Cerberus' navigation field subsided, he heard the creature in the companion-way. Desperately he checked the readouts on the consoles, and looked to the projector. Already the lines and vectors were changing; the Starliner was coming around onto a new course and gathering momentum. If he could just distract the creature for long enough, he thought, he might just be able to prevent it from realising what he was trying and stopping him.

The projector flashed warnings as the heading came around to head straight into the approaching swarm. Warning buzzers began to sound across the command deck.

"Turn that shit off," he ordered calmly.

The hologram tilted her head. "Collision risk. Recommend course change to avoid."

"Button it baby," he said, cutting her off. "And button the alarms. If you knew what I knew you would get with the programme a whole lot quicker."

The buzzers wailed once then ceased, and he smiled. Maybe the hologram was not so bad after all.

"Explain?"

"What?" He looked up and found the flickering image of the woman looking at him as if expecting a reply.

"Explain why?"

"What year do you think this is?"

"Chronometer indicates…"

He cut her off. "What I mean is, have you any idea where the last ninety years went for you, or where the crew and passengers from this hulk are? The *Cerberus* was attacked by some kind of alien. It infiltrated everything, including the ship's electronics. It killed everyone, and it's doing the same to my crew, and will keep doing it. I saw inside its mind. It assimilated part of you; surely you must have seen it too?" He looked back to the console suddenly feeling slightly stupid. How he hated holograms – too easy to treat them as human when they were nothing more than a machine limited by their programming.

She seemed to consider his words, then spoke with a faraway look on her digitised face. "There are memories with inconsistencies."

Her words seemed to falter, and he looked up. Her face seemed frozen in one expression as if half way through the sentence. For a moment he thought the programme had crashed, but a wave of static ate briefly into the image and she moved again.

She looked at him. "Course corrections accepted."

He raised an eyebrow and the frustration began to finally show through Tracker's otherwise calm exterior. "What does that mean? You're selling us out and keeping that thing alive?"

Then he realised that the projector still showed the same course he had set. The ion drive was still running; nothing had changed.

She smiled. "You speak the truth."

Before he could answer, the green haze outside the screens died away, and complete clarity returned to both the hologram's image and that on the projector.

"We've cleared the dust."

Already he could hear the scream of the creature. It seemed so close.

"Can you lock the course?" he asked desperately.

"Course set. No guarantee that it cannot be changed."

He felt his heart sink.

"However, fuel cells depleting fast. Six minutes burn time until insufficient fuel for further course corrections," she said, then she winked at him and smiled.

He felt almost taken aback. He was almost beginning to like this woman even though he knew she was not real. She was his kind of woman.

*　　　*　　　*　　　*　　　*

It came just like before; the lurch and the rending of metal as the clamps finally let go. Buzzers sang angrily on the bridge, but they ignored it. In a gut-wrenching change of gee force, the *Magellan* lurched madly away from the hull of the Starliner and began to snake wildly.

"Shit, gyro is down!" shouted Toze. He wrestled with controls.

All Dezza could do was hold on tight and watch with a sickening feeling as the slender form of the Starliner lurched in and out of vision beyond the screens.

"Check the consoles!" screamed Toze.

Fighting against the changing gee forces, Dezza pulled himself to the consoles and scanned across the display. It was hard to read as the *Magellan* lurched backwards and forwards. He could tell that there was something wrong with the ship's computer. It did not look like the gyroscope was down, but there was a problem with the relay between it and the computer. He fumbled for the access cover underneath, and it went whirling away to clang across the bulkhead, nearly hitting Toze as it went.

"Sorry!" he called out, "There's a short out in the circuits."

He pulled at circuit boards, feeling for the connectors.

"Hurry it up before I puke."

He felt the edge of the connectors in his fingers and pulled. There was no sense in feeling for anything loose, not under these conditions. The only hope was to pull them all out and hope that the computer would just shut the drive down.

The *Magellan* lurched once more, then the vibration from the ion drive died away and the gee forces diminished. For a moment there was a strange silence that descended in the command deck.

Then Toze spoke. "That was one rollercoaster ride I don't want to do again."

Dezza ignored him, studying the scopes. Every console was blank; he must have pulled the master bus. "We're running blind," he said urgently, "Where's the *Cerberus*? We have to make sure we aren't going to collide."

Toze scrambled to the bridge screens and peered out, scanning the starscape. Dezza joined him.

"Where is she?" Dezza muttered. He could feel his heart in his throat. They had already seen the dropship graze the Starliner and be destroyed. Without any early warning, they could very easily fall into the same fate.

"How far do you think we came?" asked Toze.

Dezza shrugged. "Difficult to tell. That was a bit of a bucking bronco trip."

They kept scanning; stubbornly the starscape yielded nothing. They moved to another of the bridge screens that looked out over the other side.

"I got it!" yelled Toze, pointing.

Dezza followed his finger. Just slipping out of view he saw the bulk of the Starliner slipping from view. He felt the perspiration on his back; that thing was damn close. Another few hundred yards and they would have been tangled into the antennas. In the vastness of space, that distance was a mere hair's width.

Toze breathed a sigh of relief, but Dezza was still concerned. He saw the fiery glow from the *Cerberus*' ion drive exhausts and knew that their wake would pass close by. A stream of ionised particles could cause far more damage to their systems than any amount of loose connections ever could.

"We have to pass clear of her exhaust or we are toast," he said.

"Why?"

"The particle stream is lethal to electronics. Space regulations state no vessel under ion drive propulsion may pass within two thousand metres of another vessel. We're a fraction of that. At this range she could fry everything we've got."

"What do we do?"

"Hope, and pray."

"I'm not religious."

"If that ion stream comes to close and torches the hull, you soon will be."

They scrambled back to the consoles and Dezza sank underneath to the open access panels. Luckily the pieces inside were labelled neatly. Without the shifting gee forces this would be a much easier job. He felt the connectors slide together easily one by one, and saw the lights flicker on across first one console then another.

"Give us a squirt of the ion drive. Anything to get us clear," he called out.

Toze slid into the seat at the console. He tapped firmly on the controls and they both felt the shudder as their ion drive fired once again. This time he made sure he had only manual control.

The starscape beyond the bridge screens shifted and rolled slowly, and through a bank of monitors they saw the slender hull of the Starliner seem to roll away from them. They saw the glare of the exhaust ports, and for a moment the monitors flared white then darkened to black as the computer struggled to compensate for the sudden changes in light levels. The image slowly faded back in, and the Starliner was well away into the distance.

"Did he do it?" asked Toze, glued to the images.

"I don't know."

Toze booted up the projector unit and a sphere of space flickered into view.

Dezza wrinkled his nose at the acrid smell, but said nothing. Blotches appeared one by one as the computer calculated objects and their trajectories, and reams of text began to shimmer gently in the static-laced air.

"We'll miss the meteorite storm okay," said Toze at last after scrutinising the figures.

"And the *Cerberus*?"

Toze's fingers tapped deftly on the console. The point of view of the projection changed and focused in on another blip. Vectors streamed out and numbers flickered up and down in the air.

He checked the numbers, and double-checked them. Finally he sat back and drummed his fingers together in contemplation of the results. "Looks like a collision course," he said quietly at last.

*   *   *   *   *

"Stall it as long as you can."

That had been Tracker's words to the hologram as he had backed away into the gloom of the other end of the command deck. The woman looked at him and tilted her head, and then she looked back at the companionway. It was as if she did not quite understand.

The darkness was gathering there, though with closer inspection there was more to the shadows than just an absence of light. A tentacle flopped, making a noise like wet leather and something slithered under bridge consoles. Something moved in the corner; for a moment it was almost as if something was stood there, watching. But in a moment there was nothing but a haze of white that dissipated in the blink of an eye.

"You can't run," said a voice. It sounded almost like Spanners, then it seemed to just slide in pitch and tone and evolve into the voice of Exbo.

"I'll run where I want to," retorted Tracker.

Another tentacle flopped out of the darkness and felt its way over the edge of a console. Tracker found himself drawing back further and further away until he felt the cold hard steel of the bulkhead behind him. It was the childhood closet all over again, and there was nowhere to go.

A console in the centre of the deck seemed to heave upwards. Rivets popped like speeding bullets from its stanchions and he could hear the tortured metal start to distort.

"What are you going to do? Taunt me by rearranging the furniture?" he said, pushing out the bravado. He was not going to give the creature the satisfaction of knowing that it had got to him.

252

A tentacle probed greedily towards the hologram, and the woman squealed and seemed to contort in on herself as waves of static rolled across her image. He grimaced as the squeal turned to a scream, and then the holographic woman was gone. In her place stood a middle-aged man wearing an ornate uniform that he did not recognise.

Tracker became aware that the creature had, apart from the mystery man, gone, taking with it the hologram. No more tentacles probed the deck, and no things slithered in the darkness and shadows. Only the bent console remained as evidence that the creature had been here in alien form.

"Who are you?" demanded Tracker, his voice reverberating in the now strangely quiet command deck.

The man turned to look at Tracker, regarding him with eyes that seemed as though they were seeing him for the first time. He did not answer.

"Who are you?" he repeated.

The man smiled, but still did not speak.

"Captain Paschendorf," said a familiar voice at Tracker's side.

He turned in surprise. Stood beside him, as if she had been there all along, was the hologram woman. But he saw in her eyes that it was now more alien than the ship's computer.

The captain seemed to be viewing the consoles and controls, looking for something. He turned to the projector display, and slowly poked an arm into its shimmering display in the manner that a curious child might. Instead of distorting around his arm as the displays usually did, the image seemed to suck in on itself and scrunch down onto his fingertip. It was as if he was sucking the display into himself.

Then Tracker realised that in a way, he was. The creature knew; he could sense it.

The Starliner's engines shuddered off. Finally the distant vibrations of the colossal ion drive cones at the rear of the vessel ended, and the Starliner became even more silent as the starscape beyond the screens continued to scroll by ever so slowly. For a moment the alien in its twin manifestations was silent, then the captain moved back to the central console.

"Initialise ion drive," barked the captain in an order that seemed to be directed at no-one in particular, "Course correction to starboard."

With a sinking feeling, Tracker knew that the creature had realised his plan.

"State authorisation," said the voice of the computer, speaking disembodied from a console speaker rather than through the tainted hologram.

For a moment Tracker thought that the ship's computer had done it and that the real hologram had managed to be true to her word. But the captain calmly stated his name and rank, and the computer accepted it.

"No!" he shouted at the computer's disembodied voice, "That cannot be right. That's not the real captain."

The man ignored him, but the woman at his side smiled and looked at him with those eyes that flickered dark and forebodingly. There was a rumble as the ion drives fired into action again.

Slowly the Starliner's prow began to move sideways against the starscape, beginning to change heading with agonising slowness. Tracker knew that this was his last chance. He threw himself across the command deck towards the captain and the central console. He sensed the woman move, more of a blur than a true motion. He felt the woman's hand touch him as it began to morph with sickening speed into something else. Then a blow hit him hard as the captain turned to face him. He was going to hit, but the captain seemed to dissolve and precipitate at the same time so that without actually moving he allowed Tracker to pass straight through him without flinching.

He slammed into the floor, and the creature followed. Tentacles slapped over every surface and the banshee scream came again. He shut his eyes, and braced for the pain.

The air seemed to burn as the forks of blue light zapped across the command deck. He felt his body arch with the pain as they lanced through him, and in a moment he felt again the creature probing at his mind. With surprise he realised that it was looking to know what he had done, and with a sudden feeling of determination, he realised that the creature was afraid; despite its bravado, it did not know if it could succeed.

For the first time, he felt the fear in the creature's alien mind.

The burning stopped, and the blue light faded as fast as it had come. Tracker groaned and nursed his aching head. His skin felt scorched and tingled to the touch.

At first he thought he might already be dead, but then he realised that the whole command deck was bathed in green. He heard the creature scurrying, but it was no longer coming for him. The air in front of him seemed to flicker, and he saw the image of the woman reappear. He looked into her eyes, and she looked back. For a moment he wondered whether she was still the alien, but her eyes were different again; somehow just human.

"Everybody be cool," he groaned, "You be cool."

She watched impassively as he dragged himself upright and looked through the screens. The ship's navigation field glowed bright green again; the radiation had sent the creature reeling away, driven further into the Starliner for protection. Already he could see the first heavy streaks that showed that this time there was more than just dust. As he watched a yellow streak pierced the field and gouged across the decking of the prow sending fittings cart wheeling into space in showers of white hot metal.

He suddenly remembered the course correction that the alien had made. He could still feel the ion drive shuddering through the ship. Panicked, he looked for the figure of the captain, but he was gone. He dragged himself to the central console, desperately looking for anything that would show him the course of the ship and the meteorite swarm. Infuriatingly the projector was no longer working. None of the screens seemed to be able to show him what he wanted either.

"What's our course? Where are we heading?" he demanded.

The woman appeared at his side, and smiled. "The controls are set again for the heart of the swarm. Goodbye Tracker."

Then her form flickered with the radiation one more time, and folded in on itself.

"Hey," he sighed, "I never got her name or number."

Then the rocks came faster and faster and began to pulverise the Starliner. Decks ripped open venting gases into space, and bulkheads roared as they bulged and exploded into space. A direct hit smashed through the bridge, ripping through the Starliner until it split her from stem to stern. In a showering pattern of white-hot gas, the remains twisted and exploded until only fragments remained, and even these became pulverised into dust by the ferocity of the meteorite storm.

*   *   *   *   *

By the time the debris had passed, there was nothing left to show the *Cerberus* had been anything more than a myth. Dezza gazed into the dust cloud, fist clenched, eyes watering. It was still real to him, burned into his brain for an eternity.